Spelled

BETSY SCHOW

sourcebooks
fire

Published by Sourcebooks Fire, an imprint of Sourcebooks, Inc.

P.O. Box 4410, Naperville, Illinois 60567-4410

(630) 961-3900

Fax: (630) 961-2168

www.sourcebooks.com

Library of Congress Cataloging-in-Publication Data

Schow, Betsy

Spelled / Betsy Schow.

    pages cm

    Summary: "As the crown princess of Emerald, Dorthea lives a charmed life full of Hans Christian Louboutin glass slippers and Glenda Original ball gowns. But when she unknowingly wishes upon a cursed star, all spell breaks loose and the rules of fairy tale disappear--taking Dorthea's parents with them"-- Provided by publisher.

    [1. Fairy tales. 2. Princesses--Fiction. 3. Magic--Fiction.] I. Title.

    PZ8.S3118Sp 2015

    [Fic]--dc23

                        2014046129

Printed and bound in the United States of America.

VP 19 18 17 16 15 14 13 12 11

For Melody and Stacy, ladies who are wildly creative, amazing writers, and even better friends.

"Rule #17: To rescue a princess from magical imprisonment, a handsome prince must first slay the dragon. If one is not available, a large iguana will do in a pinch."

—*Definitive Fairy-Tale Survival Guide, Volume 1*

Dragon Slaying for Dummies

S tupid princes," I muttered as I stalked down the green-flecked quartz-and-marble hallway. "Why is it that when I don't want them, they're practically popping out of the closets? But the one time, *the one time*, I actually need a knight in overpriced armor, they're nowhere to be found?"

I checked the guidebook in my hand one last time, to make sure I hadn't missed anything. My plan was perfect—so brilliant, in fact, that I was amazed none of my other ancestors had thought of it. The fact that it took *me* seventeen years to come up with it was moot. For once, I was grateful that the world of fairy tales and magic adhered to such strict rules. Still, the entire thing hinged on finding a single prince willing to help me end my lifetime of house arrest in the Emerald Palace.

So far, I'd searched through the north and west towers, the potions pantry, the arcane arcade, and the armory. Next, I'd try the main floor. On my way down the curved staircase, I had a perfect view of the one and only entrance to the palace. The double doors were made of ironwood cut from Sherwood Forest and large enough to accommodate visiting giants. Sunlight filtered through the ornate and impenetrable stained-glass side panels, casting a shimmery green-and-gold hue on my skin.

Before I reached the bottom step, the doors slid open with a whoosh. For a minute I hoped the new arrival was one of the palace's visiting princes. Unfortunately, it was just UPS (United Pegasus Service). Even worse, since I hadn't ordered anything for a few days, the delivery wasn't for me.

I waved one of the postal brownies over. "What's in the crate?"

He gave a sharp whistle, and the workers set down the box—with the arrow saying "this side up" pointing to the ground. To tell the truth, I didn't care about the contents. But it kept them busy while the double doors remained wide open. Maybe I wouldn't need a prince after all.

While the brownies unpacked, I slipped past them and headed to the one and only palace exit. As soon as I was within five feet of it, the doors slid closed with a clap.

That's the problem with automagic doors: they knew who to let in and who *not* to let out.

"Sign here please." The boss brownie either didn't notice or care about my experiment with the door. Without looking at me, he held out a quill and a parchment saying I'd received the goods undamaged, though I had no clue what it was to start with—some sort of ornate gold stand with filigree chains coming out of the center. About a dozen little glass balls hung at the end of the chains. Those seemed to be intact, so I signed and shooed the brownies to the ballroom.

Even from a room away, I could hear Queen Em—my mother—directing the servants in their preparations for tonight's holiday festivities. She commanded her battalion of party planners like a general on the battlefield, even setting up a triage corner to treat the wounded. Imagine the number of paper cuts from folding thousands of star ornaments to hang on the Story Spruce.

Year after year, I took part in the Muse Day tradition just like everybody else; I wrote my wishes on the foil stars, hoping the Storymakers above would hear my prayers and make them come true. It hadn't happened yet. Obviously as a princess, I would get my happy ending, but the Makers were taking their sweet time getting around to it, and I was tired of waiting.

Movement in the courtyard caught my eye. Still on the prince hunt, I went over to investigate, taking great pains to stay out of view of my mother. A man stood on a ladder, waving a net frantically back and forth. Though he had a bit

3

of a tummy that hung over his belt, he used to be a handsome prince. Now he was just my father, King Henry.

"What in Grimm's name are you doing, Dad?" I hurried over to stabilize the ladder as it started tipping over.

"Language, pum'kin," he chided and wobbled down the ladder. "And a Merry Muse Day to you too. Your mother sent me to gather will-o'-the-wisps for the new chandelier. I'd forgotten how tricky they were to hunt. I believe I prefer trolls."

So that's what that package was; the globes were to contain the will-o'-the-wisps' light while the chains were to keep them from getting loose. It was a smart idea after last year's glowworm fiasco. Some of my heels still had glow-gook on the bottoms.

Hummingbeeswax candles would be easier, except every heroine has her Achilles' curse: apples for Snow White, spinning wheels for Sleeping Beauty, and fire for the House of Emerald.

Our family became spelled after my ancestor pixed off two evil witch sisters. The witches' curse was supposed to doom my great-great-great grandmother to turn evil and torch the world—except the spell wasn't worded right. It didn't specify *which* Emerald princess. So ever since, all the girls in the Emerald family have been stuck inside, since there's no way to know what generation will inherit the curse.

Until we know for sure who the unlucky royal is, candles, lava lanterns, and anything with a flame is banned to keep the palace safe. As for the outside world…well, if you aren't allowed out, you don't have to worry about it. Completely lame that *I* have to suffer because one princess couldn't mind her own glammed business.

Well, *suffered*—past tense—if everything goes as planned. "Father, any chance you've seen a prince lying about? I seem to have misplaced them all."

"Well, which one are you looking for? Your date to the ball, perhaps?" He leaned in close and whispered conspiratorially, "I bet it's Hudson, right?"

Hudson was the half-giant prince and Dad's favorite of all the suitors he and Mother recently infested the palace with. Dad probably figured Hudson would make a very good hunting companion, given he was fierce looking and around the size of a boulder. Unfortunately, he also had the IQ of granite.

With a dreamy look, Father put a hand around my shoulder. "Ahhh, I remember when your mother finally accepted my suit. It took more time and patience than getting Cerberus to fetch. That's the thing about love: the best kind isn't easy or instant, and you often get roughed up a bit on the way." He winked at me. "But I suppose you know a thing or two about love yourself now."

"What in spell are you talking about?" I sighed, tired of the little *talks*, not to mention the entire game of thrones and accompanying prince parade. "I'd rather date Quasimodo than any of those royal rejects. I just need one of them for a little project I'm working on."

Father exhaled heavily and crossed his arms. "I'm guessing

I don't want to know. That way I can't get yelled at by your mother for not stopping you."

I smiled and tapped my nose, indicating he was right. Neither of us had illusions about who wore the biggest crown in the family.

"I think I saw Sterling earlier in the hall of mirrors," Father said and climbed back onto the ladder.

I groaned internally because, one, I'd missed such an obvious spot—Sterling was hardly ever without his entourage of stylists and personal mirror holders—and two, finding him meant I had to deal with his ego, which was so large I was constantly amazed he didn't pop his armor wide open.

"Thanks," I said, heading off for the south tower.

"Dorthea," my father called after me. "Try to remember it's a holiday and have a little fun tonight with your friends."

"Sure." I waved, not bothering to paste on a fake smile since he couldn't see me. Though all the major fairy-tale families were coming tonight, I wouldn't exactly call any of them friends. Aside from the once-a-year gathering, I never spoke to any of them, except the occasional chat on Flitter with Cinderella, since we shared a love of designer footwear. All the other princesses were too busy, wrapped up in their own adventures to distract me from my lack of them.

I found Sterling exactly where Dad said he'd be, flexing his muscles and making duck lips at one of his fifty reflections.

"Princess, you look as stunning as ever. To what do I owe this immense pleasure?" He gave a half bow, and I couldn't help but notice that his eyes were still darting to his own reflection. He was generically dashing but unremarkable from a lineup of a dozen other princes.

Still, he fit the bill: royal and handsome—and boy, did he know it—with a sword hanging from a sheath around his waist.

"I have something that I desperately need help with. I would be ever so grateful if you would loan me the services of your sword arm." I purposefully made the request formal, so he would be less likely to refuse.

"Of course, dearest of my heart. What manly task may I perform for you?"

"If you care for me at all, you'll slay a dragon."

"Such a simple task to prove my devotion? For you, I will gladly take up this quest. Why, by the age of ten, I had already felled my first ogre."

I spun around on my satin ballet flats and started walking, so Sterling wouldn't see me gagging as he recounted his knightly résumé for the rest of the trip through the tower's maze of spiral staircases until we reached our destination.

"Here we are. Go get 'em." I gave Sterling a little push toward the waist-high mother-of-pearl column situated in the alcove between the grand staircase and the entrance.

"That?" he asked incredulously, pointing the tip of his sword at the object resting on the column.

That was a very detailed dragon sculpture, carved painstakingly out of the highest quality emerald. The statuette was approximately eighteen crown lengths across and as high as my arm from elbow to fingertip.

"Breaking an antique is hardly a fitting feat for a knight such as I." He went over and poked the emerald dragon with his finger. "Don't you have anything bigger? Perhaps something along the lines of a great beast?"

I shook my head fervently. "Nope, it has to be this." Though it wasn't exactly what the guidebook intended, I didn't even have access to the village pet shoppe, so the dragon work of art would have to do.

Sterling sighed. "As my lady wishes." Hoisting his broad sword into the air, he sliced down, hitting the statue with a great reverberating *crack*. The noise filled the palace, much louder than it should have for the small chunk of glittering green that broke off from the dragon's spine.

The statue shuddered, lifted its head, and roared.

When Statues Attack

Sterling dropped his sword and shrieked like a milkmaid, running behind me. "It's alive! Why is it alive?"

I tried to yank the prince forward. "Quit being a puss in boots. There's your beast. Hurry and get it."

Sterling steadfastly refused to move from his cover while the dragon hopped off his pedestal and started advancing. I was about to grab Sterling's sword for myself when the creature stopped, rolled to the side, and started wailing.

"I've been wounded!" Its cries echoed throughout the grand foyer. "All these years of faithful protection and I am betrayed, stabbed in the back."

The poor thing thrashed around as if in death throes, its

hollering pitiful and loud. And if it didn't shut its snout, it was going to get me in trouble.

I crouched down beside it, retrieving the missing chunk in the process. "Shh, shh. It's no big deal. I can fix it. No need to be upset." I spoke in soothing tones and tried putting the piece back in, hoping the magic that brought it to life would put it back to sleep once it was whole.

The chunk clattered to the floor the moment I let go.

"Farewell these mortal coils!" The dragon gave one last exhale and lay still.

"Oh, Mortimer, don't get your scales in a bunch. It's just a chip."

Between the wailing and shushing, I hadn't heard anyone approach. The Emerald Sorceress's gnarled green finger, complete with razor-sharp red-tipped nails, poked me under my chin, forcing me up until I stared at her warty nose. The single, wiry hair sticking out of the wart twitched, a signal I've come to interpret as meaning *You're pixed*.

Verte was the kingdom's head sorceress, oracle, palace grump, and the only reason I hadn't died of sheer boredom. We were often partners in mischief, unless I was messing with her stuff, and then I was on my own. One time, I blew up her cauldron trying to make soup. In retaliation, she sent me a billy goat that ate my entire closet's contents.

Mortimer, the carved emerald dragon, shook his scales and sprang up to his claws, scurrying into Verte's arms. While she was cooing and stroking him like a cat, I took the opportunity to try and sneak away. Just beyond the still-cowering Sterling, the entrance to the palace stood slightly ajar, even though I was less than three feet away.

It had worked…sort of. As I inched closer, the door remained frozen, but I could almost feel it wanting to shut, like it too was alive. The opening was small, but maybe if I sucked in and shimmied sidewa—

"Dorthea Gayle Emerald! Do not take a single step outside that door."

Mortimer's caterwauling had drawn more than just Verte; the commotion had also caught the attention of my mother. She stood tall, proud, and stone-faced at the archway between the ballroom and the foyer. Every inch of her looked regal, from her sweeping velvet dress to her brown hair, braided back into a severe bun. My father stood behind her, and the servants she'd been directing poked their heads around the archway wall.

At a noticeably safe distance.

Caught red-handed, with a large audience no less, there was no use pretending it didn't look like exactly what it was. Time to use the skills that every proper princess was born with—begging, pleading, and whining until I got my way.

"*Please please please please.* I'll do anything you want if you let me outside for just a little while."

My mother's eyes narrowed and her chin squared into an even harder line. "And what of the curse? Have you forgotten? Or perhaps you think we stay inside to avoid grass allergies."

I folded my arms, refusing to budge. "Seriously, has anyone ever thought about the shelf life of this thing? That spell is as ancient as Verte and probably past its expiration date. The elemental hags are probably dead, so maybe their magic died with them." No one said anything for a few beats, so I continued, determined to win my cause. "I promise I'll be really careful and not play with matches and only go into stores that use glow crystals."

My father, ever compassionate, stepped in to help plead my case. "Em, perhaps just a few minutes with an escort wouldn't—"

Mother cut him off with a withering glare. "Henry, I believe you have other things to attend to."

In my head, I imagined the crack of a whip as my father's shoulders slumped and he went back to catching will-o'-the-wisps in the courtyard.

Mother's eyes softened a little as she walked toward me. "I'm not purposely being cruel. This is the story the Makers have given us. Were it just the possibility of an endless sleep, I might consider breaking the rules. But it's more. *Girl of Emerald, no man can tame. Burn down the world, consumed by flames.*" She placed a gentle hand on my cheek. "Can you really risk the lives of our people on a few maybes?" Anger and sadness filled her voice. After all, she was bound by the curse too.

And that's exactly why she should understand how *I* felt.

"But can't you see I won't be risking anyone?" I started to

explain my brilliant backup safety plan, which included half a dozen servants with water buckets. My words withered and died in my throat as her eyes turned steely again.

"You have already put us all at risk by breaking the dragon and thus the protection spell cast over this entire palace!" Before she turned away, I saw her unmistakable and familiar look of disappointment.

Oops didn't quite seem sufficient, but how was I supposed to know the dumb carving actually did something useful besides looking sparkly? "Sterling," my mother snapped sharply. The prince immediately stopped cowering and stood at attention. "As a favor to the throne, would you please stand guard at the door? With the barrier broken, now we must watch both what comes in and what goes out."

Sterling bowed, going on and on about his guarding pedigree as my mother walked away without giving me another look.

I gave Sterling a thorough evaluation—yeah, I could take him, but then he'd scream and the guards would have my nose in the dirt before I made it past the carriageway. But now I knew it was possible; I would just have to wait for my chance.

Almost as if the little dragon could hear me plotting against him, he stirred again and pulled his shortened foreclaw to his head in a melodramatic gesture. "I feel myself slipping away. Is that a light I see?"

Verte bopped him on the snout and ambled away. "Be

quiet, you ninny, or I'll turn you into a pair of earrings." Her voice faded down the hall.

Most of the crowd had dispersed. The final few stragglers looked at me with the all-too-common look of fear mixed with trepidation. Pix 'em. They were just servants. It wasn't like their opinion mattered.

Only one remained, watching me with open curiosity. He looked to be in his late teens or was magically enhanced to appear so. He could have been a hundred for all I knew. I'd never seen him before in my life. He was handsome enough, for a commoner, even in his worn leather pants and cracked work boots. A foreigner, his hair was unruly and dark auburn, which complemented his tanned but dirt-smudged complexion, though the tall, dark stranger vibe was ruined by his piercing pale blue eyes.

Well, I'd had enough of being a sideshow for the day. "If you're the new gardener, the hedges are overgrown and in need of a trim." I pointed in the direction of my father. "While you're there, you can help the king with the wisps."

The young man's expression clouded over, but he didn't move.

I stamped my foot and pointed more forcefully. "Off with you. Courtyard's that way. Be sure to clean those awful boots before coming back in."

"Someone told me I'd find a princess of great worth here. One with the strength to be the hero this realm needs." He stared at me with those unsettling blue eyes. They were cold, like ice water—made me shiver from head to toe. Then his gaze seemed to search even deeper. Finally, he looked through me, like I was nothing.

In brisk steps, he strode across the marble to the courtyard. But before crossing the threshold, he turned back to glare at me with his lip curled ever so slightly. "It seems she was mistaken."

Just like that, I had been sifted, weighed, and found wanting.

I felt my own lip curl in response. *How rude!* Who the Grimm was this peasant to judge me? I was wearing a Glenda original. Original! Not some fairy-godmother knockoff worn by those servant girls turned royal. I was a crown princess, for the love of fairy, and *no one* dismissed me.

Before I could put the boy in his place—down in the dirt, where he belonged—a clatter came from behind, making me nearly jump out of my shoes. I checked and was relieved that Sterling had simply dropped his sword. By the time I looked back, the gardener was gone.

After stowing his blade, Sterling held up his shield, not in defense of the entrance but so he could look at his reflection. "Clearly he's blind and doesn't know what he's talking about."

I didn't ask for Sterling's opinion, but it made me feel better.

Until he opened his mouth again.

"Worth, *pffft*. I mean, look around at all the jewels. Your palace has everything you could ever want. Honestly, I don't know what you're fussing about. Why would anyone want to leave?"

Because a cage is still a cage, no matter how big or glittering the bars are.

And I would find a way free, no matter the cost.

"Rule #43: Beware of strangers bearing gifts—especially little old ladies and cute kids."

—*Definitive Fairy-Tale Survival Guide, Volume 1*

3

When You Hex Upon a Star

E ven though I was in trouble, princess protocol required me to attend the ball. Nobody said I had to be on time though. Since I arrived fashionably late, the celebration was already in full swing.

Everyone had dressed in their finest, myself included. I'd used my StoryExpress card to buy a gown and matching cardigan shrug spun from platinum; it was softer than silkworm wings. Best of all, it was self-sizing, so the dress would fit the same before and after I made the rounds at the buffet. The couture fashion was a one-of-a-kind and practically cost my firstborn, but it was totally worth it.

But as usual, the shoes really completed the look—limited

edition silver Hans Christian Louboutin slippers, with crushed rubies covering the sole and two-inch heel. They'd been a Muse Day gift from Verte and made my feet tingle with happiness. Very few things in the world couldn't be fixed with a new pair of shoes.

Unfortunately, my mother's ire was one of those unfixable things.

I hurried past the base of the dais, hoping my parents wouldn't notice my late arrival. They did but, as usual, were too busy greeting royals and dignitaries to make time for me. For once I didn't mind though. Between the dragon incident and now, my mother had sent three page boys to fetch me, each servant more insistent than the last. I'd ignored them all, pretending to be asleep when they had yelled through my door. Whatever Mother wanted to talk about, I guarantee I didn't want to hear it.

On my way to the center of the room, I waved at Rapunzel, one of the few princesses who wasn't half bad. After all, she was a former shut-in herself. She didn't notice me, since she was busy untangling her hair from some pugnacious lady's mountain of éclairs. Above them, the will-o'-the-wisps tried to get away in their crystal balls, but the gold chains held them tethered around the wisps' middles. Their agitated flittering made the light shimmy and sparkle around the room.

In particular, the wisps' glow bounced off the foil ornaments, making the Story Spruce look like it had been dusted with glitter. I couldn't help but be drawn to it, and reached for one of the twinkling stars.

Spelled

The smell of incense overpowered the tree's wintery scent as a deep male voice whispered in my ear, "You don't need one of those to make your dreams come true."

I pivoted sharply on my heels and somehow ended up in a stranger's arms.

"Pardon me," I demurred politely and tried to take a step back. When his arms stayed firm, I said, "I'm steady. You can let go now." After that didn't work, I threw princess niceties aside with a "get off" and pushed him away.

I didn't get very far.

"A beautiful jewel such as yourself shouldn't be alone in a corner. Dance with me and shine." The anonymous Prince Smarming didn't wait for permission before twirling me onto the dance floor in time to the music. Other girls around us swooned with dreamy expressions, like they too hoped to be swept off their feet.

Understandable, since the grabby stranger looked pretty good—okay. Who was I kidding? He was gorgeous in his finely tailored suit that even I couldn't find fault with. His golden hair somehow seemed windswept, even without a breeze. And when he smiled, his sapphire-blue eyes twinkled, and his cheeks had dimples big enough to keep your gems in.

I still wasn't interested.

Though I'd never met the man before, I'd met his scent. Ever since my parents started playing matchmaker, I'd received an avalanche of love letters all doused with the same noxious sandalwood-and-rose cologne. After the first hundred, I asked Father to make the hounds guard my window to scare off the carrier doves.

I vaguely remembered the guy's name, but mostly I thought of him as *stalker*. "Look, McWhiz or something."

"I'm flattered you made the connection, even though I've been unable to introduce myself in person until now. However, the name is Mick, the Magnificent Wizard of—"

"It doesn't really matter," I interrupted. "For one, you're way too old for me. And since you're not a prince, you're not eligible to be a suitor anyway. So you can stop with the creepy fan mail."

A quick frown marred Mick's face before reversing; he blinded me with his pearly whites. "That was rather rude for a lady, but I'll forgive it this time, since I've a keen interest in you, young Dorthea of Emerald."

"That's nice," I said sarcastically and yanked on my hand, but the action only seemed to make him hold me tighter.

"You remind me of someone I used to know."

"Good, then go dance with her."

"That's not possible." He faltered on the three count of the waltz. "I made a mistake and let her slip through my fingers."

History was about to repeat itself. Mick's clinginess made it that much easier to "accidently" step on his shiny, gold-colored shoes.

Hard.

While he gasped and reached for his injured foot, I slipped away and out the ballroom doors into the courtyard.

I found a quiet place in the very back of the gardens, among the agave lilies and a few wisps that Dad seemed to have missed. The lilies were my favorite flowers, even though the blossoms came from a prickly cactus. Unfortunately, their beauty was marred because all of the nearby topiaries were so overgrown that the lion more closely resembled a hedge hippo than the lean and ferocious king of beasts.

Apparently, the gardener was not only rude, but also horrible at his job.

I wandered over to take a closer look and catalog all his mistakes; I'd already started a mental tally of all his faults, so that next time he crossed my path, I'd be prepared to return his previous insult. With interest.

My list-making ended abruptly. I was no longer alone in the leafy menagerie. A little girl stood in the moonlight, her skin pale as a china doll's, her hair sparkling like spun silver. Taking a step toward me, she nearly tripped on her too-large pewter gown. The wobble made the huge fire opal necklace she wore swing wildly across her chest.

"Are you lost?" I asked, stooping low just in case her dress-up clothes tripped her up again. "What's your name?"

"Emerald Princess, just who I was looking for." Her voice tinkled like broken crystal. "I'm an intern with the Union of Fairy Godmothers, and I have a present for you." The little girl smiled brightly and extended her hand. When she opened it, there was a delicate, white object inside.

While I was not the kind of girl to pass up any kind of gift, unless the union recently started using munchkin labor, the child was fibbing. But I remembered making up things at that age too, trying to get someone to play with me.

I went along with her game and gingerly picked the gift out of her palm, hoping it would at least be jewelry or something nice. Looking closer, the white seemed to be ivory but just broken pieces stuck together into a crude ball kind of shape. Something was inside as well. It was not ribbon—too thin. Perhaps silver thread. No chance this came from Blooming Dales. The child had probably made it herself.

"Um, thanks. This looks…" *Terrible. Chintzy.* "Like someone worked hard to make… What exactly is it?"

"It's a Muse Day wishing star, made just for you. But you can't show anyone," she said with a serious face.

I placed the "star" gently into the pocket of my silk shrug; I could ditch it when she wasn't watching. "I'll keep it out of sight."

"Good," the kid said, sounding satisfied at my promise. "Wish on it well, so you'll get exactly what you deserve."

Before I could ask what she meant by that, the girl vanished—thin-air style.

Maybe she had a bit of fairy godmother in her after all.

4

Hate at Second Sight

Where the spell did she go?" I asked as if the night air might answer.

"Are you blinder than all three mice? I'm right here," Verte answered and ambled toward me, her emerald staff making a *thunk-shuffle-shuffle* sound.

"Not you, the… Oh never mind."

Tonight Verte wore her finest black muumuu with a matching pointy, and slightly crinkled, hat. She was also decked out in magic, from her staff to a silver belt inset with a giant emerald, intricately carved into the shape of an eye. The belt has given me nightmares since I was five, when I finally got the courage to wink at it—and it winked back.

"I've been asked to inform you that the king and queen want to introduce you to a new prince. There, consider yourself informed." Task finished, Verte shuffled away, grumbling in low tones. "One of the most powerful sorceresses in all of story, reduced to a secretary, of all bubbling…"

She thumped her emerald cane against the stones that paved the garden paths. The stones brightened and glittered, illuminating the way back to the ballroom.

Fairy fudge. I should've known that's what all those messengers were about. I hurried to catch up with Verte. "So, who is it this time?"

"Who's on what time?" Verte said absently, focusing on a slight rustle in the bushes.

I swear, I've known cats that had longer attention spans than Verte. "The prince. Who's the royal reject they want me to meet now?"

"There." Verte's hand struck out between my legs and under the bush at a speed that shouldn't be achievable by hunched old ladies. I squeaked in surprise as she drew back with a frog in hand. It uttered a pathetic and alarmed croak in protest. Verte studied the frog and then nodded in apparent satisfaction, turning her focus back to me.

"Is that the prince?" If so, he was on his own. There was no way in spell I was going to let my first kiss be with an honest-to-fairy-godmother slime ball.

Verte made a rude noise. "Don't be addled. This is Rexi, the kitchen girl. She shorted me on my frog legs yesterday.

Had to get 'em another way." She shoved Rexi under her hat. "Your prince and one true love is inside." She puckered her lips a bit and waggled her hairy caterpillarlike eyebrows.

I screwed up my face. "Mother of Grimm!"

It was an extremely un-princesslike curse, one that could have gotten me turned me into Rexi's froggy friend for a week. I didn't care; I had bigger fairies to fry. Up until now, I had been dragging my silver-and-ruby heels back toward the party, but this had to stop. I began a brisk and determined stomp down the cobbled walkway.

Behind me, Verte breathed heavily and clip-clopped at a frantic pace, trying to keep up. "Wait one newt's tail, Dot. I'm not two hundred anymore."

The childhood nickname gave me pause, just like it always did. But I stopped dead when a faraway look crossed her green face and the emerald eye turned cloudy. The air filled with the smell of overbaked bread, her signature magical scent—sure signs she was seeing something that no one else could. Which usually meant trouble.

"The pages are turning and there is more at stake than one girl's happiness. You'll have to make a choice and someone will lose. So for Grimm's sake, use your head." She gave a resigned huff and bonked my forehead with her staff.

I *really* hated when she did that, went all "fortune cookie" on me. As if I didn't have enough to worry about.

Frustrated, I jammed my fists into my pockets in an attempt to calm myself. A sharp poke rewarded my efforts. The child's gift, still inside my cardigan, apparently had jagged edges that cut my palm. Ruby-red drops of blood stood in stark contrast to the brilliant white of the star.

The wind picked up slightly and chills inched their way up my spine. Cue creepy feeling that I was being watched— and not just by the frog, who was giving me the evil eye from under Verte's hat. I looked around, hoping to find the boogeyman that had caused my chills. Sure enough, staring at me through the ballroom window was quite possibly the most fearsome creature in all the realm—my mother. She shot me a look from atop her gold- and jewel-encrusted throne, which practically screamed that her patience was thinner than my father's hair.

Leaving Verte behind, I wove my way through the party, which was well past its prime. I had a little trouble getting by Snow White's little friends floundering around the punch bowl. One of them was trying to pry off Cindy's glass slipper. I'm not sure if he wanted to play prince charming or try on the high heel himself.

Once I maneuvered past them, I walked up the plush red carpeting, and my queenly mother ushered away all the lingering servants with a wave of her royal hand.

Standing up straight, I squared my shoulders and put all those years of princess training to good use. I hoped. "Mother, Father, I must insist that you stop all of this prince nonsense," I started. Clear, concise, and with authority. "After tonight, there's no point in inviting any more of them to the palace."

Before going on, I looked to my dad first to see how I was doing. If rubbing your temples with a grimace was a good thing, I was set. Mom's expression was more difficult to decipher—part bemused, part shark.

She rose from her throne and stalked toward me. "I agree. In fact, that's what I wanted to talk to you about all afternoon."

"Really?" I squeaked.

She placed an arm around my shoulders. "Yes. You see, that love at first sight you hear naive princesses go on about is not real."

Wow, two *talks* in one day. This must be a record. But as long as it got me what I wanted, I'd bear it.

Her voice turned soft. "True love is a lot like those lilies you favor. At first glance, it can be prickly and ugly. But with time and care, a precious blossom can grow. Unfortunately, we have neither at the moment."

I wasn't really sure where this was going. "So just to be clear, you don't expect me to fall crown over heels for one of these princes I just met?"

"Correct. But civility and an open mind make a very good start." The queen spun me around until I faced a young man with blue eyes. Not sapphire, like the stalker's—this color blue was much colder. Like ice water. The rest of his expression looked frosty to match.

"You!" I stomped toward him. He'd changed his clothes and combed his hair a bit, but I was still definitely staring down the gardener from before.

"Yes, and most unfortunately you as well." He sighed and crossed his arms. "After meeting you earlier, I'd hoped you had a twin sister with a better temperament."

My mother's cough sounded an awful lot like a laugh. "I see you've already met Prince Kato. That should make this a lot easier."

"Or harder," Father mumbled.

"Did you all drink the punch? Just look at him. This guy is no royal. Unless he's Lord of the Stableboys or something." I corrected my previous judgment and wrinkled my nose since, up close, he smelled more like animal musk than dirt.

The air around him cooled, and with almost no movement, his posture changed. He hadn't grown an inch, yet the *prince* towered over me with a wry smirk. "Then you'd better get used to being Lady of the Stableboys."

I turned to my mother, hoping for an explanation, but knowing I wasn't going to like it.

She sighed heavily and held her head like she was getting a migraine. "Perhaps you understand why I tried to do this earlier in a more private setting." She turned her glare at Kato. "The king and I had hoped to *gently* let everyone come to terms with the idea—"

"That would change nothing," the prince said, daring to cut the queen off. "The wedding is in one month and I will return the day before. She has that much time to get used to it."

I couldn't breathe. "Wedding...month?" I managed to wheeze out.

No way. I would rather lick a toad. I would let a wicked old hag bake me into gingerbread before I married this son of a basilisk who had the gall to look amused while I hyperventilated.

Kato motioned to a nearby footstool. "You should sit down before you fall over and embarrass yourself further."

My palm was in the air before I had even made a conscious decision to smack the smug off his face.

But it never landed.

His grip felt strong around my wrist. His hand was chapped and rough—from hard labor, I'm sure. And his fingernails were black. Not painted black. Actually black. One of them was even broken off in a contemptuous lack of good hygiene.

"You are a disgusting beast," I snarled.

Instead of holding me off, he yanked me closer and lowered his lips to my ear so only I could hear what he was saying.

"And you are a useless princess who knows absolutely nothing of the real world. You would be the very last person I'd choose to chain myself to. But apparently both our kingdoms—no. The whole realm needs this alliance, so what we want doesn't matter. I will do what I have to do, regardless of my personal feelings, and *you will* do the same. So sit down, grow up, and start acting like the kind of princess your people deserve." He snapped off the last syllable and abruptly let go at the same time so that I stumbled backward.

That was it. Politics or not, he was going down.

I launched myself at the prince, and the next thing I knew, my feet were in the air and my father's arm was around my waist, most likely preventing an interkingdom incident. He hauled me back and dumped me unceremoniously on his oversized throne.

"If you'll excuse us for a moment, Prince Kato," Mother said while Father held me down. "I need a word with my daughter."

"By all means." The prince bowed low and retreated. "Perhaps you will have more luck."

"What has gotten into you, young lady?" my father demanded in a hushed yet urgent tone, a stern look frozen on his face—a look I was used to seeing from my mom but not from him. He was usually the nice one.

I made a big, round gesture meant to imply *everything*. "What is that beastly prince talking about with alliances, and how could I be engaged anyway? I never agreed to anything. I'm pretty sure betrothal involves both an asking and an acceptance."

My mother chose to respond. "There was. Prince Kato explained why he needs you, and in your absence, we accepted on your behalf."

"What?!" My jaw dropped. This made no sense. Why would he need me? He didn't even like me. Both he and my parents were out of their fairy-lovin' minds. Out loud, I said, "Is that even legal?"

My mother scoffed and pointed to her emerald crown. Oh yeah. The queen of the Emerald realm could do whatever she glam well pleased. "Once we explain everything to you in detail later—"

"No, I want to know now!" If my *fiancé* (bleh) could interrupt her, then so could I. "What's so important that nobody cared how I would feel?"

Father at least had the decency to look mildly ashamed. "Well, you see, it's rather complicated. But we figured you wouldn't mind, since you never showed any interest in the other princes—"

"Maybe I have no interest in getting married. To anyone. Ever. I mean, look how well yours turned out. You do everything she tells you, and then go hunting for weeks to hide while we're stuck in this gilded cage. No thanks. If I want to boss someone around, I'll get a dog."

Immediately I knew I had gone too far. Even if both my parents hadn't gasped from the barbs of my sharpened tongue, my own heart was ashamed to beat within my chest. Before I could take it back, my mother hardened her face and gave me the look she was famous for—the one that caused grown men to fall on their knees and beg forgiveness before they were sentenced to death.

Her nose came within an inch of mine. "Contrary to your spoiled little beliefs, this is not all about you. This alliance is necessary for the safety of the entire realm. If, as crown princess, you do not feel a responsibility to protect your kingdom, then by Grimm, you will follow the rules of this land and obey your queen."

What started out as a rumble in my mother's throat had ended in a roar. Before, only those close to the thrones could hear what was going on; now, everyone in the room went quiet and still as statues.

My face heated—from shame, anger, humiliation, frustration... Pick one. There had to be a way out of this. Tears threatened along the edges of my lashes, but I willed them away. I'd rather be boiled and feathered than let them all see me cry.

Every eye turned to me as I rose to regal height with my nose ever so slightly in the air. On the outside, I was as cold and unfeeling as a block of ice. Inside, a fire of indignation burned brighter and hotter than the three suns.

I walked away from my parents. Each step brought me closer to a confrontation with the prince, who stared at me with pity now, instead of his usual disdain.

I searched for something, anything, to ground me and keep me from running away. Once again, the twinkling stars on the Story Spruce caught my eye. Wishing had never worked before, but then again, I'd never been this desperate. With the tree too far away, I reached in my pocket for the next best thing. My hand clenched around the child's star, the earlier cut flaring to life.

I wish I didn't have to do this, that the rules and everything else governing this stupid world would just disappear, and I'd never have to listen to my parents ever again.

The ache in my hand shifted from a prickle to a burn. I pulled it out of my pocket to take a closer look. It was glowing. Well, my hand wasn't glowing, but the star was. I opened my palm, and rays of light shot out from the gift. Dots seared my vision.

I was light blind. Unfortunately, I could still hear, but the noise made me wish I was deaf as well.

Glass cracking. Someone screamed. And roaring?

What in Grimm's name was going on?

"Rule #23: If you keep a storybook villain talking long enough, they will never fail to spill all the details of their evil plan. Some might even draw you a diagram."

—*Definitive Fairy-Tale Survival Guide, Volume 2: Villains*

A Nightmare Is a Wish Your Heart Makes

When my vision cleared, I had no idea where I was. Surely it could not be the same party. It looked like a war zone. The floating chandelier had crashed and shattered on the dance floor, freeing the now-dark floating orbs. People ran madly for the exit. Some were being chased by pickax-wielding dwarves, to say nothing of the ogres. The floor was littered with frogs. Hopefully they weren't enchanted princes, because some of them were getting squished by the mob.

I looked around for familiar faces. The beautiful people I had known since birth had changed or twisted into things nearly unrecognizable. Rapunzel remained by the treat tables, her hair now lying completely in the éclairs, with not a strand atop her bald head. By the punch bowl was a giant pumpkin—wearing glass slippers. A ferocious growl drew my gaze to the back of the room, where a hairy beast wore a yellow ball gown. I tried to block out the memory of Beauty in that dress earlier this evening.

Shutting my eyes, I shoved the star back into my pocket and willed everything to go away. This had to be a nightmare. Any minute now, I was going to wake up in bed, under my golden-goose down comforter. There would be no party, no beasts, and no engagement.

I needed to wake up. Then I needed therapy.

What was it that you're supposed to do—pinch yourself? Somebody did it for me. My eyes snapped open from the needle-sharp pricks to my toes. "Ow! That…"

A little ball of fur chewed on my slippers, not caring that my feet were still inside. I'd never seen another creature like it. It had the auburn-colored body of a lion cub, but it also had nubby horns, wings, and a dragon's tail. Its little black talons scratched at my leg; then it stared at me with accusatory ice-water blue eyes.

"No pixing way! Prince Kato?"

The look of disdain the little fuzz bucket gave me was all the proof I needed.

This was all too crazy to be real, but the pain debunked the whole nightmare idea. But maybe there was an upside to this. There was no way I could marry Prince Kato now. I just had to show my parents…

Where were my parents?

They were gone. The only signs they'd ever been there were their two emerald crowns still spinning on the ground.

Nothing else mattered. I'm not sure how long I stood there frozen—seconds, minutes, hours. I was semi-aware of Kato tugging my gown and growling. *Too bad, runt.* My attention stayed focused on the spot where I'd last seen my parents.

Until the clapping.

My head reared in surprise. The sound sliced through the chaos, clear and crisp and completely out of place. Making her way up to the dais was the little girl from the garden. The opal necklace flashed with brilliant orange and red streaks against her pale skin.

She ceased her clapping long enough to scoop up my mother's fallen crown and place it on her head. But it was much too large and fell down over her eyes and ears.

My back stiffened automatically in response. Nobody touched my parents' stuff. "Freeze, you freaky munchkin. You've got two seconds to drop my mother's crown."

"I suppose this child has outlived its usefulness," she said in that broken-crystal voice. Her eyes narrowed and flashed silver; they were slitted like a serpent's. Her lips set into a thin line while she made some complicated hand gesture and uttered a few words under her breath. Then she disappeared into a puff of metallically specked gray smoke.

When the smoke cleared, instead of a child, a tall, lithe woman stood in front of me, her oversized pewter gown fit like snakeskin now. The woman still resembled the kid, with her porcelain-pale skin and silvery hair, but she was all grown up, and her ageless beauty was mesmerizing. Looking at her was like being hypnotized by a siren—right before she capsized your ship.

Kato was not impressed. He gave a low grumble in his throat that snapped me out of my stupor.

"Who the spell are you, and what did you do with my parents?" I demanded.

The woman ignored my question and casually pulled a looking glass out of thin air, admiring her reflection in it. After her magical growth spurt, the crown fit perfectly.

"You may call me Queen Griz," she finally answered with a satisfied smile. She stopped preening and focused her attention to me. "Thank you for cracking open the barrier, by the way. I've been meaning to stop by for ages but never had the chance until now. It's such a shame I have to kill you. You would have made an excellent villain. After all, you've caused more damage in one afternoon than most henchmen do in a lifetime. And I didn't touch your parents. The blame for their loss lies squarely on your shoulders." She punctuated the *your* by pointing the mirror in my direction.

Instinctively, my body recoiled from her and her accusations. "Liar," I snarled. "I have no magic."

"Tsk, tsk." Griz let go of the mirror, where it stayed suspended as if held by strings. Now that her hand was empty, she made a few more hand gestures, and I felt my cardigan lift.

Panicked, I held my clothes down, afraid she was trying to magically strip me. But she wasn't interested in swiping my designer clothes to go along with the stolen crown—just the contents of my custom-made pockets.

The star that Griz's previous incarnation had given me floated up and away, into the air. As if some glamour had been pulled away, I saw the gift as it really was—not a poorly made child's craft project but a grisly magical artifact.

"Bone, hair, and blood. I hadn't factored in the blood. The star should have just killed you outright as the cost for granting the first shallow wish that came to mind, but whatever's in your veins protected you and reflected the hex outward a hundredfold. Little wish, big consequences." She smiled wickedly and flung the star back at me.

I caught it just before it smashed into my face. The word *wish* echoed in my ears. I hadn't wished for this, not really. All I had wanted was a way out of the stupid arranged marriage. I was just tired of the rules, tired of being told what I could and couldn't do.

I'm absolutely sure I hadn't wished for this disaster.

An ill-worded wish is worse than a curse, the old adage whispered in my mind.

Not helping, I thought back. It would be okay. I'd just take it back. That's how these things worked. I closed my eyes and gave it a try. When I reopened them, my world was still in pieces.

Maybe the dumb thing needed more juice. I squeezed the star and allowed the jagged part to cut my skin again. Then

I shook it for good measure. That always helped when my spellphone was on the fritz. "I wish to unwish it."

Nothing happened.

Hunched over in high-pitched, off-key laughter, Griz fell back and collapsed on my mother's throne. "Oh, you are just too precious. You can't take it back. You've already ripped the fabric of magic. The threads of fate are unraveling as we speak. Even if I were so inclined, I'd have no idea where to begin stitching it back together." She wiped tears of mirth from the corners of her eyes.

My heart broke. Add it to the list of things that couldn't be stitched back together.

Glancing around for some means of escape, I could see that the room was mostly cleared. None of the other guests who had stuck around seemed inclined to help me. Beauty looked ready to eat me herself.

Griz stood up again and smoothed her dress before advancing on me. Making a dramatic show of large, circular movements with her arms, she gathered a mercuric ball of lightning. "Finally, it is time for the House of Emerald to fall."

"Why?" I said, stalling for more time, stepping slowly in reverse. It was a dumb question, but the bad guy *always* takes time to explain their whole wicked plan, giving the hero a chance to save the day.

Apparently, that rule of story had disappeared as well.

"Nothing to worry your pretty little head over. You won't have it long enough," she said and hurled the stormball.

My life flashed before my eyes, and sadly it looked a lot like an infomercial, since my existence had been mostly filled with things—jewelry, shoes, dresses, shoes. Very few people. Mom, Dad, Verte… "Kato!"

I tripped over the little fur ball, and my feet went flying. As I landed on my royal derriere, the stormball sailed harmlessly overhead.

Well, harmless to me. Not so much for the north wall. It was toast.

Looking annoyed but still deathly determined, Griz raised her arms again to gather the silver lightning.

Her lightning wouldn't miss twice, meaning my time was up. Kato knew it too. He let out a high-pitched whine and scratched my hand with his paw.

"Sorry," I said. It was inadequate, but it's all I had. I closed my eyes and waited for oblivion to claim us.

It didn't. Griz gave a frustrated wail.

Opening one eye tentatively, I saw a shimmering green film forming a wall between me and Griz. The silver storm glob trickled down it.

"Well, don't just sit there, pup. Get. It's not like I can hold off the Gray Witch all day."

Verte stood behind me with her emerald staff held out in front of her, a bead of sweat forming on her slightly mustached upper lip. Whatever magic she was doing was difficult and probably wouldn't last long.

I stood up and ran over to her, about to burst with

41

questions. Griz flung balls and sharpened lightning bolts more quickly now, trying to break the shield. Verte flinched with each blow. I tried to help steady her, but she shook me off.

"Why are you still here? Run. Leave the palace," Verte said irritably.

My body jerked like I'd been slapped. Leave the palace? The idea of actually being ordered to do so was inconceivable. "What about the curse? Where will I go?"

"Your only hope is the spring over the rainbow." Verte nodded over her shoulder, toward the hallway. "Rexi will help get you there. Then wait someplace safe nearby it and I'll find you."

I hadn't seen the girl standing in the hall. Short, blond hair poked out every which way but down. My escape guide didn't look too excited about her new job. She stuffed her fists into her trousers, eyes narrowed and jaw set. But then she nodded in agreement and motioned for me to join her.

For so long I had pined for freedom from these walls, but now I was hesitant to take it.

Of course, the crack forming in Verte's green wall made me a little less hesitant.

Making sure not to trip over the broken debris, Kato and I ran toward the girl and away from Griz.

From behind me, Verte yelled a few final words of advice. "Stay away from fire. Use your head. And for Grimm's sake, *don't lose your shoes.*"

That stopped me in my tracks. I loved my shoes, but come on. Priorities. I was about to say something when another of Griz's stormballs smashed through Verte's shield, causing part of the ceiling to collapse.

Right. Priorities. Escape now. Questions later.

From the hallway, I heard Griz scream, "I'll get you, my princess. And your little fur ball too."

"Rule #74: When escaping into the wilderness, be sure to pack your magical bag with clean undergarments. And bread crumbs."

—Definitive Fairy-Tale Survival Guide, Volume 3: Enchanted Forests

6

There's No Place Like Home

After running to my room, the servant girl dove under my bed and grabbed a wicker basket in the name of packing provisions.

"How do you know about my snacks?" The stash was supposed to be a secret. It was stuffed 'round the clock with my favorite treats—you never knew when you might want some midnight cake.

She stopped her frantic pace a split second to roll her eyes at me. "Just how do you think that basket gets stocked? Magic?" With a disgusted huff, she opened the lid. "Half-full, even though I stocked it this morning. It'll have to do."

The click in my brain was almost audible. Rexi…the kitchen girl. "Weren't you just a frog?"

"Yeah, well, thanks to you and your friends, it's been a busy night." Her point was emphasized by the continued crashing from the ballroom. She sighed and started to leave.

"Where are you going?" I made a move to follow her.

She scoffed audibly and looked me up and down. "You think you can run in that dress? You'd get caught before we made it ten troll's lengths. I'm going to swipe that green wench's Dust Devil."

Last year, Verte had upgraded her old broomstick for the state-of-the-art vacuum. All her friends at Swampy Acres Home for Retired Witches had one.

"You have exactly three minutes to pack whatever you can carry. Then I'm leaving." Rexi shook her head slightly, expression tight. "I'm not going to die so you can stuff a few extra jewels down your corset."

"That would be a dumb place to put…" Rexi couldn't hear me; she was already halfway down the hall—a prime example of why I don't like to hang out with other people.

"Doesn't she know that's what purses are for?" I muttered to myself and grabbed my enchanted handbag. Best accessory ever—the size of a book on the outside with the space of a small storage unit on the inside.

I stood looking around my room for a moment. What should I take? I'd never stayed at a friend's for a sleepover, never been on vacation. I'd only seen the outside world through magic mirrors.

The battle for the ballroom raged on. There was more banging and the sound of things breaking and cracking. At this rate, the whole castle would be glittering rubble in a matter of minutes. A noise came from the closet floor. It was a cross between a growl, a whine, and a purr. At first glance, nobody was there—until I looked down, ankle level, and saw what looked like a mini-lion hiding from the witch—in my wardrobe. I couldn't know for sure what he was trying to say, but I had a decent idea.

"The answer is no. You're not coming with us. Go find your own parents."

The word *parents* ended with a sharp stab to the chest. I told myself they weren't gone. They were just missing. Missing I could deal with. *Missing* could be found.

More crashing from downstairs. Closer this time.

"Look," I said, bending down nose-to-muzzle with Kato. "Don't give me those puppy eyes. You are not a dog. I don't know what you are, but if you're not gone by the time I come back, I'll take you to the window and see if those wings are just for show."

Even at the size of a bread box, Kato still had the evil glare down pat.

"Good, glad we understand each other," I said dismissively and took my bag to the closet, shoving everything inside that wasn't nailed down or dry clean only. By the time I turned back around, the doorway was empty.

The floor rumbled beneath my feet.

Rexi ran back into my room, pockets bulging while lugging the heavy red vacuum. "Time to go."

She ran back to the bed to retrieve the food while I inspected the Dust Devil. "Are you sure this can carry the two of us?"

She snorted. "That blasted sorceress weighs more than us both combined." She hefted the basket. "But this thing weighs a ton. How can you keep eating all this and not get fat?"

Some things don't deserve a response.

Stepping onto the vacuum, I settled onto the front. Rexi moved in close behind. I tapped the top like I'd seen Verte do countless times.

Nothing happened. "Where the spell is the owner's manual for this contraption?" I muttered, looking around the red machine.

Footsteps.

Someone was coming up the stairs, and there was a fifty-fifty chance that it wasn't my Emerald Sorceress.

I've never been very lucky.

The Gray Witch rounded the banister. "Did you really think you could run fast enough or far enough to get away?" She was at the doorway now. There was plaster in her hair, and her dress was ripped in several places.

"On...on...where's the Grimm-galled on button?" I panicked.

"Hurry! Figure it out!" my backseat passenger shouted.

"If you thought you could do better, you should've driven."

"I'm going to enjoy this." Griz readied her stormball.

Oh, pix that.

I needed this contraption to work now! When in doubt, push every button in sight and then whack it for good measure. The vacuum began to rise. It also started living up to its name. Sparkling dust swirled around me in a cyclonic pattern. My things blew around the room. One of my boots hit Griz in the side of head, knocking her stormball off course.

The stray ball took out the west wall.

"All right. Exit point established. Now how do you steer this thing?"

Once again, when in doubt…

I hit the yellow button and the cyclone tripled in size. The vacuum pitched forward and took off. Rexi squished against me, pushing the handle deep into my stomach.

I would have liked to see Griz's angry face as we flew away, but everything not nailed down whirled around us and obscured the view.

Rexi's screaming I could hear though. "Slow down!"

And exactly how was I supposed to do that? The blasted vacuum wasn't working right, and the wind was too strong. Dust grit blinded me. I reached to push some more buttons.

Something snapped.

Before, we'd been going so fast that my cheeks felt like they'd been pushed back to my ears. Now my guts were twirling around like a jester's cartwheels inside my body.

Don't hurl. Don't hurl. The Dust Devil clunked and

sputtered. Within seconds, the cyclone stopped spinning—in midair. My stomach dropped. We were falling. *Don't die. Don't die.*

"Do something!" Rexi's nails pierced my shoulders.

With the ground approaching, I said a quick prayer to the Storymakers and ripped off the front plastic panel. The emergency vacuum bag inflated, acting as a parachute. I inhaled a deep lungful of dust, relieved at least that part still worked. *Thank Grimm.*

When I looked down, I noticed the specks on the ground were getting larger at an alarming rate.

I'd acted too late. We were going to crash.

I came to lying in mud. I knew all my body parts were attached because all of them hurt.

Groan.

That wasn't me.

"Get off me, you pixing cow!" Rexi's hands pushed at me roughly.

I took my time. And I might have *accidentally* shoved my elbows in her ribs trying to get up.

Once standing, I surveyed the plastic and metal debris around me. The Dust Devil was grounded—permanently. One of the clanking sounds I'd heard had probably been the wire thingy falling off. With my handbag inside. All my stuff, gone.

The godmother of luck hadn't totally abandoned us though; the food basket lay a few feet away. Grateful, I scrambled over to check the contents, to see what, if anything, had spilled during the flight.

When I opened the basket, I did not see bread, cheesecake, or even my emergency stash of Chocolate Wands with fudge and caramel centers. I saw tufts of fur and a pair of ice-water blue eyes. I was really starting to hate the color blue.

Flipping the basket over, I unceremoniously dumped Kato out on his horny little head. I shook the basket a few times, but only a couple of wrappers fell out.

Stunned, I plopped down in the muck. "You. Ate. Everything."

He burped.

Rexi pulled herself out of the mud with a slurping sound. "I'm gonna kill you!"

Looking like a swamp monster, Rexi chased Kato, trying to beat him to a bloody pulp. After a minute, she gave up and collapsed back to the ground. "Just so you know, when I get hungry, I have no qualms about eating you."

Kato answered by taking care of some business on a golden leaf fig tree.

Yet another item for his list of negatives. "Ugh, so disgusting." I shuddered and looked away.

Wait. Emerald Kingdom got its name from trees with green gems. We didn't have golden ones.

I jumped up, even though every muscle in my battered body protested. My head whipped around frantically while

I tried to get my bearings. Not a trace of the springy green meadows of my home. In the predawn hours, the sky brightened with purple and orange. Logos, the first sun, was just about to rise over the mountain range to the east.

We didn't have any mountains.

"Dear Grimm, we're not in Emerald anymore." I started to hyperventilate.

Rexi remained sprawled on her back. She barely opened an eye at my hysterics. "Duh."

It's a Big World After All

Sometimes the body works its own kind of magic. Take adrenaline, for example. In the heat of battle, a mortal wound feels like a scratch. A mother whose child is threatened has the strength of ten ogres. And a princess chased by a witch can abandon the only home she's ever known.

Adrenaline had kept me going and put a big piece of tape around the things that were broken. Now the rush was gone, and so was the stuff that held me together.

I fell apart.

My parents were gone. There was a good chance my home was a glittering green crater. I was out in the middle of nowhere with no food, water, or wardrobe change. Oh, and I was stuck with a snarky servant and an unwanted furry fiancé.

Through my tears, I gave Kato a look that would have done my mother proud. "I hate you. This is *your* fault. I only made a wish to escape you. My life was just fine before you showed up with your freaky black fingernails. Now everything's ruined. All my stuff is gone with the wind."

"Typical." Rexi stood up and brushed off the seat of her pants. "We're probably gonna die, and you're worried about losing the new spring fashions and blaming everyone else for your troubles."

I stood, infuriated at her uncaring attitude. "Excuse me? You can't talk to me that way."

She whirled around, hand on hip. "And why not? Are you going to throw me in the dungeon? Oh wait, you don't have one anymore."

I got in her face and looked down on her. "What is your problem with me?"

Her eyes got wide, her nostrils flared, and she pushed her finger right into my chest. "I don't have a problem *with* you. My problem *is* you. You and all your high-and-mighty storybook buddies. You think you're *so* special, that you can do or have anything you want. You don't care who wakes up at two when you want a snack, or how many elves it took to make those shoes you only wear once then throw away."

I knocked her hand away. "That's not true. I would never throw away shoes—"

"Ahhhh!" she interrupted and spun away from me. "That is exactly my point. How self-absorbed can one ditz be? It's all about *you*. Everything *you've* lost. What about everybody *you* just royally hexed? Not that I care, but fuzz ball here doesn't seem too happy with the new look *you* gave him."

My defenses immediately went up. This wasn't *my* fault. "But I didn't mean—"

Rexi threw her hands up. "Of course you didn't. Well, the road to hell is paved with the golden bricks of good intentions. And while I'm here yelling at you, we're sitting swans for the Gray Witch. So stop thinking about *you* and help me figure out where we are."

In my opinion, Rexi was being unnecessarily harsh, but she was right about one thing—if we didn't get moving, Griz would wipe us out.

While I had never been traveling, I considered myself something of an expert on precious metals and gems. "Midas is the only place where gold literally grows on trees," I said. The land of Midas was named after its mad king, who ran around turning everything into gold with his touch. For obvious reasons, it was scarcely inhabited. I didn't want to risk becoming a 24-karat statue either.

Rexi shook her head and reached into her pockets, then growled as she turned them out. They were empty. Stomping over to a tree, she snapped off a glittery branch and drew a makeshift map that looked an awful lot like a doughnut. But then again, maybe I was just hungry.

Running around, she collected broken bits of the vacuum to symbolize different kingdoms.

"This is where we started." She put Emerald in the doughnut center, using the Dust Devil's handle for the tower—then stomped on it a few times just to drive the point home. "Midas is on the very eastern edge of the Realm of Fairy Tales." She chucked the shiny engine fob on the outer doughnut rim.

"Yeah, I get Fable Channels on the telemirror. So what's your point?"

She drew a line from busted Emerald to chromed Midas. "It's too far. That would mean we moved through a dozen storybook settings in the space of a five-minute cyclone. Plus, Midas has huge golden forests because it rains there, like eleven out of twelve chapters."

Our landing spot had a few withered gold trees with rotting figs sprinkled across tons of faintly glittered dirt. It hadn't seen any water in ages, like someone had sucked the moisture out of the ground with a straw. The mud pit probably used to be a lake.

Hopefully this wasn't Midas, because if it was, I was a loooong way from home and the damage caused by Griz's cursed star stretched out much farther than I imagined. But no need to panic. I was the heroine in this story, so everything would get fixed somehow. I'd been good—mostly. I'd done my part and followed all the rules the Storymakers had laid out. The Emerald Sorceress would come to the rescue with my happy ending in tow.

I just needed to tolerate these circumstances until then.

"All right, Rexi. You're supposed to be my guide, so take me to this spring on the other side of the rainbow. Where is it?" I waved my hand toward her makeshift map, waiting for her to mark it out.

She snorted. "Like I'm supposed to know what that old bat was talking about? But when I see a rainbow, I'll be sure to toss you over it."

"So what exactly are we supposed do until we find it?"

"*Mrow Mgrow,*" Kato replied and started digging a hole, messing up Rexi's map while kicking up mud onto her breeches.

"If it gets cold, I can always make a fur coat." Rexi sneered down at him.

He flipped his spiked tail straight into the air in what could only be interpreted as an obscene gesture.

Rexi duplicated it in human form. "Right back atcha."

I sighed and thought back to what Verte had said on my way out of the ballroom. *Find a safe place somewhere over the rainbow. Stay away from fire. Use your head. Don't lose your shoes.*

Well, I still had my silver and ruby slippers, and I had no intention of risking the curse by getting anywhere near fire—so I was two for four. My head wasn't getting me anything but a migraine. And from the looks of this drought, I'd be waiting awhile before a rainbow showed up. So, by default: keep walking until I find a rainbow or until the Emerald Sorceress finds me, whichever comes first.

I was putting my jewels on the latter.

When I was little, I would force Verte into games of hide and seek by stealing her staff. She had an uncanny knack for finding me, so the games never lasted long. Usually her ability drove me batty and got me into endless trouble. Now I was counting on it to save the day. She would use that freaky emerald eye of hers to come get me. Though she was ancient now, back in her heyday, she was supposedly one of the most powerful sorceresses the Storymakers had ever created. She would know how to put everything to rights again.

Hopefully before I found out if there was any truth to the whole Emerald-curse thing.

Think happy thoughts. Uh, yeah right. Because there is so much to be happy about right now. Maybe I needed to try and make up happy thoughts. Daydreaming—my favorite pastime, next to buying stuff on the Castle Shopping Network.

I would stumble upon a Bibbity-Bobbity Boutique and Spa while I waited for Verte to deal with Griz. By the time I was done with a mani-pedi, it'd be time to go home. My parents would have found their way back from wherever by then. Ooooooh. Maybe I accidently sent them to a deserted island paradise. Or even better, to the spring Verte was going on about—like a hot spring resort. Good for them; they deserved a vacation.

A hand waved in front of my nose. "Hellooo? Anybody in there, or did you zone out for a mental shopping trip?"

Kind of, but I wasn't about to tell her that. "No," I said

and sniffed indignantly. "I was just thinking about finding a safe place so Verte can find us." It wasn't a total lie.

"Well, we better get going, then, though I wouldn't hold my breath on that one."

Rexi didn't know what she was talking about. The Emerald Sorceress would come. She had to.

Even before I was taller than a garden gnome, my mother was always busy running the kingdom, so Verte had been there to look after me. She was much better and more reliable than any prince.

I looked over at the proof of that last thought; Kato growled and pounced on a fallen tree.

Rexi rolled her eyes and walked away from us. "Hey, genius, it's a log."

I hurried after her, expecting Kato to follow, since I hadn't been able to get rid of him yet. But he didn't, and after about twenty yards, I stopped and looked back. He was still obsessing over the dumb log.

I tugged on Rexi's arm, pulling her to stop. "We can't leave him. He'll be troll chow by nightfall."

"And?" Rexi made no move to turn around. But she didn't keep going either. "He's your problem. You deal with him. Plus, I hear using pets as accessories is all the rage." She snorted and tossed a shiny chrome fob up into the air, then shoved it in her pocket.

She'd probably swiped that metal piece from the vacuum's corpse—and that fashion tidbit from the stack of *Fairy Vogue* in my room that managed to magically get smaller every time I added the latest issue. I suppose if my being tricked into that wish made him into a creature, I should make sure he didn't get turned into a meal. I could be the bigger person and take responsibility, even if the situation wasn't entirely my doing. Plus, after the things Kato said to me, a very wicked part of my heart would take an ironic joy in commanding *him* to sit.

As I walked back to get Kato, it dawned on me that, for the first time in my life, I had someone to protect. For the record, Sammy the salamander didn't count, may he rest in peace.

I stopped near Kato and patted my leg. "Come on, Kato. You may not look like it right now, but you're a prince. So stop this useless nonsense and act like it."

I'd chosen my words to goad him, but he didn't rise to the bait. He sat by the log with his head down, like he was hiding something. I looked closer.

Were those legs sticking out of his mouth?

"The Rule of Favor: Save a life and it's yours for the taking."

—Thomason's Tips to Ruthless Ruling

8

Lollipop Guild

I stomped my foot. "That is not a lollipop. Spit it out. Right now!" Where was a rolled-up scroll when you needed one?

Kato looked at me, and I could almost hear his raised eye whiskers say, *Make me.*

Sinking down, I worked on prying open his muzzle. "You just ate a week's worth of food." *Grunt.* "You're going…to get…fat." Ugh. For such a little thing, he had jaws of steel. Last-ditch effort. "It could be poisonous."

That got his attention. The hack he gave sounded exactly like Verte's cat when it coughed up a hairball. Instead of a wad of fur, out came a small, wooden person. It looked like the love child of a bug and a stick. I didn't know what it was, but I don't think it was slimy naturally. Most likely it was just covered in Kato slobber.

And it was not happy.

"Big-footed booby, good for glammed giants. Pix yourselves off to the ever after and fimfammed your dwarf-dunged…"

I pride myself on using colorful expressions when the occasion arises, but this tiny thing had a bigger vocabulary of swears than any person I'd ever met. When he got around to describing Tinkerbell's thong, my ears started to burn.

Disregarding the threat of poison, Kato lunged for the little man—and I say "man," because with that language, the bug had to be male. I moved a pinch faster and scooped Kato up before his jaws snapped the rude twig in half.

Earlier, I'd only been joking about Kato getting fat, but hauling him up around his middle, I noticed he was bigger—and heavier—than he'd been at the palace.

"Bad whatever-beast-you-are. Leave the fairy alone!" I exclaimed, struggling to keep a squirming Kato in my arms.

"Fairy? First your mutt thinks I'm a lollipop, and now you think I'm a *fairy*? Do you see any wings, you pixing, pox-ridden prat?" the man said rudely, with great indignation.

Though I was tempted to set Kato down and let him have his snack, this was the first sign of semi-intelligent life I had come across, and I needed answers.

Time to brush up on princess charm-school training.

Lesson #2: Always use your best manners when greeting an unfamiliar creature or person in a distant land. Rude princesses get turned to stone or reptiles much more often than polite ones.

"My sincerest apologies, sir. I meant no disrespect. I'm afraid I'm lost and have never come across one such as yourself. Could you please help me?" I batted my eyelashes in an attempt to appear damsel-in-distress-y.

Even twenty yards away, I could hear Rexi groan.

The bundle of fur under my arms stilled and looked at me, dumbfounded. His mouth hung open, and he blinked as if seeing me for the first time. Hey, I could be polite and have social skills when the situation called for it, though I was a tad out of practice, and I might have been laying it on a little thick.

The little man picked off some of the slobbery mucus and harrumphed. "Well, I'm a Bumpkin, and you're a buggin' primpitch. You'll get no help outta me."

Okay. Nice hadn't worked; it was time to get royal on his bumpy butt.

Crouching down to Bumpkin level, I spoke with the regal tone I'd heard my parents use when they were being official. "I invoke the Rule of Favor. I saved your life and now you are indebted to me. As payment, I demand you guide me to the rainbow spring."

The Bumpkin turned his back…and mooned me.

I so didn't need that white hairy bum burned into my retinas. Fine, if the rule of favor was out of service, I was not above a little intimidation. Desperate times called for less than ladylike measures.

The Bumpkin gave a high-pitched squeak when I snatched him from the log. "Look, you nasty little *fairy*. I asked nicely. I appealed to your honor. Let's try your survival instincts. You can help me, or you can play cat and mouse with Kato here." I dangled him over my furry companion's open maw.

"You wouldn't." His eyes narrowed, assessing me.

"Try me."

"I'll make you pay for this, hag bait."

"You and what army?"

As if on cue, the log started shifting and changing shape. What looked like knots in the wood unfolded and became more Bumpkins. Now I got it. They probably got their name because they looked like bumps on a log.

And that log was really bumpy.

Kato and I backed away from the swarm. One four-inch creature wasn't scary. Hundreds of the little buggers were another matter. Think wooden cockroaches. With sharp sticks. And pointy teeth.

A stinging bite from the Bumpkin in my hand startled me into dropping him.

"Charge!"

Within seconds, my legs were covered in Bumpkins. Kato tried to swat them like flies with his tail, but they were remarkably resilient. Definitely related to cockroaches.

For every one I brushed off, two more took its place. Aside

from the creepy-crawly feeling of little feet all over me, I was being stung repeatedly as well.

Great. I'd dodged stormballs and survived a vacuum crash, but now I was facing torture at the hands of magical bugs.

One of them had a stick aimed for my eye when a sharp whistle brought them to a halt. And just like that, it was over. The swarm of Bumpkins retreated, bowing in front of what remained of the log. The log shook and stood, the bark shivering and becoming a full gown. The twigs became arms and the largest knot became facelike. If I didn't miss my guess, I was about to meet the queen of the Bumpkins.

"Why have you woken me?" She spoke haughtily, like I was beneath her, even though she was less than a gnome's height.

I searched for an answer, but I was still blown away by the whole talking-log thing. Turned out, she wasn't talking to me anyway. The Bumpkin with the foul mouth, and I knew it was him because his pants were still in half-moon position, addressed his queen. The story he told was missing a few parts, but the guts were all there.

"And you attacked, even after she saved your life," Queen Bump said in a flat tone that gave no clue whether that was a good or bad thing.

"Well, she's—"

"*Silence.* I know exactly who she is. And if the rule of favor no longer compels, you should follow the will of your Maker." She turned away from Moony in what seemed like rebuke or dismissal.

That put her knobby gaze focused squarely on me. "I do not know the rainbow's current location. Leave my children be and go west. Under the metal spire, you will find Black Crow. She will take care of you."

Without any pleasantries, the queen folded into herself— her arms becoming twigs, her dress re-forming into bark. Her "children" gathered around her and resumed their places as bumps and knots. The last to do so was Moony. Before taking his place, he gave me a look full of scorn that threatened retribution.

"Well, that was easy." Rexi now stood right behind me.

"Easy? Where were you?"

Rexi's face colored, and she looked down at her sensible brown shoes. "I was coming...but it was over before I got here."

"Uh-huh." Kato and I wore matching expressions of disbelief.

"Whatever." She turned and stalked away. "I don't do bugs."

"Approach lost animals gently, so you don't scare them away. With the right touch, they'll follow you home forever."

—Bo Peep's Guide to Enchanted Animal Care

Bumpkins, Toadstools, and Puppies...Oh My!

A few hours' walk from the Bumpkins, my feet were killing me. I was used to wearing heels all the time—I lived in them—but this was the farthest I'd ever traveled, period. This was also the longest I'd ever gone without food. My stomach cramped around the nothingness. "I'm starving," I complained to no one in particular.

"Okay, well, I nominate you to find some food for us," Rexi said, still making sure to stay a few steps ahead.

I made a face at her green tunic. "Sure, I'll put that on my to-do list. Right under *find parents, fix magic,* and *try not to end the world in a big ball of fire.*"

"Well, if you're hungry, you can always try one of the figs.

They haven't killed your pet yet. Unfortunately." Rexi pointed to Kato, who was scarfing down more of the rotting fruit.

I wasn't that hungry.

Watching him whack the tree trunks with his spiky tail, I could see that my earlier observations had been spot on. He was getting bigger fast and wasn't a baby fuzz ball anymore. He was more like a gawky tween fuzz ball with paws the size of milk saucers. When he was done growing, he would be a big boy.

Rexi hollered from a little ways in front. "Hey, Dorkea."

I moved a little faster to hear better, and so I could smack her if the opportunity arose. "Excuse me…what did you say?"

Rexi coughed into her hand. "I said, 'Hey, Dorthea.'"

Yeah right.

"So I've always wanted to ask. What's the deal with that whole curse business anyway? Are you like a ticking time bomb now or something?" She matched my pace, then looked me up and down as if assessing my threat level.

She was the first servant to ever ask; everyone else had always kept their distance. Better safe than crispy, I suppose.

"It's possible." I gave her a sly smile. "So you probably better be careful and stop pixing me off."

Rexi snorted and rolled her eyes, her favorite mode of expression. "Bring it on. You look pretty harmless."

A blumerang bird flew directly between us, then stopped to stretch its gossamer wings on top of a giant purple-spotted toadstool a few yards away. Before it had a chance to take off again, the toadstool opened its cap and swallowed the bird whole. The only evidence that the bird had ever existed were two feathers floating to the base of the fungi.

Rexi laughed uncomfortably. I wondered if she was rethinking that whole "harmless" idea. I know I was.

I turned around, but something stood in my path. It was small, about the size Kato had started out as but definitely not the same type of creature. This one looked nearly identical to the golden retriever pups the game master raised in the kennels. It had its eyes down, its tail tucked under, and light yellow fur that looked so soft it begged to be touched.

Who could resist?

"Aww, aren't you just the cutest widdle thing?" I said, petting the pup. "Are you lost too, sweet pea?"

Kato made a gagging sound behind me.

I steadfastly ignored him. "Don't wisten to mean old Kato. He's just jealous 'cause he's a stupid beast and you're so much cuter."

Rexi made a gagging sound nearly identical to Kato's. "What is it with you and attracting useless furry things? Let's move. We're getting nowhere slow."

Whatever. I was a princess, supposedly a natural with small woodland creatures and the like—though I'd never figured out how to get any of the castle canaries to clean my room.

A distant rumbling snapped me to my feet. I looked to the sky. It was clear. Thunder heralded a storm. And a storm reminded me of…

Kato circled around me, growling as if he too sensed the

danger approaching. We'd just lost whatever lead the cyclone had given us, and now it was time to go. Rexi and I made eye contact.

"We need a place to hide." She looked over her shoulder. "There!"

There was a dense grove of golden fig trees. The leaves were fuller than the other trees so far, creating a shiny canopy. They could keep us out of view if the witch came from overhead.

Kato's growl pitched lower, turning more intense.

I turned back to grab the puppy and make a run for the trees, but Kato hadn't been growling at the sky.

He stood between me and the puppy, back arched in a protective stance. The puppy was still small and fluffy— except for its ginormous batlike wings. That, plus its glowing demon-red eyes kind of ruined the whole cuddly effect.

"What the hex?" Rexi shuffled back, colliding with me.

Extending its leathery, black wings, the pup howled up at the suns. A chorus of howls replied.

"Great. I think it just called for backup," I said, looking around for the rest of the pack.

Thunder rumbled through the sky again, closer this time. The pup continued to howl, giving away our position.

Turning to make a run for the forest, a tree exploded into flames directly to my right. Smoke tendrils curled from the puppy's nostrils as it hovered a few inches off the ground.

I sighed. "Of course it's *a fire-breathing*, flying demon puppy."

Rexi looked back and forth between Kato and the puppy. "No fair. Why did we get stuck with the defective sidekick whose only special power is eating things?"

The howls were getting closer, but we couldn't go anywhere until this puppy was neutralized.

The dog's belly expanded, most likely gathering enough air to barbecue us. This was it. I'd avoided fire my whole life, and this was how the curse would come true. I was about to become the Girl of Emerald, bathed in flames.

Faster than my eyes could track, Kato whipped around, using his barbed tail to smack the puppy into the air like a ball. The fur ball flew…right into the purple-spotted toadstool. The puppy didn't even have a chance to look surprised before the giant mushroom gobbled it up and burped out a spare piece of fluff.

"I stand corrected," Rexi admitted.

Astonished, I looked at our super-awesome sidekick. "Let me guess, you meant to do that."

Kato shrugged his feathered wings modestly.

The approaching howls broke off any further praise I might have given him. Looking to the sky, I could just make out the horde of flying puppies and their leader, riding on a thundercloud—the Gray Witch.

"We've gotta move," I said and sprinted past the flaming tree. The gold dripped off the leaves like wax from a candle.

The thunder boomed directly overhead. Once we reached the grove of figs, I figured we'd be safe and unseen.

One problem: you don't necessarily need to see something to destroy it.

Stormballs crashed through the golden canopy, creating large holes that allowed light to filter in. So far, they were way off target, but all it took was one lucky shot, right?

In between the booms of thunder, Griz cackled and taunted, "Come out, come out, wherever you are. I have a present for you."

Yeah, like that was going to happen. Did she think I would yell out, "Ooohh goodie, a present! Gimme, gimme"? I might be shallow, but I'm not dumb. The gift thing may have worked once, but if I fell for it a second time, I deserved to be zapped into oblivion.

Rexi motioned for me and Kato to stop. "Maybe if we stay put, Griz will keep flying ahead," she whispered.

Stormball after stormball crashed through the grove, then nothing. After a solid minute with no new strikes, I whispered, "Maybe she's moved on."

There was a slight rustle in the trees just behind us. I looked up and found tiny pinprick holes appearing in the canopy.

What in Grimm's name was going on now?

Stupidly, I went over to investigate. Face tilted to the sky, I felt a drop on my cheek. I hissed quietly in pain because it burned. Like acid. Somehow the witch was making it rain acid, and it was coming down through the trees. A yip right above me. So not Griz, but the puppies.

I really didn't want to think about where the acid was

coming from. I prayed it was drool. The alternative was too gross to think about.

The puppies spread out in a scatter pattern, making their acid melt through the trees. Rexi's eyes bugged out and she made weird hand signals.

I mouthed, *What?*

She exhaled heavily and shook her head. *We have to move*, she mouthed back.

Right then, some splatter landed on Kato's wing. With a mighty roar, Kato let the world know his pain.

And our location.

I didn't think; I just moved, shoving Kato out of the way. Milliseconds later, a stormball crashed in the exact spot where he had been standing.

"I see you," Griz singsonged directly above us on her cloud.

"Go!" Rexi grabbed my hand and took off.

The world became a blur of gold as leaves whipped past my face. The trees behind us burst into flames, driving us forward. The grove was getting lighter, a sure sign that it was coming to an end.

I pointed to the tree line in front of us. "Split up as soon as we're out!"

Rexi nodded. We broke through the trees, and I aimed to veer right. My foot hit air.

We had run off a cliff.

"*Rule #14: For protection, a princess should never carry something as unladylike as a sword. Kitchen utensils are handy in a pinch.*"

—*Definitive Fairy-Tale Survival Guide, Volume 1*

10

If I Only Had a Head

My dress plumed out around me, but it did nothing to slow my descent. Rexi and I fell like shrieking stones, still holding hands. Kato spread his wings and caught the wind.

I grabbed his paw and prayed to the Storymakers for a miracle. In answer to my prayer, we hovered for a moment. Then we sank again. Kato's wings weren't strong enough to support all of our weight.

I let go of him.

Spinning wildly, turning end over end, the force ripped Rexi and I apart.

In my somersaults, I caught glimpses of the earth below. It

was blue. My last thoughts before I hit were, *Hooray, water is better than jagged rocks,* and then, *I don't know how to swim.*

The air whooshed out of my lungs as I performed a spectacular belly flop. Momentarily stunned, my head became submerged. When my body decided to obey my brain's commands again, it was too late. The weight of my dress pulled me down as effectively as any anchor.

The water was cold, and my fingers started to freeze up. I struggled with the pearl buttons at my back. If I could only get this Grimm-forsaken dress off.

My chest burned. The desire to take a breath was nearly overwhelming. As my vision closed in, something hit the water with a big splash. Probably a stormball. Maybe it would get me before I drowned.

Just when I thought I would give in to the urge to inhale, something pushed me to the surface. I started breathing a half beat before my mouth met air. Coughing the water back out of my lungs, I noticed that my hacking echoed. It looked like I had emerged under a shelf in a canyon's wall.

Starting to sink again, I flailed around in the water for something to grab. My hand hit horn behind me. I grabbed it and turned in the water to see what I hoped was my rescuer. It was Kato. He hadn't flown off and left me. I wondered if his cannonball dive was the result of a failed attempt at flight or if it had been intentional when my head hadn't resurfaced. Didn't matter. On my mental score sheet, I had to add a plus column.

Rule of favor or not, I owed him my life.

Lightning cracked through the sky, electrifying the very air. Thunder boomed as evidence of Griz's temper tantrum. Out of sight, she screamed in rage from above. "Do yourself a favor and drown, little princess. Because that will be a much kinder fate than what you'll get the next time I find you."

A light spot in the dark water caught my eye. It was Rexi's blond head. She looked totally different with her hair plastered to her head instead of sticking straight up. "Let's not do that again, okay?" she said, panting and swimming toward us.

"Sounds like a plan." I grabbed her green sleeve and helped pull her to us. Each of us hanging on to one of Kato's horns, we floated down the river and kept ourselves hidden under the cliff's rocky shelf. An hour of floating later, both Griz and our hiding place were gone. The high canyon walls ended abruptly, the depth turning shallow as we floated up to a beach.

I desperately wanted to get out of the water. My skin was beginning to resemble the withered figs. Clawing through the sand, I hauled myself onto the beach. *Blessed land.* I closed my eyes and savored the feel of the fine grains beneath my hands. "Thank Grimm."

When I opened them again, a pair of sightless, milky-white eyes held captive in a wrinkly and decapitated head stared back at me.

"Excuse me," the head said. "Could you give me a hand? I seem to have lost mine."

Shrieking, I scrambled back into the water—away from the

grotesque head—treading over Rexi and dunking her underwater in the process.

"What is with you?" she sputtered.

I raised a shaky hand and pointed. "It talked. How can it be talking? It's a *dead* head."

Rexi shoved me off her. "Obviously not too dead if it's talking."

Minor details. I turned away and froggy-paddled down the shallow part a bit. "I think I'll float a little farther downstream and find another head-free beach."

"Helloooo? A little help if you please?" the head cried plaintively.

Against my better judgment, I looked back. While I was freaking out, Kato had jumped out of the water and gone to play on the beach. He was batting the head back and forth between his two massive paws.

Rexi shrugged. "At least he's not trying to eat it."

"I'm getting quite dizzy," the head complained, the milky eyes rolling around, probably not on purpose.

With the poutiest lips, I gave Rexi a pleading look. No effect. I switched to what I hoped was a steely yet regal glare.

She shook her head. "Sorry, but I don't work for you anymore. Your High and Mightiness will just have to clean up after her own *pet* this time."

"But I really, *really* don't want to." While claiming ownership of him earlier, this was not what I had had in mind.

Though I'd gained fifty pounds in the form of my

waterlogged dress, I reluctantly slogged up the beach again. Grimacing, I picked up the head by its scraggly, sand lice–infested gray hair.

"Um, is there someplace in particular you'd like me to put you, Ms. Head?" I wrinkled my nose and held it out as far as my arm would stretch.

"Call me Hydra. If you would be a dear, my cottage is just up the beach a bit." Her milky eyes still rattled around the sockets a bit.

My whole outlook perked up at the thought of a place to rest. It helped me combat the *ick* factor by dreaming of hot tea and getting dry in Hydra's nice, warm cottage.

Turns out "cottage" was a bit of a euphemism. *Shack* probably would have been a wee bit closer to the truth. There was a small stovepipe coming out of the roof. Most roofs are similar in shape to a witch's hat—this one looked a bit more like a bowl because the point was sagging down in the middle. There were windows on either side of the building with shutters hanging mostly off—attached by a single piece of gum. The door looked like it had been carved directly out of the tree, and it was open.

A frumpy headless body in a housecoat ambled out, whacking into the door on its way.

"Holy hex!" Rexi splashed back into the water. "I'm just gonna stay way over here, if that's all right with you." She looked at the body and shuddered. "And if it's not, I'm *still* gonna stay over here."

"Coward!" I shouted, secretly desperate to do the exact same thing.

"Better than being zombie takeout."

Kato used one of his wings and herded the body in our direction.

"There you are. Poor dear. Did those mean doggies hurt you?" Hydra consoled her hunchbacked body as it wandered blindly toward us.

The body hefted the Hydra head onto its shoulders. Nothing magically knit the two back together, and I couldn't see a zipper or anything. There was only a slurpy sucking noise, and if you asked me, the head still looked wobbly at best.

"That's just wrong," Rexi called from the water.

Yeah, I didn't need the observation, thank you—I had the full, creepy view up close. I threw Rexi a weary look. "If you're not going to help, you're not allowed to comment."

Though part of me hoped she'd come up just so she could keep making snappy quips, Rexi held up her hands and mimed sealing her lips.

Hydra finished checking over her newly found extremities and wandered farther up the path.

I followed at a safe distance, in case the head lost its balance or something. Polite conversation tamped down my urge to run away, screaming. "I heard you say something about dogs. Did they do…um"—how to say this delicately?—"did they knock your head off?"

"Heavens no. What a silly idea." Hydra rooted around in

a weed-infested garden. She pulled some bloodroot from the ground and ambled back in my general direction, using a broken garden hoe like a walking stick. "It was a witch who played croquet with my head. The dogs just rolled me down to the beach."

"Did you happen to see what direction they went?" I hoped the answer was, *Way the spell away from here.*

"Well, obviously I didn't see anything." Hydra pointed to her sightless eyes. "But if you'll come with me I can ask the others."

"Others?"

She gestured me over. "Up at the house. Be a dear and guide me." Her nails were long overdue for a manicure. They were yellow and gnarled, and they bit into my arm as I led her up the wilted garden path.

Kato gave the area a thorough search. Probably hungry *again*. When he approached the garden, he looked back at me like he was asking for permission—guess he'd learned his lesson with the Bumpkins. I shook my head, since I recognized a few of the plants from Verte's garden—the cursed and poisonous section.

He gave a last mopey look at the plants and trotted to keep pace with me. I ruffled the fur between Kato's horns to reward his obedience. For a moment, he seemed to enjoy it; then he smacked my hand away with his tail. I suppose he'd decided he was too noble for head scratches—good thing I hadn't tried to rub his tummy. My stinging hand served as an excellent reminder that underneath the soft, comforting fur still lurked the Kato that liked to knock me down a peg.

Taking off at a gallop, he beat me to the half-hanging cottage door and ambled in—then nearly knocked me over backing out.

"Big baby."

Even though Kato might be a prince, he'd started off grubby enough that he didn't have much room to judge Hydra's housekeeping. And surely it couldn't be *that* messy in there. While he was being hypocritical, I was quite proud of myself for being so helpful and humble.

As I walked through the door, I gave myself a little pat on the back—and then froze.

I'd been prepared for a hovel. I might have even been okay with a house full of magically trained circus mice. I was not prepared for the *others*.

Heads lined the floor-to-ceiling shelving. Different sizes, different species—all of them looked lifeless. Some had clearly passed their expiration date. Several looked freshly harvested. One still had a faint flush to its cheeks.

And wouldn't you know, there was an empty spot on the shelf, just the right size for my royal head.

Following Kato's example, I backed up toward the door. "You know what? On second thought, it doesn't really matter which way Griz went. We have to go west anyway. I'll just see myself out."

For a fragile blind lady, her grip was surprisingly strong.

"You definitely don't want to be heading west. I can help, and there's so much I have to tell you. I'm afraid I must insist you and your friends stay here."

Spell no.

I squirmed, trying to get free, and cursed myself for not staying on the beach in the first place. This freaky hag made Gretel's gingerbread witch look like a sweet, harmless baker. Probably the only thing Hydra wanted to help me with was removing my head. Well, that wasn't gonna happen. Groping blindly to the side, I grabbed the first thing I could get a handle on.

Ah, frying pans—the preferred weapon of princesses everywhere.

Hefting the pan from the sink, I whacked Hydra's head from her shoulders, sending it flying into a shelf, where it fell to the ground with all the *others*.

Hydra's gnarly hands instinctively flew to the spot where her head had just been, releasing her grasp on me but snagging the cardigan on my shoulders. I dropped down and out of the jacket. Then, planting my bejeweled heel on her crusty behind, I sent her body to join the heads on the floor. For good measure, I chucked the skillet at her and booked it out the door.

It wasn't until I was outside that I remembered the wishing star had been in my pocket. But nothing could have made me go back in there again. Besides, the stupid thing was busted anyway.

As if to confirm the wisdom in my decision, Hydra's body came ambling out the door again. I bolted.

My companions were waiting for me farther down the beach at the border of the woods.

"Zombie?" Rexi shouted as I ran past.

Close enough.

"The Rule of Diplomacy: A royal should never get their hands dirty. If you can't reach a compromise, use an assassin. It's called diplomacy."

—*Thomason's Tips to Ruthless Ruling*

The Haunted Acre Wood

How can you run in those ridiculous shoes?" Rexi huffed and puffed behind me.

Ignoring the barb, I kept running. Plus, I didn't have enough breath to respond anyway. Wanting as much distance as possible from the headhunter, I jogged until a tree root seemed to reach up out of the ground to send me sprawling.

First, I spit out a mouthful of dirt. Then, I screamed at the sky. "That's it! I've had it! Everything is trying to kill me! All I did was make one stupid wish. Aladdin made *three*. I'm the hero of this story, so where's my happy ending, already? It's not fair."

Rexi bent over, trying to catch her breath. "You know

what's not fair? Spending Muse Day as a toad just because the kitchen ran out of frog legs. Or being volunteered for this little journey. So build a bridge, then make like a billy goat and get over it already because no one is listening."

"I wouldn't expect you to understand, since you never had much to start with." I sniffed. "Besides, you should be thanking me, since my wish is the only reason you're not still covered in slimy warts."

"You worthless piece of fluff!" Rexi launched herself at me. "Look around you! Your wishful thinking ruined everyone's life."

She pinned me against the ground, pulling my hair and scratching my face in the process. I threw up my arms instinctively. Aside from "How to Give an Open-Handed Slap," the proper way to fight had not been in the princess charm-school curriculum.

With a flurry of hands, I swatted at the space in front me. "I order you to get off!"

Rexi growled in response, yanking my shoulders up before slamming them back down. "Not until you admit it. You're more worried about replacing your wardrobe than getting your parents back."

The world seemed to go quiet, like it was holding its breath. Kato had been about to intervene but now backed away from the invisible line that Rexi had just crossed. I no longer gave a bubbling cauldron about how a princess *should* fight. Instead, I let my fear and fury take over and started hitting back. Using my legs for leverage, I bucked up and flipped her over. The sparkle of my ruby heel caught my eye. I yanked it out from under the tree root and raised it high.

"Take. It. Back."

For the first time, Rexi looked at me with fear in her eyes— and not just because a curse said I might end the world.

Her mouth moved but nothing came out.

"I can't hear you."

"I'm—" Her eyes widened and she pointed behind me. "Look!"

"Try again."

"No really, I swear," she said earnestly.

"If she moves, eat her," I instructed Kato.

I looked to the treetops where Rexi pointed. According to her makeshift map, we should have been in the Sherwood Forest. If that was true, then the wish had struck here as well; the usually rigid ironwood oaks were now gnarled and twisted. The treetops rustled and swayed like they were alive, but only one at a time. In a pattern. That was moving closer. Fast.

Weapon—wicked heel—already in hand, I faced the trees and stood my ground to confront our next opponent. With one fight under my sash, I felt a little more prepared to defend myself. Kato joined me, tail swinging high, ready to use like a whip. Rexi got up off the dirt and leaves to complete our defensive line. Well, more like defensive triangle since she stood noticeably behind Kato and I.

"There." She pointed at a sparkle of gold moving through the branches.

I squinted to focus in on any details. My heart stilled, then beat wildly. I could just make out a big, bulky black lump riding a sputtering and clunking broomstick.

I bounced up and down unevenly on one shoe. "It's Verte!" It had to be. *Please be.* "Over here," I cried, waving my arms.

"Shhh," someone chided and whacked my back. I turned, ready to let Rexi have it, but she held up her hands.

"The dog did it."

Sure. Only in this case, she might be right. Kato poked me in the side with his horns, growling a strange combination of gargling and hissing. *Wait, when did he get big enough to be waist height?*

"Bad Kato." I shook my shoe in front of his nose. "Help is here."

The broom and its rider crashed down through the trees. Joy leaped through me at the initial sight of black, wiry hair; the feeling quickly dissipated. Verte's hair only covered her head and maybe a bit under her lip and arms—not her entire body. She also favored the pointiest hat she could find, rather than the boxy gold fez that rolled to my feet.

"This is help?" Rexi scoffed behind me. "It's a flying monkey."

The party crasher was not technically a monkey, but a gorilla in a finely made tuxedo. Wearing those kind of clothes, he must have been human before...

Spelled

Before you and your wish came along, a little voice in my head whispered. It sounded remarkably like a certain snarky servant.

"Those who were very recently toads have no room to mock," I countered over my shoulder to the real Rexi, to combat the imaginary Rexi in my head.

The large gorilla bowed low. "Lady Emerald."

A smile tugged on my lips. "Well, it's about time we met someone with manners—*eep*."

My sentiment was cut short as the gorilla changed his formal greeting into a forward rush, scooping up his hat—and me with it. Before I knew it, he'd flipped me over onto his back like a mountain troll with the catch of the day.

"Forgive me, but we must make haste," he said over my shriek while bounding away. "The magical infection has spread to the trees, and we are all in danger of being bushwhacked."

I stopped beating him with my shoe long enough to look back at where I'd stood. The knots in the trees trunks made a pattern in the bark, like faces. Angry ones. And the branches, having lost their broomstick-flying prey from the sky, silently bent low and reached out for what was on the ground. Clawlike twigs and branches flexed hungrily, making the Bumpkins seem like cheery woodland sprites.

"Move!" I yelled.

Kato was already roaring and chasing after me, though at my holler, he looked behind him. Then he ran faster.

Rexi stayed put with her arms folded. "I'm done rescuing dimwits in distress."

Why do I even bother? I thought to myself.

Out loud, I yelled, "You're about to get a splinter the size of a broadsword, SO DUCK!"

For once, she obeyed without arguing and barely missed being skewered. "AHHH! Why didn't you warn me sooner?" She scrambled away from a slashing branch.

The four of us sprinted through the forest—well, technically three, since I was a reduced to bouncing cargo. My ride was fast, much faster than my companions, who trailed farther and farther behind. With nothing else to do, I could only watch helplessly as the trees pulled up their roots and closed in around them.

Kato tried to hit an oncoming branch attack with his tail, but these trees were not the withered ones from Midas. The ironwood sprouted metal thorns that ripped through Kato's dragon-hide tail. He howled at the same time Rexi screamed after barely avoiding an impossibly fast acorn bullet.

I buried my face in the gorilla's fur. It was bad enough to watch them get hurt knowing I could do nothing—it was soul rending to watch and know the cause of the "magical infection."

I wish—no. I'd never wish again. Instead, I offered a broken prayer in the hopes that the Storymakers or the powers of magic itself would hear my plea. *Someone…please help them.*

Something sliced up the top of my calf. I inhaled sharply

from pain. The fur I'd buried my nose in smelled like animal musk, sandalwood, and roses. The wind picked up harshly and brought the scent of burning wood with it.

Crackling and popping sounds came from overhead. I looked up, half-afraid of what I might find. A smoking twig claw retreated backward, the tree it belonged to stood tall again instead of stooping low to attack. Normally, I'd freak with anything associated with fire, but it was working in our favor this time.

The rest of the trees stopped advancing as well and formed a semicircle border behind us. Once they had re-rooted themselves to the ground, they froze in place.

"What are they doing?" I muttered to myself.

The gorilla answered, "It would seem you are not very tasty. And they are most likely petrified, since a Maker's workshop chose to appear in their forest."

"Huh?" Confused, I twisted my back to look where we were going instead of where we'd been. At the same time, the gorilla stopped running and let go of me. I fell to the ground and landed nose to nose with some sort of worm. It had a green body the size of my fist, a salt-and-pepper mustache, and wore large, round spectacles. He blinked at me and, seemingly unimpressed with what he saw, inched back to a tower of books stacked by *half* of a stone building. If this was the workshop that supposedly "appeared," the other half didn't make the trip.

"Why are we stopping? I thought stopping equaled dying,"

Rexi huffed. She and Kato staggered into the magical clearing, out of breath. "Hey, was this thing here a minute ago?"

"'Chose to appear.' That's what…" I realized I didn't know the ape's name. There hadn't been time for introductions. *Would I have bothered to ask even if there had been time? How long has Rexi worked as the kitchen girl and I just learned her name yesterday?*

"What's your name?" I whispered, so Rexi wouldn't hear and say something to embarrass me further.

"Nikko," he answered just as quietly before righting the fez atop his head again and peering up at me gratefully.

"'Chose to appear' is what Nikko said."

"Every wizard has a workshop," he clarified. "The more powerful the wizard, the more magical the workshop. And a Maker bends magic and fate at will, so it's not surprising that their workshops can too. Although this one does seem to be in a state of disrepair."

"Understatement," Rexi grumbled under her breath.

Bookshelves lined the two and a half walls, and the layer of dust was every bit as thick as the books it covered. Still, the workshop was proof a Maker had heard my prayer.

"I think it's, um, charming, and we should just be grateful it popped up and not be so quick to judge by appearances," I said.

Rexi opened her mouth to mock but a tail whack upside the head cut off whatever unpleasant thing she might have said. Instead, she switched her focus off me and narrowed her eyes at Nikko. "Not that I believe for a second that this place is what you claim, but how do you know so much about wizards, Makers, and magic? I don't think you found us by accident."

"Of course not," Nikko said brightly, unaware or uncaring of Rexi's implied meaning. "I've been sent to bring the Emerald Princess home." He offered me his arm. "Shall we go?"

Suddenly, it felt like the three suns would come out tomorrow after all, that birds were chirping again instead of being eaten by fungi, and surely, my happy ever after was right around the corner waiting for me.

"Sent by who?" Rexi asked, not buying it.

"By Mick, the Magnificent Wizard of—"

"That's why you smelled like that yucky incense," I interrupted, making the connection.

"So you know who he's talking about?" Rexi asked me.

"Yeah. Remember all those singing telegrams and gifts baskets that started showing up about six months ago?"

"I think so," Rexi said slowly. "Did they smell like someone dumped a bucket of perfume on them?"

"Yup, those were from Mick. He might have some obsession issues, but he's also a wizard, so maybe he's teamed up with Verte back at the palace to help undo the whole wish thing."

Maybe they'd even already managed to bring back my parents.

Rexi gave a wary look to the vicious yet still unmoving trees, then shrugged. "Okay, then what are we waiting for?"

Nikko put a hand out, stopping Rexi. "I'm sorry, I should have been clearer. The princess and I are going alone."

"When invited over to a tea party, the only acceptable behavior is to eat every last crumb and drop. Then, even if it turns you big or small, don't forget to say thank you with a tip of the hat."

—*Hatter's Mad Manners*

12

Friends of a Feather

Everything got a whole lot louder as the three of us yelled at Nikko. Or roared in Kato's case. Nikko slowly backed away from the very real possibility that he might be eaten by the ever-growing beast.

"It's not by my choice, I assure you," Nikko said.

I positioned myself between ape and winged dragon mutt. Probably not the smartest place to be, but I was too pixed to care.

"Whose choice is it then? My palace, my rules. And I say we go home *together*."

"That's right," Rexi said while slowly scooting closer to the building of books and out of Kato-tail range. "Tell him who's boss."

Great. Now she recognizes my position.

Nikko turned his fez over in his hands. "My apologies, Princess, but it's not your palace we're going to. We're off to see the wizard at the Ivory Tower. It's not far, but my master was most insistent that I only bring you."

Normally I'd yell and scream until I got my way, but I had a feeling that wouldn't work here. Nikko was just following orders, and you do not disobey someone who has the power to turn you into slimy green things. Just ask Rexi.

So instead, I held my tongue and thought about what to do: Stick to Verte's more dangerous plan, or stay safely in a tower and wait to be rescued? Chasing rainbows hadn't worked out so well and the wizard might be able to just *poof* my parents back. But I couldn't leave Rexi and Kato behind on a *might*.

Well, I could, and it would serve Rexi right for attacking me. But then Kato would probably eat her, and then he'd get indigestion…

I sighed. "If you're positive that we all can't go, then you'll have to go to the Ivory Tower without me too."

"I knew you'd ditch us…" Rexi spat out, then paused mid-stomp. "Wait…really?"

"Yes, really."

"Oh. Hmph." Rexi suddenly became very interested in the scrolls along the closest shelf.

Kato sat on his haunches and growled at me. I had no clue what that meant.

Nikko smiled and patted my arm. "Loyalty is a noble quality, so I won't ask you again to betray it. Thank you for invoking the protection of Oz back at the trees." He looked off in the distance and shuddered. "Now to deliver the news to *him*." Nikko ran away, even faster now that he wasn't carrying me. *What was he talking about? I didn't do anything.* "Hey, wait!" I called, but he was already gone. I took two steps and realized I'd lost my shoes after my last fall. One ruby heel was within reach, the other had—

"Ew, get away from that one-of-a-kind Hans Christian Louboutin shoe!" The bibliobug or whatever had its slimy green body wrapped around my right heel. I reached down to pry it off, but when I touched the worm, it puffed out a little cloud of green dust that smelled like moldy bread.

Now I had the overwhelming desire to sneeze. To my embarrassment, the sound that came out was nothing even remotely close to a ladylike *achoo*. It was more like howling hurricane-force gusts—including the spray.

"Nice one, Sneezy," Rexi chortled.

She should know better than to mess with me in the middle of a shoe crisis, so I replied with the well-recognized dwarf hand sign telling her to heigh-ho herself off a cliff.

"Fine, Princess. Walk barefoot for all I care, but let's get going before these trees snap out of their trance and shish kebab us. Besides, it'll be dark soon."

Finding a shelter, with four walls no less, made perfect sense. So why did I not want to budge? "I don't think they'll come any closer. Maybe we should stay. I have this feeling that we're supposed to be here."

Rexi threw her hands up in the air. "And I have this feeling you're delusional, probably delirious from shopping withdrawal and hunger."

A very loud grumble from Kato's stomach put him firmly in agreement. Even my traitorous tummy cramped and reminded me of its emptiness.

Rexi started walking "First food, then sleep. Tomorrow we can keep looking for that rainbow and your moldy green witch."

Without proof that the trees would stay petrified or a steak dinner would magically appear, I couldn't convince them to stay. And just like I didn't want to leave them behind, I didn't want to get left behind either.

When I didn't argue, Kato took that as a sign to get going. Or he got tired of listening and too hungry to care. He put his nose to the ground and padded off to the west faster than any of Dad's hunting hounds.

I took one last look at the piles of books and the bespectacled bug. He puffed another little cloud of dust and went back to munching the quill pictured on a leather tome. The image had been engraved in sparkly red ink. Guess the bugger really liked red.

Rexi whistled. "Are you coming?"

"Yeah," I said and hurriedly reclaimed my shoes while the bibliobug was busy with his snack.

Keeping her back to me, she started talking before I reached her. "So I'm sure that you just wanted someone to boss around, but that was kinda cool. You know, not ditching us and stuff. You might not be entirely worthless." Without waiting for a response, she ran to catch up with Kato.

It was not even remotely close to an apology but better than a punch in the face or a dagger in the back.

The moment Kato smelled something, his whole posture changed. First he went rigid; then he pranced circles around Rexi and I, trying to get us to move faster. A sweet smell wafted on the wind just as the three of us stumbled to the cusp of the meadow that housed the big black spike. The aged, spiraling metal came out of a greenhouse full of plants, flowers, and flutterbeaks. There was also a modest house in the midst of periwinkle blue wildflowers. It gave off a much better vibe than Hydra's little shack of horrors.

The perfection was marred by high-pitched trills. Someone was singing—badly. A short woman with a rather round middle sang while she hung laundry on a line. Black, feathery hair hung down her back. Everything else about her—scarf to ankle boots—was pink. Even her skin was rosy in its coloring.

"We are in the west. There's a spire. Do you think this is Black Crow? The name sounds ominous, but I'd say the whole bubblegum theme makes her look nice and cheery," I whispered to Rexi, since I knew it was pointless to ask Kato. His dripping saliva answered for him.

A pie wafted delicious-smelling steam from an open

window. That clenched the decision for everyone. After over a day with no food, we had devolved into creatures ruled by our stomachs. Kato's rumbled extremely loudly as way of introduction.

"Who's there?" The woman turned around, startled enough that she dropped the hot-pink knickers she'd been hanging on the line.

Either we looked really scary, or we smelled really scary. Most likely we just looked like we'd been to spell and back. Kato, in particular, was starting to look less cuddly and more wild beast.

The woman gathered her hot-pink poodle skirt and ran toward us, getting within touching distance of Kato. She pulled her hand back at the last second. "May I?"

I thought she was addressing me, but her gaze was honed in on Kato. He, in turn, looked at me and shrugged his wings as if saying, *Do you think she'll feed me if I let her?*

"Um, he doesn't talk, but I think it's okay if you touch him," I said, trying to get the woman's attention.

She looked at me for the first time, her eyes large and magnified through Fairy Fizz Bottle glasses.

Her attention to me was brief, and then it was all about Kato again. Instead of petting him, she clinically pulled back his lips and examined his fangs, turned his head this way and that, and even looked up his nose. I'm surprised he didn't bite her. "Fascinating," she murmured. "A fine adolescent chimera such as yourself should be able to speak."

"A what?"

"Pardon?" the woman said distractedly.

Rexi stopped staring at the pie and looked at the woman. "You called him something. I've just been calling him fur ball, but is there really a name for what he is? As in, there's more than one of him out there?"

"Fur ball," the woman snorted in disdain, talking to me and ignoring Rexi entirely. I liked her already. "This noble creature is a chimera. Very rare and clannish. I've never heard of one this far from the mountains." She looked me up and down with renewed interest. "You must tell me how you enchanted him. Slavery spell? Potion? Or did you somehow manage to smuggle out his egg before he was hatched?"

I leaned in to talk to Black Crow, hoping to make her an offer she couldn't refuse, considering her obvious interest in Kato. "You are Black Crow, right? I'll make you a deal. If you share some of your food and drink with us, I'll tell you all about my friend here."

She squinted into her thick glasses. "Do I know you? Have you attended one of my Spider's Webinars or perhaps read my latest bog post on potions?"

"Actually, I heard about you from the Queen of the Bumpkins."

"Hemlock?" Black Crow said.

"Never caught her name." In my head, I'd just been calling her "icky bug creature" or "queen of the cockroaches."

Rexi butt in to close the deal. "So, about that food?"

Crow stepped back, and her eyes widened, getting even bigger, as if she was taking in the whole picture for the first time. "Oh. Oh, forgive me. I don't get a lot of visitors and I'm not really good with social situations. Come in, come in." Her hands flitted about, and she blinked rapidly. "You probably do need help. After all, you look terrible."

"Not good in social situations? You don't say," Rexi muttered.

Black Crow didn't act like she'd heard and waddled toward her home. I gave Rexi a look, warning her not to blow this. Kato did me one better and whacked her with his tail.

Crow ushered us inside her home, apologizing for the nonexistent mess.

We all took a seat at the little white dinette set—well, Kato sat under it, so big now that he lifted it up just a smidge— and I explained our chance encounter with the Bumpkins and how that led us to her door.

"How odd," she said, stirring a little honey into a gaudy pink-rose teacup before she handed it to me. "The rule of favor is broken, you say. I wonder how that happened."

The tea was sweet with just the slightest tang, like it had a little bite to it. At first my stomach protested the intrusion after being empty for so long. Then it was nice and happy, and it demanded more. It's like that bedtime story *If You Give a Princess Some Tea, She'll Ask for a Cookie to Go with It.*

"I don't suppose you have any chocolate wands, do you?" I asked when she refilled both mine and Rexi's mugs.

She blinked her big eyes behind her thick glasses. "Gracious, no. Why would I have a chocolate wand? They'd melt at the very first spell. Terrible thing to make a magical instrument out of. I do have a fine one made of wormwood if you've lost yours." Her nose scrunched, and she looked me over again. "I didn't take you for a practitioner."

"Foooood," Rexi croaked, looking groggy and very near to passing out.

Crow gave Rexi and me a piece of pie, then put the rest of the tin on the ground for Kato. I was fed, so it wasn't worth explaining what a chocolate wand was and extolling its magically delicious virtues. She looked at me expectantly though. Like it was my turn to give up the goods.

"I'm not a magic user. At least not on purpose." I settled in and told my story, starting with the odd, porcelainlike child, the gift, and the wish. Things popped out of my mouth that I had no intention of saying—like my initial hatred of Kato, though he was kind of okay now. At least for a pet. Then I went on about the issues with my parents and how much I was beginning to hate rainbows. Soon, I couldn't even remember what I was saying seconds after I said it.

In my mouth, my tongue grew thick and slow. Pink spots danced across my vision, twirling and spinning.

"'Scuze me. Can you point me to the little princess's room?" I slurred.

Crow gave me a friendly smile and patted my head. "Of course, dearie. It's just down the hall. Take your time. I was just going to spell a pot and make a call."

Her hand made my head feel heavy(er). "Oh, thaz nize." I got up and stepped over Rexi, who had slipped off her chair to the floor. That made me giggle.

I ambled off in the direction Crow had pointed, and Kato wobbled behind. I placed a hand on the counter. "Why do I feel zo weird?"

Kato whispered, "I dunno. I think we should go."

"Hey, tha rhymed. Thaz funny." I broke into a fit of giggles again. "Wait, you can talk?"

I stumbled back into the kitchen, wanting to share my new discovery with Black Crow since she seemed so interested in chimeras. I only made it a few steps before my feet fell off— or at least, I couldn't feel them anymore.

Ah well, the floor seemed like as good a place as any to take a nap—just ask Rexi.

Black Crow was still on her spellphone, so she didn't notice me. *She probably wouldn't mind,* I thought as I yawned and closed my eyes.

While I drifted off, my ears still worked. My brain couldn't make much sense of it though.

"You can have the girls. All I ask is to keep the chimera."

Thunder rumbled in the background, and a voice spoke that reminded me of broken glass.

"Done."

Someday My Witch Will Come

I woke up in a strange bed with a pounding headache. Ugh. Where was I, and who the spell had been using my head as a bongo?

There was a really nasty taste in the back of my throat. A little drool came out of the corner of my mouth and dropped onto a needlepoint pillow that said, "As the Crow Flies." I went to wipe the spittle from my cheek, but my hand wasn't cooperating. That's because it was tied to my other hand behind my back. A quick kick proved my ankles were tied too.

I looked around the room for an explanation—like maybe there was an ocean of alligators on the floor and Black Crow was worried that I'd fall out of bed if I weren't restrained.

Yeah right.

Didn't see any alligators, just ugly pink floral carpeting. The whole room was decorated with girly pink and white furniture, and every square inch of it was covered in knick-knacks and trophies—science fair awards, spelling bees, an Achievement in Alchemy crystal. Clearly, Black Crow was a bit of a brain. The walls were mostly bare, but I did see a nice plaque on the closest one: Hex Salesman of the Year. And under it was a picture of Black Crow shaking hands and accepting the plaque from none other than Griz, the Gray Witch.

"Bedknobs and broomsticks. That pixing Bumpkin and his Grimm-glammed queen set me up." I kicked the metal post with a clang of frustration at being so naive.

I tried to calm myself down. Maybe I was wrong. Perhaps it was an honest mistake and the Bumpkins had really been trying to help. Then I remembered the look of knowing and retribution that Moony had given me—and how easily the queen had given me directions, even though I was trying to squish her children. What were her words again? *Black Crow will take care of you.*

Yep, she was sure taking care of me all right.

"How could I be so stupid? She probably pixie dusted the pie."

I thrashed around on the bed to get myself up.

"Shhhh."

Now what? The shushing came from the sitting room off to

the side of the bedroom. Trying to get a peek proved a little harder than I thought, considering I was trussed up like a solstice day game hen.

Kato looked so calm, sitting there all nice and comfy next to a glass armoire filled with potions. A large, plush pet bed lay next to his clawed feet. Where were *his* manacles? If Black Crow left him free, she must have thought she could trust him. I couldn't help but notice he had a new fashion accessory—a hot-pink rhinestone collar.

"Traitor," I spat in disgust. "I was beginning to think that maybe you weren't so bad. But no, she feeds you and now you're *her* pet?"

Kato huffed and repositioned himself. "Can you for once go beyond the obvious? Look…" He used his tail to bat one of the yarn balls that Crow had so thoughtfully provided for him. It flew toward me and hit an unseen barrier. Vaporized on contact.

Huh. So he was a prisoner just like me.

"Sorry," I muttered. "But what was I supposed to think?" I hated being wrong—and yet lately, it happened so often. "In my defense, you are wearing a very nice collar with a medal hanging down." Hopefully it said something stupid, like Fluffy or Spot. Would serve him right for taking on such a superior tone of voice with me again.

Wait a minute.

I raised myself up as high as I could to take a good look at Kato. "You talked just now. Am I still dusted?"

"Yes, so go back to sleep." His voice had a deep, gruff quality, but even as an animal, he sounded condescending.

I liked him better when he couldn't talk.

"You know, for supposedly being a prince, you really lack a sense of finesse. Both your words and tail use force to get what you want. Maybe if you had tried a softer approach from the start, we wouldn't be here now."

"Yes, things would be different if only I'd given you poetry and a mountain of shoes." Kato did a very un-chimeralike eye roll. Then again, maybe chimeras did eye rolls all the time. How should I know? "In my domain, being soft will get you killed. Subjects respond to strength, not fine clothes and false pretty words."

"They also respond well to someone who bathes regularly," I muttered, then, louder, "How come you can talk now? Was it something in the pie?"

His tailed twitched and thumped against the glass case, rattling and clinking the potions together. "More than likely it was something in your wish that kept me from speaking until the spell matured."

"Well, now that you've *mattered*"— I tried to match his high and mighty tone—"maybe we can figure out a way to break that barrier." I had a little experience with that sort of thing, though the dragon at the Emerald palace was not only prettier but much less violent than Crow's see-through vaporizer.

"Don't worry. I already have a plan." He put his head down and gnawed on something.

I tried to straighten my back and crane my neck just enough to see what the spell Kato was doing. "That's great. I don't suppose you'd mind filling me in on said plan? Are you going to chew your way out? Or smack open a wall with your tail?"

"I said...don't worry about it. I don't need anyone else's help. I've got...it...under...control." He struggled to break whatever he was chewing on free.

A thought occurred to me—even with Kato talking, it was awfully quiet in here. "Hey, have you seen Rexi?"

Kato growled around a full mouth. "Quit bothering me. I'm...*mrph*...busy."

I tried really hard not to feel like I was being dismissed. I failed miserably. Being home, being here...it was all the same. Every time I wanted to have a picnic or a girl day with my mom, I heard the same thing. Well, it was closer to, *Come back later. I'm busy running every teeny tiny detail of everyone's life.* I'd known stepmothers that spent more time with family than the queen found for me. And if she'd let me, I probably could have helped—or at least not messed it up so badly that Verte couldn't fix it after.

"At last," Kato said triumphantly, spitting a black piece of something out of his mouth. It was hard to tell from the angle and distance, but it looked like he'd gnawed off one of his black talons.

I propped myself up again, high enough that he could see the full displeasure on my face. "So, let me get this straight. We're being held prisoner, awaiting death, dismemberment, or torture by off-key show tunes, and you think the best plan is to give yourself a manicure?"

We were completely pixed.

Behind the white door, two voices sounded like they were getting closer.

"Pretend to be asleep," Kato instructed.

Controlling little beast. Still, he didn't have to tell me twice. My head hit the pillow an instant before the door swung open. I deepened my breaths to look more asleep—and to keep from hyperventilating. My eyes were mere slits, so that I could see just enough to move before death hit me.

"I told you it was her. We're agreed on the payment, then?" Black Crow stayed back in the door frame. Her robust shape barred the way to the exit even if my feet had been untied. She stood next to the Gray Witch.

I lowered my lashes so she couldn't see that I was awake.

"Yes, yes. Five hundred and you can keep the bespelled ball of fur." Griz's voice was way too close for my liking. I could feel her breath on my cheek. In my mind, I envisioned her crouching low to look over her purchase—me.

"He's a chimera. Very ra—"

"Spare me, Crow."

Silence, but the hot air stayed on my face.

"Really, I expected more from the long-awaited Girl of Emerald. Maybe you're just a simple child after all."

It was all I could do not to jump a foot in the air when a hand brushed the hair off my face.

"So delicate," Griz said softly into my ear. Something sharp pressed against my neck. "So fragile."

The pressure increased but pulled back suddenly at the introduction of a new sound. The first few bars from the Wrong Direction's hit song, "My Spell's What Makes You Beautiful," came from somewhere close by.

Saved by the spellphone, though I hadn't taken either lady for a fan of Munchkin music. Apparently Griz was the one with the guilty pleasure, because she's the one who answered.

"What is it? I'm busy," she said in clipped tones.

I couldn't hear the voice on the other end very clearly, but it sounded like they said, *She's awake.*

"Are you absolutely sure?" The seriousness of Griz's voice indicated very bad things if the caller was not.

Since Griz was no longer breathing on my neck, I took a chance and opened my eyes to slits again. She walked away from me and closer to the door, so I had no chance of hearing the mystery caller's reply. Whatever it was, it satisfied Griz. She snapped the phone closed.

"Something's come up. Prepare me a spelled opal to use on the commoner, and I'll send Tinman to collect everything. In the meantime, don't you dare say a word to the wizard," Griz informed Crow, her back to me. "I've seen him skulking around, and I won't give him the chance to double-cross me again. He's always had a soft spot for those infernal Emerald girls." By the time she finished the statement, her voice had turned from thoughtful to bitter.

"What's so important about them?"

"None of your concern. Just keep our little transaction confidential. It's imperative that this blasted girl stays here and away from anything even remotely associated with Oz." Griz walked to the door and pushed the heavy woman out of the way. "That meddling fool has a tendency to pop up where you least expect him."

Oz? I thought his name was Mick. Oz must be his magical specialty…or where he lived in his Ivory Tower. I never did catch what he was the wizard of…

My thoughts froze when I caught a glimpse of something that changed everything.

Before rushing out the front door, Griz grabbed a staff from the kitchen. An emerald staff.

Verte's emerald staff.

Verte wasn't coming. She would never be coming.

"At the end of the day, it's all about having the newest, latest, and greatest. Save your business today by spicing up old products with fresh ingredients."

—Orbes Magical Business Magazine

14

Put a Spell on You

With Griz gone, Black Crow headed back our way. Quickly, I shut my eyes.

"No need to fuss on my account," Crow clucked. "I can see from the tears on your face that you're awake."

Since my hands were tied behind my back, I couldn't wipe them off. Didn't want to anyway. I reopened my eyes and glared at Black Crow, imagining what would happen if looks really could kill.

"So, what's on the agenda now? Painful death or more of your awful singing that makes me long for painful death?"

Snark is a fabulous defense mechanism.

Black Crow looked genuinely surprised and wounded at

my comments. "You don't have to be mean. I'm not evil or anything. I've been nice to you—fed you, took you in. I even used silk ropes."

"Which you used to gift wrap me for Griz." I pulled on the ropes to give her a little demonstration. "Very thoughtful of you."

"Oh, you're not a gift," she said matter-of-factly, completely missing the point. "You're merchandise."

And that was so much better.

"I figure you owed me compensation for the loss of my business," she continued, fidgeting with the pink ribbon on her dress.

"How do you figure? I've never even met you," I protested.

"True, but your little wish has thrown off the balance of magic. None of my potions work correctly anymore. Forgetting hexes bring eternal knowledge. Glamour salves make the skin curdle like milk. You've ruined my reputation," she sniffed.

"How inconsiderate of me," I said drily.

"I know. So glad you understand." Crow apparently wasn't too familiar with sarcasm. She also seemed to unequivocally believe what she said: that she wasn't being a bad person for handing me over to the mother of all evil. She was just conducting a simple business transaction. Righting a wrong. Since it was my wrong, I had to pay. In a delusional sort of way, it kind of made sense.

Evil is tough to override, because it's ingrained in the soul.

Nutcases, however, I could work with, and this lady was off her toadstool. I changed my facial expression to one that I hoped looked honest and repentant. "I am so very sorry I have inconvenienced you, but surely we can resolve this. Isn't there some other way I can repay you?"

Black Crow appeared to give this a bit of thought. All at once, her face lit up and she scurried off to the kitchen.

Did I miss something? I glanced over at Kato, still sitting on his pillow, looking as clueless as I was. When Black Crow came back into the room, she was carrying a syringe and a small vial. It was empty.

The problem with empty vials is that something has to go in them.

"Grizelda mentioned something about your blood being special. So it makes a reasonable hypothesis that if I added a drop or two to each potion, they could work correctly again. Perhaps even better!" She sounded way too chipper at the prospect of taking my blood.

I tried to sound enthusiastic too. "Hey, that's a great idea. If you untie my arm, you can get a good vein."

Crow considered for a moment. "You're not going to try anything, are you?"

I smiled, probably showing all my teeth. "I just want to pay you back, that's all."

Crow went around to untie my wrists. Kato sat up, ears perked, watching closely to see what I was going to do. Black Crow tapped my now-free left arm a few times to get the blood to rise to the surface. Just before the needle went in, I decided to strike.

My left fist arched across the space between Crow and me, making a perfect landing on her jaw. "*Ow!*" we both said in unison. The blow knocked her glasses off her face, and she bent over to grab them.

Now to make a run for it. Of course, running usually required the use of two feet, and mine were still bound together. Planning FAIL.

Gravity worked its magic, and my nose met carpet in a spectacular face-plant. Though the pink rosette rug looked plush, it wasn't soft enough to keep me from breaking my nose.

Propping myself up on my elbows, I saw blood streaming down my face and onto the floor, creating a new abstract rosette. I rolled away from it, trying to stem the bleeding with one hand. Now I was flat on my back and Black Crow stood directly over me. Her glasses were askew, adding to the craziness in her eyes.

She pulled one of the black feathers from her hair. Feathers are generally known to be soft; that's why they made good stuffing for pillows. Crow's were downy on one end and razor sharp at the other. The feather looked like a deadly quill.

I scooted backward on my elbows, trying to squirm away from her. "Hey, wasn't that thoughtful of me to provide all this blood? See, it's dripping. May as well catch it and make good use, right?"

She didn't grab her vial like I'd hoped. Instead, she

advanced with the lethal feather, pointy end first. "You are not a nice girl. You lied to me." She wiped the blood from her own split lip. "I think you owe me more blood."

"Sure. Get it while it's hot." I laughed weakly.

Her eyes flashed with madness. "All of it."

She dropped to her knees, straddling me, squeezing my arms to my sides, effectively binding me again. She must use a Thighmaster or something, because I couldn't break away. She grabbed my wrist and pressed the feather into the hollow.

"Wait!"

Both mine and Crow's head snapped over to the chimera in the corner. Sadly, the quill stayed in place; the slightest pressure would pierce the skin.

"So you *can* talk." The madness receded slightly, and the more scholarly Crow emerged again.

"Yes, it's a little difficult to adjust to this voice box. I could tell you all about it." Kato neared the door frame, stopping just shy of where the barrier was.

Crow leaned back a little bit, shifting her considerable weight, which allowed me to breathe a little easier.

Silently, I willed Kato to keep her talking. If she would get off me, I could untie my feet and knock the nut job out. But it was gonna have to be fast. I was getting woozy, and my nose was leaking everywhere.

"Why don't you come over here?" Kato kept his voice calm and smooth. "It will be nice to talk to someone with a brain for once, instead of that useless princess. In fact, she might actually be the reason I couldn't speak before—lack of intelligent conversation to engage in."

"She is a bit shallow, isn't she?" Crow concluded as I tried my best to look harmless and stupid. Not a tough feat when you're scared out of your mind.

"I've read nursery rhymes with more depth," Kato confided.

Kato and Crow had a laugh at my expense while I covertly untied my feet. And even though I knew he was on my side, what Kato said still hurt. *He's just acting—playing a part.* But did he have to play it so well?

Or maybe that was how he really felt. Even if he was on my side, Kato didn't do pretty lies, just ugly truths. This wasn't the first time he'd called me a useless princess either.

Well, why should I care what he thought?

I don't. I'm not useless, and I'll prove it by getting out of this mess all by myself.

I rushed her, surprise on my side.

Unfortunately, she had the crystal prism from the desk on hers.

My head exploded into visions of twinkling stars, but I don't think any of them would grant my wish. Blood poured off my forehead and into my eyes. The world was awash with red. Kato roared, going wild and breaking things. When the bottles of potions started hitting the invisible barrier, Black Crow freaked out.

"My work!"

Spelled

For an alchemist and businesswoman, the loss of so much research and product drove the last bit of sanity away from Crow. She screamed a nonsense word, and the next potion didn't stop—it sailed through the doorway.

Directly at me.

The green, liquid-filled orb broke against my skull.

Nothing happened.

I inhaled in a moment of cool relief. Then I burst into flame.

"Power is a worm that crawls into your heart and eats away your soul. Finally, when there's nothing left—that's when the good part starts."

—Malevolent, *Dungeon Confessions*

A Case of Heartburn

Starting at the point of impact, the fire devoured me, burning away my hair before traveling to the rest of my body. I felt a flash of intense searing pain before my nerves thankfully singed away.

Black Crow backed away from my nightmare and covered her nose to escape the stench. Her back hit the dresser, bumping the mirror so that it tilted in such a way that I could see the fiery angel I had become.

The angel's arms—my arms—came up, and the fire shifted, burning white, then green. Where the green fire burned, the skin reknit itself. In moments, I was healed and renewed—like a phoenix rising from the ashes of my former self.

That couldn't possibly be me, could it?

Girl of Emerald, no man can tame. Burn down the world, consumed by flames.

Seeing part of the Emerald curse come to life should have scared me hexless. But I felt strong and powerful. Like I could take on the world. The feeling was intoxicating. I wanted more. I *needed* more.

A brown blur streaked across the room, snapping me out of my trance and knocking me over. Kato's tawny wings felt like ice as they covered me, smothering the flames. Continuing to pat me, he cried, "Dorthea, are you okay?"

The euphoria of the intoxication was gone, and I felt frozen, physically trapped under the weight of the chimera. Mentally and emotionally, I seized up in shock. This was clearly another pixie dust–induced hallucination.

"It's amazing. I've never seen anything like it." Black Crow looked at me like you might look at a three-eyed toad.

That couldn't be a good thing.

"Take a look in the mirror." Her earlier craziness completely gave way to her curiosity. Well, maybe that wasn't true. She still looked utterly mad but more like a mad scientist.

I pushed Kato off me and walked to the mirror. Before looking in it, I glanced back at him. The look on his face was indecipherable, and I don't think it was just the furriness obscuring his thoughts. I had the feeling that his human face would have been just as difficult to read. His overall body language looked wary.

But of me or Black Crow?

I didn't want to look. I was afraid of what I would see. The girl of Emerald consumed by flames? A burned-black husk? Finally, I took a deep breath and stared in the mirror. My nose was no longer bleeding, swollen, or broken. All my earlier wounds were completely healed.

And my hair was still on fire.

Bright orange tendrils of flame weaved and swirled over my shoulders as if directed by the wind. The tips of my hair ended in emerald-green flickers.

"Get it out! Get it out!" I screamed. I beat at my head to tamp out the flames. They didn't go out, but they didn't burn my palms either.

"A living flame. I've only ever read about it in myths. I didn't think it could actually be achieved," Black Crow said with a tone of reverence.

"Where's a bucket of water?" I looked around frantically for the bathroom, ready to dunk my head in a toilet if I had to.

Crow grabbed my wrist. "I wouldn't do that if I were you. Living flame is life magic." Taking her razor feather, she cut off one of the emerald sparks and stuffed it into the empty vial.

"Hey! Give that back." I tried to swipe the vial, but she danced away. "And what does that mean, anyway?"

Kato spoke quietly. "The magic is tied to your life. Put simply, if those green flames die, so do you."

That little fact made me stop playing keep away and stare back into the mirror.

Crow prattled on, examining the vial. Turning it this way and that. "Quite right. Glad one of you has a brain. I still don't know how it was done though. The potion itself was a simple explosion hex, but I suppose when it mixed with the blood from your head wound... Well, look at the results. Do you understand what this means? How much money I could make using your blood with the rest of my potions?"

Black Crow paced, going on and on about possible combinations, but I mostly tuned her out. I stood transfixed by what I saw in the mirror. There was no pain—I wasn't getting burned. My fingers twirled the tendrils of flame unharmed.

Was it permanent? Could I ever shower again? What if I got caught in a rainstorm?

"—and maybe if Grizelda had given me a little bit of warning about your blood, I would have crafted the wishing star differently."

"You would have what?" My voice hardened, unrecognizable even to my own ears. The ends of my hair flared a brighter green.

Black Crow blinked a few times, trying to adjust to my abrupt change in attitude. "The star. I would have made—"

"You did this. You ruined my life. You made my parents disappear. You killed Verte."

"Now...I...d-d-don't...think," she stuttered, backing away from me.

The living flame turned inward, burning away nearly all rational thought. It honed my pain, my focus, and my rage onto one central point: Black Crow.

"Bring. Them. Back."

Crow's eyes went impossibly wide and her mouth went slack. She looked like she had seen the devil, and maybe she had. Backing farther away, she offered more denials, but her excuses fell on deaf ears. I could only hear a little voice whispering to me in the back of my head. It no longer chirped like a cricket. Now it slithered through my consciousness like a snake.

This woman has taken everything from you, just to make a quick buck. She deserves to pay. You could make her pay.

Yeah, I should make her pay. But first she was going to tell me how to undo this spell.

I sent my hands out to snatch her, but green flames burst from my palms instead. They slammed into Black Crow, knocking her into the potions case. All the remaining vials and bottles broke, spilling their contents onto her.

She didn't burst into flames like I had. Her skin turned a sallow yellow and bubbled, dripping like hot wax. One eye drooped down her cheek; the other pleaded with me. Her mouth tilted into a sickening mockery of a grin. Her limbs flattened and went boneless.

Without a doubt, the most horrifying thing I had ever seen.

And I had done it.

My earlier rage was extinguished immediately, replaced with a shame deep enough to bury a giant. "Oh my Grimm. I'm… I didn't…"

Her hand stretched out to me, and I rushed to it. Before I had a chance to help her, she slashed across my palm with a razored feather. Blood flowed freely from the almost surgical slice. I sat motionless as she applied my blood to her melting skin.

Within the room, the air changed. Something was happening but probably not what she wanted.

The puddling stopped and her skin re-formed into a solid state. She got a little taller and stiffer, the surface of her skin taking a clothlike appearance. Her face looked flat, like someone had painted all her features on. Her limbs got bulbous and lumpy, as though they were stuffed with straw. When the magic finished with her, the only thing that remained was a scarecrow.

The horror in front of me would not compute. I could have blamed a lot of things, but deep inside, I'd wanted this. Not *this* per se. But I'd needed Crow to pay, and she had. In full.

Mentally, I added Verte's and Black Crow's names to the tally of things I had a hand in destroying.

The list kept growing.

Kato sat by the bed; he had been ever since putting out the fire, quietly watching the events unfold. He hadn't reacted at all, and that just seemed wrong. Spell's bells, he still wasn't reacting at all to the fact that *I had just changed a living being into a scarecrow.*

He calmly stood and padded to the door.

"We can't leave. We have to do something." My voice cracked.

"There's nothing we can do for her. And she doesn't deserve your pity. Don't forget she tried to kill you and keep me for a pet."

"I don't need the reminder, thanks." Crow was in league with the wicked witch of the west, but right now, I felt like the bigger monster.

"Maybe you do. Evil needs to be stopped, whatever the cost."

The crackle of shattering glass came from outside, and the floor shook from some sort of impact.

"It's time for us to go." Kato turned again to leave.

"I'm staying. Rexi might still be here somewhere. And maybe I can help—" That plan went out the window. Or rather out the roof.

With a loud creaking sound, a large metallic gigan, with an equally large ax, sliced the roof off from the house. He peered down at us with empty black eyes and a nose that poked out crookedly, like the tip of an oilcan. Shiny, pieced-together tin plates made up the rest of his enormous body—including the hand that reaching down into the room.

Who Needs Fairy Dust to Fly?

R un!" Kato roared over the shrill creaking of the gigan.

Like I really needed that little piece of advice. I was already down the hall. "What the spell is that?" I shouted behind me.

"My guess would be the Tinman."

We ran out the front door and headlong into a different giant monster.

We were trapped. And I was out of ideas. "Glam it all. Isn't this a tad bit of overkill?"

"You wanted to know the plan, well, this is the plan," Kato sniped at me, then yelled up to the huge creature. "Bobbledandrophous, can you carry both of us on your back?"

The beast looked down in surprise. He was easily the size of the house, and now that I looked past the huge legs and really sharp talons, I could see that he bore a striking resemblance to Kato: lion head, ram horns, dragon tail, and ginormous wings. Oh, fairy fudge. Had I turned Kato's entire family into chimeras?

His voice boomed. "My Lord? How did—"

"Later. Escape now."

The beast lowered himself and allowed us to climb onto his back. "Yes, my lord. Is that little human yours as well?" The big chimera nodded to the side.

The little human was Rexi, tied to the laundry line with hot-pink panty hose. Her eyes were closed, but she stirred a little, so at least she was alive. Of course, if she opened her eyes and saw a massive chimera and a metal giant about to step on her, she might have a heart attack.

Tinman's creaking was ear-shattering, worse than finger-nails running down a cauldron. It made a great early warning system though. Bigger-version-of-Kato flapped his enormous black, feathery wings and took to the sky as the Tinman swung his ax in an attempt to bring us down.

"No!" I shouted. "We have to get Rexi." She wasn't much, but with Verte gone, she was the only tie I had left to Emerald.

A scream sounded from the ground below. Rexi was awake.

"What would you have me do, Highness?" asked our ride.

I started to reprimand the chimera when I realized that I was not the *Highness* the he was referring to.

"We don't have time for this, but leaving her here would give the Gray Witch the upper hand. Bank left and use the gigan's higher center of gravity to knock him over. Then fly swiftly and snatch up the line." Kato spoke with confidence and grace, giving directions with ease.

I'd had my doubts about Kato's claim to royalty—understandable given his earlier appearance, then kittenish nature after the change. That playfulness disappeared the more he grew, and there was no mistaking the air of authority he now wielded. Furry or not, he was a prince and not my pet.

The larger chimera did exactly as he was told, swooping low and using his tail to swat the Tinman.

That saying, *the bigger they are, the harder they fall*? Totally true. The Tinman flew back and landed right on the house, squishing it flat. He looked like a silver turtle stuck on its back, unable to flip itself over.

We took advantage of our fallen foe and flew back over to the clothesline. The chimera gingerly gathered the poles in his mouth, letting the line—and Rexi—hang down. If screaming and cursing were any indication, Rexi was not happy with her mode of rescue.

The Tinman creaked and groaned as he rolled off to the side, readying himself to stand.

"Fly, Bobbledandrophous! Take us home," Kato ordered.

Bobblewhatshisbucket curved sharply and flew away, hitting and denting the tin gigan with his barbed tail.

The chimera flew quickly, and I watched Crow's house and the Tinman grow rapidly smaller. Soon, I no longer heard his scraping sound, just Rexi's shrill shrieks as she kicked and flailed helplessly in midair.

"Shouldn't we get her up now?" I said.

Kato looked sheepish—and on a lion's face, that is something to see. "Do we have to? It might do her some good, you know."

"It might, but she'll also scream herself hoarse."

"I'm not hearing a downside."

I smacked his furry side. "Do I have to try and do it myself?"

Kato's cool blue eyes stared into mine.

"What?" I squirmed, suddenly feeling very self-conscious in my extremely expensive dress/now rag.

"I don't understand you. If you wanted, you could have that girl executed for treason for striking you. You lost an opportunity to get help from the wizard because you were too soft. Even Crow manage to garner your concern. You think personal accountability is something to do with your pocketbook, yet for some reason you still keep attempting to help people that don't deserve it."

"Thanks, I think."

He shook his head. "It's not a compliment, Dot."

My chest felt like it was being shredded by the shards of glass that still littered the big chimera's fur. *Dot.* That was the nickname Verte had given me as a child.

Kato huffed in his growing mane. "At best it's slightly

noble. At worse it's dangerous and puts everyone around you at risk. You mean well, but that won't keep us alive." He turned away, carefully padding his way up to speak to his friend and figure out a way to better secure Rexi.

I felt anything but secure. Sitting alone, I had nothing left to distract me from…me. Or what Kato said. Was he right? From playing with a lost child in the garden, to giving Crow information for food, my best intentions had brought nothing but ruins.

Soaring high in the clouds, my thoughts weighed me down like lead balloons. Everything was…wrong. This wasn't the way my life should be written. The Storymakers had made a misstep somewhere. Verte couldn't really, truly be gone. She had to be missing, just like my parents.

But she had been my one hope to setting the whole mess right-side up again. And now I had no idea what to do or where to go—or if I should go anywhere. Maybe with the curse, the world would be safer if I was dropped in a deep fireproof pit somewhere.

Kato and our beast pilot must have argued during their talk because as the enchanted prince made his way back down the larger chimera's back, his face looked like he'd sucked down a gallon of rotten curds and whey. I did my best to push all thoughts of the curse out of my head before he reached me. Denial, thy new princess is Dorthea.

Kato approached and shrugged his wings. "The best Bobbledandrophous can do is lower her down into his paws. It would be too risky to try and bring her up here midflight. She'll be fine…probably." He tilted his head and narrowed his eyes before plopping down in a big heap. On my lap.

"Ahh!" I tried to use his horns to pick his head up, but even that part of him weighed a ton. "What are you doing? Did you just die?"

"No," he growled and turned his face up, pursing his lips in total seriousness. "I've recently been advised that you might find the cute and fuzzy approach much less threatening. Supposedly it's also more endearing."

"I hate to tell you, but that Jolly Roger has sailed, sunk, and been eaten by ticking crocodiles." I tried to stifle a laugh, but it was too large to contain. Kato really had zero skill at manipulation, but at least he was honest.

"I told him it was a stupid idea," he grumbled and rolled off me.

"What gives? You've gone more than five minutes without finding some new way to call me incompetent."

Shaking his head, he swiped a paw across his face to hide what looked like a smile. "I can't decide if the Storymakers are brilliant or mad as hares for bringing us together as partners."

"*Partner* is an awfully strong word. Let's go with *associates for a brief duration until the ever-after part.*"

He sighed. "Well, I suppose that's an improvement over *disgusting beast.*" Finally he looked me in the eye. His glacial stare was serious but neutral and without disapproval—an improvement of its own. "We need to talk."

"Good, I'll go first." I sucked in the biggest breath possible to blurt out all the questions on my mind before Kato had a chance to change the subject. "The way I figure it, you seem to know a lot about me while I know next to nothing about you. Why is that? Were you friends with my parents? And what's this big threat thing to both our kingdoms? And where is your kingdom anyway? I've never ever heard of a chimera or seen pictures. Bob here looks like something out of a nightmare, especially the big pointy fangs."

"Bob?" Kato's muzzle quirked up in amusement. "He's not so scary, and he'd do anything to keep me from harm. And now you too."

"Avoiding the more important part of that rant."

Kato huffed and sat on his haunches across from me. His eyebrows drew together while he unfurled his right wing out wide. "That's where I'm from." He gestured to the mountain we were rapidly approaching. "Even though I lived a day's flight away, you could see the tall, glittering green towers to the South. I'd never been there or met your parents before Muse Day though. In fact, I rarely needed to venture away from my domain."

Instinctively, I scanned the skyline for the towers of Emerald City. They weren't there anymore.

He continued. "My home is nothing like yours. And I'll give you bit of warning now that you would be wise not to make a fuss about..." His face scrunched up as he searched until he found the term he was looking for. "The decor."

I stiffened in defense at the insinuation, but I really didn't have room to talk. When we first met, I had thought I was better than him because my clothes were designer and he had dirt smudges on his.

His tail poked my back in what I think was supposed to be a reassuring pat. "But don't feel too bad about not being in the know about chimeras. My *people* are a well-kept secret." He craned his neck and looked at the horizon. "You'll see soon enough though. We're almost there." He rose to all fours and turned away. "I'll be right back."

"Wait. Almost where?" I yelled and leaned forward as far as I dared. Before I could get any answers, he'd already kind of hopped, skipped, and flew back up to the top. I still didn't understand why he pushed for the *alliance*. (A much better word than *engagement*.) And what exactly did he mean, his "people"? What kind of kingdom was Kato prince to?

"Hang on, my lady," Bob bellowed. That's all the warning I got before he arched into a steep swan dive on a crash course with the mountain.

I did the only thing I could—took a death grip on his fur and joined Rexi in screaming my head off. As the mountain got closer and we hadn't slowed, I closed my eyes. I didn't need to know which jagged edge was going to rupture my spleen.

My first clue that we didn't hit the mountain was the lack

of a bone-crunching splat. The second was a little more subtle—our screams echoed back at me. I'd missed it because my eyes were shut, but we must have flown into a cavern or tunnel or something.

No, that wasn't right either. I think we were somehow *inside* the mountain.

Everything was pitch-black; the only light came from my flaming hair. The sinking in the pit of my stomach told me that we were headed down. I saw a warm, red glow bouncing off the walls ahead. The closer we got, the hotter the temperature.

Please, Grimm, don't let us be traveling to the pits of hell.

The rocky chute ended abruptly, dumping us into a surreal new world. My first thought was, *There is no way all of this could fit inside of a mountain.* My second was, *Of course it has to be made up almost completely of fire.*

A Whole New Hotter World

A river of bubbling lava bisected the ground. On the right half was a meadow of sorts. Bright flowers bloomed up from the solid obsidian ground. Not your ordinary tulips though. These blossoms reminded me of the fireworks the kingdom shot off on festival days. They glowed and crackled, making starbursts of colorful flames—red, blue, purple, yellow, orange, white...every color but green.

What exactly did you call a large group of chimeras? A flock? A parliament? A pride? Whatever you called it, that's what was on the other side of the lava flow—lots and lots of chimeras. With their overgrown wings tucked around them, they reminded me of nesting birds, except their nests looked like giant hearths. Great rings of glowing red embers made the perfect bed for a chimera apparently.

Most of them were sleeping, and I was all about letting sleeping chimeras lie. If Kato's penchant for eating everything that wasn't nailed down was a common chimera trait, then I didn't want to be close at hand when they awoke for supper.

Luckily, our ride banked off to the right, coasting to a stop amid the colorful blooms. I slid down his back, anxious to be on solid ground again.

"Dot, wait!" Kato shouted right as my feet squished one of the blooms.

When I craned my neck to look up at him, he was staring at the flowers, aghast. My silver slippers reflected the light from the fire blossoms. "Sorry," I said. "Are they important?"

Kato flapped down to me awkwardly. He was still getting used to the whole flying bit. "You shouldn't be able to stand. Fire flowers are thousands of degrees. No human can survive them."

"Nice of you tell me *now* as opposed to *before* I hopped off into a floral minefield." But I couldn't be too mad, since I was no worse for wear. "My toes feel a little warm, but that's it." I picked up my feet, one at a time, and looked down at my ruby-soled heels. They were top quality, but I'm pretty sure they weren't designed with heat resistance in mind. They had been a gift from Verte. Maybe she'd added a little something *extra* to the original design.

I looked them over with a whole new appreciation. "Enchanted shoes. Awesome."

Rexi had stopped screaming herself hoarse the minute Kato yelled, "Wait!" Now she stepped out of Bob's paws and walked lightly on tippy toes around the fiery meadow. Then she bopped Kato on the nose the moment he got within range.

Kato flinched from the blow. "*Ow!* You can't do that to me in my own kingdom."

"Yes, I can. Because you keep trying to *kill* me. First, you dangle me like a worm from a giant bird's beak, and now you drop me down someplace that's supposed to melt my feet off." Rexi stopped, straightened the wrinkles in her tunic, and jerked her thumb in my direction, not really looking at me. "Dorky's glammed lucky her shoe fetish finally paid off, but indentured servitude doesn't exactly pay for magical footwear." She made a fist as if to bop him again, but he flapped himself out of range.

Rexi was really starting—okay, not *starting*, more like continuing—to pix me off. The big piece of hair draped over my shoulder sparked and flared, mirroring my irritation. Before that, the bright glow had died down a bit, almost making the pieces I could see look like they came from a natural redhead—with green tips.

Guess it brought a whole meaning to the idea of a temper flare.

The flash drew Rexi's attention, and she walked, carefully,

over to me. She peered closer around my head, apparently noticing it for the first time. "What happened to your hair? New fashion trend or something else equally stupid? Because I've got to tell you, it doesn't really suit you."

"For Grimm's sake, will you shut your mouth for one fairy-loving minute," I snapped, losing the last sliver of patience I had.

She jerked back as if I'd slapped her. I'd have to worry about her hurt feelings later, because right now, we had other problems. We were about to have guests.

Curious chimeras flew over the lava flow to see what all the fuss was. They conferred and whispered with one another, pointing at us with their tails. A shiver racked my body, traveling up my spine. Some of their tails were serpentlike—with actual serpent heads.

I couldn't make out what anyone was saying though, and not just because they were whispering. Have you ever heard a one-ton beast whisper? It's not very quiet. No, it was all the voices talking at once that created a buzz so that no one voice could be easily picked out from the group.

Kato launched himself in the air and landed on the nearest outcropping of rock. He let out what was probably meant to be a mighty roar, but it came out more like a squeak. The room full of chimeras guffawed and heckled him.

"Whose hatchling is that?"

"From the belly, pup. Ha ha, try again. From the belly."

Kato did not take to being mocked very well. He sent them

all frostbite-worthy looks, but the other beasts paid him no mind. To them, he was a pipsqueak who had left the hatchery too soon. Kato's voice could not rise above the din.

Chimeras surrounded us. Rexi jostled into me, and I took a step back, my heel landing on something squishy. Angry hissing rose from the floor and traveled up the length of my body until the forked tongue from a serpent tail licked along my arm. I followed the line of the tail up to its chimera owner. His body was patched with scars interrupting his fur, his wings looked like they were molting, and one of his horns was broken off. The other was sharper than any sword I've seen. Both the chimera and his snake tail raised part of their lip in a snarl, exposing fangs.

"Enough!"

I looked up at Kato, grateful that he had finally found his voice. But it wasn't him speaking.

Bob parted the circle and walked toward Rexi and me, fire flowers falling victim to each step. "How dare you mock our lord?"

Bob was the largest of the bunch, but not by much. He also seemed to be well respected because the other chimeras backed off. Most of them, anyway. The chimera that owned the stepped-on tail got in Bob's face.

"Our lord is not here. He abandoned us to go collect some child bride. I only see a walking matchstick girl and her mouthy human. I, for one, am tired of outsiders coming into our home. First the green witch, and now this piece of kindling." Using his snake-headed tail, he gestured over to me in disgust.

I skipped over the insults and focused on the really important part. Verte had been here. Why and when? I wanted to go over and beat it out of him, but even I wasn't that stupid.

Kato flew haltingly next to me, staring fearlessly up at the bully, even though the tips of Kato's horns only came up to the bully's armpits. "Grifflespontus, I suggest that you apologize to your future queen. And then you may apologize to me."

I thought I'd been pretty clear with him and itched to argue about the whole "future queen" part of that, but now didn't seem like the right time.

Griff was a little slow on the uptake. He didn't notice the other chimeras gasp and hurriedly bow on their forepaws. He lowered himself muzzle to muzzle with Kato. "And why should I apologize to a runt like you?"

Kato's ice-blue eyes honed in on Griff. "Because I am your liege, and if you don't, I will continue to freeze you where you stand."

I looked down at the bully's paws. They were covered in frost crystals.

Rexi scooted away from me to get a closer look. "Whoa. Is fur ball doing that? When did he get that little nifty trick?" She shook her head in disgust. "Typical, everyone else gets cool magic and all I get is tied up with old lady tights."

Whatever he was doing, it didn't look easy. I don't think anyone else noticed because they were all looking at the ice growing up Griff's legs, but Kato's shoulders held a fine tremor. He swayed slightly, unsteady on his feet.

I walked over and laid a hand on his back, which now rested just above my waist. "Enough."

Kato continued to do his icy stare but whispered, just barely audible, "Stay out of it. This isn't your concern."

I leaned into his ear. "I'm saving your tail before you fall over on it from exhaustion. Remember, finesse over force." Loud enough for all to hear, I said in my best princess voice, "Please spare this poor fool. He obviously could not recognize you in your new form."

Rexi may have rolled her eyes at the change in my tone, but the bully was not as dumb as he looked. He grabbed on to the lifeline I offered him. "Forgive me," he said through chattering fangs. "I could never have expected to see the future Beast King as a beast himself."

Griff let out one more frosted breath before Kato released him, apparently accepting his quasi-apology. I let out the breath I was holding too, relieved that this little confrontation was over and that everyone was still standing—and uneaten.

Bob, however, wasn't going to let Griff get off that easy. "You forgot the priestess." He pushed his way through to stand next to me.

Rexi didn't take too well with being pushed aside. "Look, Bob, I don't know what baby fur ball over here"—she stuck her thumb out at Kato—"has been telling you. But she's no priestess. Just a delusional princess with major hair issues."

And here I thought *I* had trouble knowing when to keep my thoughts to myself. Bob stared down at Rexi. I couldn't see the look on his face, but it must have been scary because it made her shrink a few inches and hastily mutter something that might have been a sorry.

Bob turned back to face the other chimera. "Your turn now. Apologize."

"Apologize to a human?" said Griff haughtily. Apparently arrogance was a natural chimera trait.

"Use your eyes. No mere human stands before you. See the emerald sparks in her living flame? That is not mere magic. That is the sign of the Fire Priestess come to deliver us."

Oh spell. Now Bob had done it. I had no idea what he was going on about (Kato had conveniently left that out of our *talk*), but I didn't get the chance to correct him. If Griff had offered an apology, which was doubtful, I wouldn't have been able to hear, because every chimera started shouting at once. A few muzzles got very up close and personal, trying to examine Bob's claims for themselves.

"Silence!" Kato bellowed and the temperature in the room dropped significantly, causing the crowd to still. "Bobbledandrapous, not another word. Please see our guests to my chambers, where they can rest." He turned and focused his icy glare on me. "I will speak to the council and join you shortly. Don't do *anything* until then."

Kato was in full Lord of the Universe mode. So much for being equals. I didn't want to be led to some room. While it was nice to have found a safe place—if you could call a mountain filled with lava and large beasts safe—the situation had changed. With Verte captured or worse, nobody was coming to the rescue. We all needed to come up with a new plan to find my parents and put back the rules of fairy tale. What did Kato have to deal with that could be more important than that?

I stepped to him. "Can't I—?"

"No." Kato turned away and stalked off toward an opening near the hearths. The remaining chimeras followed him or went back to their nests until it was just Rexi, me, Bob, and Griff. Griff looked over me like I imagined trolls looked over billy goats.

Sneering, he turned and flew away. As he raced into the sky, his tail hissed menacingly. The stress must be getting to me, because I could have sworn it sounded like, "Sssleep with both eyesss open."

"There's really nothing to fear but fear itself. And trolls. Fear and trolls. Oh, and I guess gigans and dragons too. And can't forget wicked witches. Yeah, I guess there really is a lot to fear."

—*Prince Charming*, excerpt from an interview in *Hero Beat*

18

Blanc Stare

While Bob led us through the claw-carved corridors, Rexi quizzed me on what had happened at Black Crow's. I gave her the back-of-the-book version. Crow sold us off to Griz. Kato learned to talk. I got hit in the head with a potion and now had hair you could toast marshmallows on. The end.

"So what happened to Black Crow? Is she going to come after us again?" Rexi asked, her voice tight.

My heart stopped for a moment and so did my feet.

I coughed to cover my unease. "No. I think she's dead. After all, the Tinman and a house fell on her."

No one else needed to know what happened to Crow before that.

"Good riddance." Rexi's whole body exhaled, the tension disappearing. "Ding dong, the bi—"

"Are you two even listening? I feel like I'm talking to myself," Bob interrupted.

Both of us assured him that he had our utmost attention.

"Good." He turned and continued on, apparently satisfied. "And on your left, you'll see the original hearth where Pufflepotomous the First slept."

"I'm not sure what's more surprising, the fact that chimeras preserved a centuries' old nest or that there was more than one named Pufflepotomous," Rexi whispered, nudging me.

"Shhh," I whispered, but gave her a small smile to let her know I appreciated being included on a joke that I wasn't the target of for once.

I was still miffed at Kato for running off and leaving Bob to play tour guide when we had way more pressing concerns. But since there was nothing to be done about it now, I might as well make the most of it and pump Bob for information. I hurried forward to catch his attention before he could launch into a discussion about how he was Horanthamum the Third's second to last cousin. Twice removed. "So, Bob, was this Puff the Magic Chimera the founder of…whatever this is?"

He stopped and used a wing to gesture all around him. "Not exactly. Pufflepotomus was the first alpha to nest in this home. But it was the magnificent Bestiamimickos who combined the clans and claimed the title as King of Beasts. And the clans have been united here ever since, keeping watch of the White One…tending the flames… I probably shouldn't have said that." He quickened his pace to leave us behind.

Not happening.

"Keeping watch over what? The white what?" I asked.

"I can't say. We are not to speak of her to outsiders." Bob looked at us with wide eyes, practically begging us not to say anything to Kato.

I wouldn't, and he'd kind of accidentally answered my question anyway. The white one was a *her*. Of course, that opened up a whole 'nother can of questions.

I tried bugging and badgering him with them, but he steadfastly refused to utter another word about the White One or the whole Fire Priestess thing. He tried to distract me with details about Kato and his family, like that his parents had died a few years ago—meaning we were both orphans, although my state of orphan-hood was just temporary— and that his mom was the Frost Queen, which is where the snow cone trick Kato pulled earlier had come from.

We stopped at the entrance to a smaller cave, one that had a human-sized entrance—clearly Kato's room, since there was no way for a chimera to fit. Even Kato probably wouldn't fit anymore. Apparently this was our stop, but I wasn't ready to let Bob go yet. I still had questions. I wanted to know what kind of prince Kato was, why the chimeras were ruled by a human, and what had brought Kato to Emerald in the first place.

Rexi was apparently on the same wavelength, which was disturbing. "Hey, Bob, why do you guys follow Kato anyway? He's less than a quarter of your size, and as a human, he's even less impressive."

Bob shifted his weight uncomfortably from paw to paw. It almost looked like he had to use the little chimera's room.

I decided to add some pressure, because I wanted to know the answer too. "If I'm supposed to be this priestess, shouldn't I know these things?" I crossed my arms and looked at Bob expectantly.

Rexi nodded appreciatively and leaned close to whisper, "Very manipulative. I like it."

Bob still looked distressed. "I don't know... He made it very clear that I wasn't to say any more about it and that he'd rather tell you himself." The dilemma must have deflated him, because he let out a great big sigh and slumped to the ground in front of us. With his chin on the floor, the top of his head was just a pinch higher than mine. If I stood tall and reached, I could probably touch his ears tufts.

Bob glanced around nervously, checking to make sure we wouldn't be overheard. It reminded me of when the chambermaids gossiped with each other in the hallway when they thought no one was looking.

Someone was always looking.

"I'm just passing along what I've heard. Bestiamimickos was the greatest chimera to ever live, but he was in love with a human princess. So he begged the Storymakers to transform him so they could be together. And ever since, the Beast Kings have been human, including Lord Kato. But he can't claim the title for himself until after he's married, although with his mother's command of ice and his father's power over beasts, he's powerful enough to fend off any challenges for the title for a little while. Although now with you at his side, all the dissenters will follow him because—" Bob's muzzle remained open and his eyes widened perceptibly.

I started to ask if he was okay, but all I got was dust in my mouth as Bob flew down the hall. He sped off as if the Big Bad Wolf were knocking on his door. I'm pretty sure he wasn't scared of me or Rexi, soooo…

"There's someone behind me, isn't there?"

"Yup."

"Is he small and fluffy or big and ugly?"

Rexi squinted and weighed her answer. "That's a matter of perspective."

I finally turned to face Kato, and he was not a happy chimera. He looked like he had aged ten years while he was with the council. In fact, my mother often had that same worn-out face after she spoke with her advisors.

His tail tapped the floor. "I thought I told you to rest and stop asking questions."

"Sheesh, Mr. Bossypants," I said under my breath. "You were much cuter when you couldn't talk and chased your tail."

Rexi coughed into her hand.

Kato didn't share our amusement. "You wanted to know

what threatened our realms and why I needed an alliance with Emerald. You're about to get your wish." He turned and padded down the hall, clearly expecting us to follow.

The way he phrased that last sentence did not sit well with me. I didn't want to wish for anything ever again. Maybe I was better off not knowing anything.

But it's probably helpful to know what to be scared of as opposed to waiting and finding out when it bites you in the rump. I ran to catch up, picking up my skirts and matching my two-legged stride to his four-legged one.

"He looks pixed at you. I am so not missing this." Rexi hastily followed, with, if I wasn't mistaken, a skip in her step.

"Where are we going?" I said breathlessly.

"To meet Blanc."

"What's a blanc?"

"Not what. Who."

"Okay. *Who* is Blanc?"

Kato stopped so suddenly that I ran into him. "*That* is Blanc," he said, lowering his head and using his horns to gesture in front of us.

In the far corner was a giant furnace of some sort—a big metal box with a wall of flame in front and two chimeras taking turns spitting molten lava into the sides.

Within the box stood the most beautiful woman I had ever seen. She had long white hair—not white blond, pure-snow white. She wore a simple shift that was, you guessed it, white. Everything about her was empty, lacking in color or personality. Except her eyes. They were silver, and they pleaded.

I ran a few feet toward her before the heat from the flames pushed me back.

"Holy Mother of Grimm. You're cooking virgins or something else cultish," Rexi said from behind me.

Kato snorted. "Do you see her screaming in agony? No. Up until a few days ago, she'd been in a magical slumber for the last two centuries." He walked over and sat in front of the wall of fire. "We're not cooking her. We are guarding her."

I stared at the woman, transfixed. She seemed frozen—all but her entreating stare. "Guarding her from what?"

"Guarding the world *from* her."

I whipped around. The tumblers in my brain started to click. "She's the White One." I gestured over to the chimeras shoveling the coal. "And your whole 'kingdom'"—I made little quotation marks around the word—"is all about keeping her imprisoned."

Rexi ventured closer to the furnace prison and stilled, seeming to get into a staring contest with the woman. "So what did she do? Try to bake children into gingerbread cookies? Send a huntsman to kill off her much better-looking stepdaughter?" Rexi tilted her head to the right and to the left, like she was studying one of the animals at the palace menagerie.

She had asked, not so eloquently, exactly what I had been thinking. What could Blanc have done to deserve this?

155

I studied the woman, trying to spot the flaw, the sign of her crimes.

"Let me tell you two a story." Kato sat on his haunches, extending his paw over to a desk along the wall. He still used very humanlike gestures that I hadn't seen the other chimeras use. "It even has pictures," he said snidely in Rexi's direction.

Rexi was busy flipping Kato off, so I got to the desk with its single chair and took a seat first. The desk had a few papers, but it was mostly bare, except for a thick tome. The cover was bound in some kind of hide and had curly letters written in platinum across the front: *Blanc Pages*.

I opened the book to a random spot. There were no words, just a large picture. It was of a younger Blanc, and she was happy and smiling.

"What is that?" Rexi brushed against my back, startling me.

"It's a book," Kato said wryly.

"Well, I can see that, gnome nuts, but why are the pictures moving?"

Rexi was right; it was like watching a magic mirror or a play transformed onto the page. I'd only seen one other like it before, an ebook—the *e* short for *enchanted*. They were extremely rare, and some said they could only be made by the Storymakers themselves.

Kato might have answered Rexi. I don't know. I was too transfixed on what I saw on the page. The girl sat on the edge of a lake next to a boy. The water danced and spun through the air, performing acrobatics.

Kato cleared his throat. "Once upon a time, there was a family of powerful, evil elemental mages. Their eldest daughter was a water sorceress with no interest in villainy. She vowed to be good, left her parents and sister, and then fell in love with a handsome prince—but his parents didn't approve." The images changed along with Kato's words. The happy scene of the two lovebirds shifted into one that looked like Blanc arguing with a man and a woman. I could see her mouth moving but couldn't hear the words.

I glanced over my shoulder at Kato. "Why isn't there sound?"

He shrugged his wings. "Probably the same reason everything else magic is a little glitchy."

Oh yeah, me. I turned back and watched the book some more.

Kato continued. "The king and queen didn't think Blanc was good enough for the prince because of who she was and who her parents were." He'd brushed on a touchy subject, and I could practically feel Rexi stiffening beside me. "So the king enlisted the help of a warlock to curse her, but it backfired." And that brushed on a touchy subject for me.

Kato didn't say anything else and the book took over. The images bounced and sometimes broke with a little static, but it was still clear what was happening. Blanc and her prince held hands and took a stroll in the forest, but a dark figure lurked under a nearby tree. He offered the couple a beautiful white blossom, which the prince accepted and then gave to Blanc. Shifting again, the picture changed to a close-up of the prince kissing Blanc. That's when things went wrong. The prince started sputtering and coughing. Water trickled from his lips, slow at first, then gushing out. Blanc watched him with a look of helpless horror as he drowned.

I gasped sharply, and I'm sure my expression matched Blanc's almost exactly. "This can't be right. The handsome prince *never* dies. That's not how it works."

"Oh wake up," Rexi said, slamming her hand against the wood. "When are you going to move past your sheltered little palace mind-set and realize that your precious Storymakers aren't real? They're stories told to little children so they won't be afraid of the Jabberwock under the bed and will have nice dreams of happy ever afters. It's time to grow up. Bad things happen, parents sell their children to pay taxes, dreams only come true if you have enough money, and there's no one up there answering my prayers. Or yours." She stormed out of the room.

There was nothing I could do or say to stop her, because in that moment, I realized I knew nothing about Rexi or what pain had scarred her enough to bear such hatred toward her creators.

But she was wrong. She had to be wrong. Life made no sense otherwise. Someone had to author the rules that we lived by. As long as you followed those, the Makers made sure it all worked out. If no one else was guiding this story, then that meant... My home. My parents. Who would bring them back?

19

Princess and the Beast

Rexi's rant upset and unbalanced me more than I let show on the outside. I tried to match my expression to the woman in the corner: stoic and blank.

Neither one of us followed after Rexi, and when she didn't come back, Kato scooted into her spot and continued the story. "Like *almost* everyone, Blanc had worshipped and prayed to the Storymakers her whole life. Now she blamed them for how her story turned out. She lashed out, using the curse and her magic to take revenge." In the picture, Blanc no longer smiled or laughed. The white, which previously seemed bright and innocent, now looked stark and empty. She stalked toward the shadowy man hiding in the tree. The warlock appeared to beg and plead, but she drew him in and kissed him. Within moments, the warlock lay on the ground—drowned in the middle of the forest.

I had seen enough and turned away.

Clearing his throat softly, Kato brought my attention back to him. "But she wasn't done yet." Kato nudged me back to face the book. "Still unhappy, she decided to find the Storymakers and force them to rewrite her story. But to do that, she would need a lot more power and help. She found an ally in a powerful chimera, Bestiamimickos, who was also unhappy with his story. He loved a princess who would not love him back since he wasn't human royalty. So Blanc showed him how to use life magic to control beasts and named him king of them all. In return, he brought an army of chimeras to make war on the Storymakers and, together, to force them to revise their fates."

I'd already heard Bob's history of the first Beast King, and I liked that version, the lovey-dovey one, better. I watched what Kato and the book wanted to show me anyway. The images moved rapidly. Blanc, along with other witches and the chimeras, burned through villages—and Blanc no longer had to kill by kiss. Somehow, she was able to draw all the water out of a person, leaving them mummified.

"She began stealing magic, at first only taking from the wicked. But it twisted her soul. When she realized that the strongest power came from life magic, she started stealing life instead. Drunk on her new power, she decided that the only way to correct her story and bring back her prince was to erase

Spelled

everything and start again. She proclaimed herself the empress of all story and wiped away entire species, whole fairy tales."

I looked over at the real live Blanc again, behind her wall of flames. There was no evidence of the young girl who wanted to be good despite what her parents were. She had twisted into something else. Maybe the curse had tainted her. Maybe she had always been destined to be evil. I understood a little bit about loss and pain, about pushing and fighting against your destiny. But to take it out on everyday people... "What kind of villain does that?"

"All of them," Kato said, his tail hitting the cave wall.

Unbidden, the image of Beauty becoming the Beast came to mind. I shook my head. That was different. I didn't mean to screw up anybody's story. I was different.

Wasn't I?

"How did she end up here?" I turned to the book and watched the story unfold through the pictures and Kato's words.

"Supposedly, the Beast King finally caught a Storymaker and forced the Maker to transform him into a human." On the page, a group of chimeras stood next to an older man with odd clothes and a curled mustache. The man touched the one with golden horns, and the chimera became human. My guess was that he was the Beast King, but that would make the other man...

"That can't be a Storymaker." I leaned in closer to try and get a better look. "He doesn't look all-powerful. Just old."

161

Kato shrugged his haunches. "I find it hard to believe myself. But that is the story that has been passed down for centuries. After becoming human, Bestiamimickos returned to his princess and realized he had been tricked—no matter what form he took on the outside, the princess could never love someone who had caused such suffering to other stories."

Now the book showed a young girl. She looked plain, her clothes had few frills, but her brown hair was braided into a crown of green and gold.

"As a magical empress, Blanc had so much power, she became basically immortal. Nothing could kill her. But she still needed to be stopped. The princess demanded that the Beast King make amends for his crimes by betraying Blanc and sacrificing his power to imprison her."

The picture showed the supposed Storymaker writing in a book with a quill on the cover. Now-human Besti-Mc-whatever-his-name held Blanc down while the princess put gold bands around Blanc's neck and wrists.

"With those, the Storymaker, princess, and King of Beasts bound Blanc's powers, trapping the evil sorceress in magical flame."

I hadn't noticed the gold jewelry before, so I looked at the real Blanc again. Sure enough, a glint of gold barely peeked out from under her bell sleeves and high neckline.

"So then what happened? As far as happy endings go, I've seen better. Your king didn't get the girl, and Blanc didn't suddenly see the error of her ways and become a good white witch."

Kato tilted his head to the side, tapping his chin with his tail. "Well, I suppose the story isn't over yet. The Beast King vowed to someday deserve the princess's love. Until then, he exiled himself, but first, he ordered the chimeras to spend eternity watching over Blanc, keeping the flames burning in punishment for the sins they committed for the sorceress. The ritual of life magic to control beasts was passed down to each future generation to crown a new Beast King. That, of course, includes me. The sole purpose of my life has been to rule over the chimeras, watch the White One, and keep the flames. That is, until yesterday."

I waited for the book to show me what happened to the princess, but the picture jumped and filled with static. Finally the whole page turned dark, with only a white, half-eaten, poisoned apple in the center.

I shifted my body around to watch Kato, since the book had broken. "What changed?" I asked.

"You did, Dot."

I fell right off the edge of my seat.

Kato wiped a paw across his face, another humanlike gesture. "My best guess is that your wish affected the magic that kept her asleep. The fire is going out and nothing we're doing is working. She'll be free in a matter of weeks. Then Grimm save us all."

The weight of the air tripled and landed squarely on my

shoulders. This was bigger than making vacuums fly screwy or trees wither and turn cannibalistic. Seeing Blanc's story unfold pulled away the final pieces of wool I'd used to cover my eyes. Denial was no longer an option. But I couldn't remember what had been going through my head when I'd wished the world away. Had I just been spouting off because my temper had gotten the best of me again? Or had I, somewhere deep in my subconscious, known the wish would work this way? Did it even matter? I was still responsible whether it was on purpose or not.

True, but one makes you a monster. The other one just makes you an idiot. Which one is it?

"What are you going to do?" I asked quietly and got up off the floor, dusting off my scorched and tattered dress.

Kato stretched and paced. I couldn't help but notice he was moving away from the other chimeras—and from Blanc. "Over the years, a sort of legend about Blanc's weakness has been passed down with the power. I never put any stock in it." He paused for effect. "Until now."

I rolled my eyes, taking a page from Rexi. "Overdramatic much? Just tell me what the legend said already."

Kato continued pacing, talking to himself now more than me. "I mean, it sounded like a bunch of fairy dust. Why would changing the color of the flames matter? But for generations, we've tried everything anyway—tried feeding the fire with gemstones and magic, crossbred until we had dozens of different colors and species of fireflowers, but we could never get flame like the one the legend described."

You know that feeling that you get in the pit in your stomach? The one that goes along with the warning bells ringing in your head that screams, *Don't ask! You don't want to know.* Yeah, I had that feeling.

"What color?"

Kato stopped pacing and used the full power of his ice-blue stare. He winced, as if saying it would hurt. But hurt him or me?

"Emerald. The legend says that only emerald flames can free us from our vows."

I said nothing, waiting for the ax to drop.

"Dot, you need to kill Blanc."

Mirror, Mirror, Broken on the Wall

Even while my mind balked at the idea, Emerald flames leaped to my fingertips. My vision clouded over, and Blanc glowed like a flare.

All that power. Yours for the taking. Make the world the way you want it. Make yourself into a real hero.

So easy. I could be strong and no one would call me useless again.

Heat danced across my palm.

"Are you okay?" Kato flicked his tail against my leg.

The thump returned my vision and senses to normal. The flames disappeared, but I still felt an oily residue where they'd been. Not a physical coating, but the kind of stain that would never go away, no matter how many times I washed them.

"No," I answered simply.

"No, you're not okay? Or no, you won't fulfill our alliance and eliminate Blanc?"

"Both," I said and walked away.

I thought about going back to "my room," but I needed some time…just…away from everyone. After watching Blanc's story, then feeling the lure of my own flames, an unwelcome theory started to form in my mind, an explanation for why the story had skewed so far off course.

Maybe I wasn't the hero.

Maybe I was the villain.

I roamed the vast network of caverns for a long time, trying very hard *not* to think or glance at my fiery reflection in the shiny obsidian walls. Unfortunately, that meant I paid no attention to where I was going. All the pointy rock things looked the same, and I was lost.

More than just directionally.

I slumped to the ground and put my head in my hands. *Someone tell me what to do.*

Mom and I had our issues. Mainly because she wasn't content running the whole kingdom; she had to rule everything about my life too. Though it was a trait I hated, I could use her take-charge attitude about now.

I really miss her.

Someone snorted. *Has to be Rexi.* I looked up.

She was leaning against one of the caves many turns, munching on some sort of steaming red fruit. "You're going the wrong way if you're looking for food. And before you even ask, no, I'm not sharing mine. Get your own." Somewhere, she'd found a knapsack, and she clutched it protectively to her chest.

Food of any kind sounded pretty good. I stood and headed the direction she indicated. Her footsteps shadowed mine.

I paused and said, "Didn't you hoard enough food? Because I figure I'd be about the last person you wanted to tag along with."

"True if we're talking *people*. But when the alternative is dozens of giant, hungry beasts, believe it or not, you're better company."

"So why don't you leave the mountain? You've gotta have family somewhere. Haven't you gotten the memo? I pixed up the whole world order. There's no more Emerald Palace. No dishes to wash. No princess to serve. You don't owe me anything, and you don't have to stay with me anymore."

"Sheesh. What happened to you that you are willing to admit that?" She crossed her arms. "Still, where else am I gonna go? I'm not exactly on good terms with my folks, and like you said, you pixed the world. Everything you've done up to this point has gotten us into more trouble. Odds are you're going to do something right soon, and since I've already put up with all the zip-a-dee-doo-*doo*, I'd like to be there when the good stuff finally happens."

That probably wouldn't be anytime soon.

Tiny tremors shook the ground beneath my feet. I'd felt them on and off earlier and learned to ignore them. This time they didn't stop and rumbled louder in a steady rhythm—the cadence of a two-ton chimera running down the cavern full speed.

Bob saw us a little late and dragged his tail in an attempt to brake. He veered right and stopped—after busting through a wall.

"Priestess," he called breathlessly. "My hearth warms seeing that you are all right."

"I'm fine too, not that you care," Rexi muttered.

Bob ignored her. "My lord ordered me to find you and confirm your safety."

Undeterred, Rexi asked, "Why couldn't the Lord of the Fleas come?"

I knew Bob wouldn't answer her, so I rephrased, "Where exactly is Kato?"

"There's been an incident. Nothing major." Bob avoided my gaze by turning tail. Literally.

I couldn't keep up with the chimera's stride, so I called out, "Is he okay?"

Bob froze in his tracks. He faced me and tilted his head to one side. "You are having concerned feelings for him?"

"Yes, of course."

Bob smiled all the way to his horns and gave a smug nod. "Good, then you will be queen after all."

"Not those kinds of feelings." I sighed. "It's complicated."

Bob nudged me and winked. "Say no more. I was a hatchling once myself. True love is like a stalactite meeting a stalagmite. Complete opposites, but with time, calcium, and a healthy drip system, they meet in the middle. Or one crushes the other. It really depends." He continued on his path a little slower but with a happy spring in his step. "Fear not, future mistress. Your love will be fine, I'm sure. In the worst case, he'll only have to break one talon. Seven will still be intact."

I nearly tripped over my own feet. "Kato couldn't be bothered to look for me because he's having nail issues?" Stupid pox-prattled…

"Wow, and I thought you were vain." Rexi took a bite of steaming fruit. "Or is this his solution to our problems?" *Munch munch.* "He's making a claw dagger?" *Munch munch.* "Or does the Gray Witch have some horrible fear of bad manicures?"

Bob looked at me like, *She's your responsibility; you handle her.*

Too bad, in this case, I happened to agree with the snark queen. "Yeah, what she said."

Bob gave an exasperated sigh. "Really, do you know nothing about your true love?"

I chose not dignify that with a response, unless you counted the withering look I gave him.

"Each prince of the Beast King's line has some natural influence over beasts. But to use that power over a great distance or to compel someone to do something against their will, he must tap directly into the source of his life magic." Bob held up his paw.

"That's how he called you to rescue us yesterday. He used life magic." Life magic…What had Black Crow said about life magic? Comprehension dawned. "His life is within his fingernails? Do they grow back?"

Bob shook his head sadly. "No, Priestess. When all his nails are broken, he will die."

A giggle escaped from Rexi. She slapped a hand over her mouth. "You can't get a haircut, and he can't have a manicure. Death by salon visit," she managed to stammer out behind her hand.

It was a horribly inappropriate comment, considering the gravity of the situation. Not that I expected anything else from Rexi. So my only excuse for joining in was that laughter is terribly contagious.

Bob shook his head and shuffled away, muttering, "I don't understand younglings these days. Follow me to your new chambers."

"Wait." My laughter died in an instant. "Why do we need *new* chambers? What happened to the *old* one?" My mind caught hold of that line of thought and started racing. "In fact, what sort of incident would make Kato use his life magic?"

Apparently, Bob found the ceiling fascinating, because he wouldn't look down at me. "My lord said he had it all under control and has instructed me not to worry you so—"

"Now," I ordered in a serious tone that demanded be obeyed.

Bob covered his eyes with one paw and pointed down a side hall with the other. "Grifflespontus caused the royal chambers to erupt in an act of mutiny."

"What?" Rexi said while I started running.

"I knew I heard that stupid snake tail talk," I grumbled to myself. "Minor incident my royal…"

As soon as I turned the corner, the temperature dropped below zero. Rubble already filled the corridor, but in the cold, the falling ash looked like snow. The human-sized entry was gone—and so was most of the wall and room. A miniature volcano took up most of the floor space, though there was still part of a bed lying nearby. At least I thought it used to be a bed.

Glad I went for a walk instead of coming back here for a nap.

Moving on, I headed toward a dull roar I recognized as Kato's.

I found him in a large cavern that reminded me of the throne room at the Emerald Palace, except everything here was carved from rock and not precious metals or jewels. Mirrors, stuck in glowing embers on the wall, refracted light around the room. And Kato was ordering a few guard beasts to move a set of chimera ice sculptures.

Though ice sculptures weren't usually that scarred and ugly—nor did they have moving eyes. In fact, I recognized one of the serpent tails frozen in mid-hiss.

"Dot!" Kato called and stumbled over. "Where have you been? It was dangerous to go off by yourself."

"Are you seriously going to lecture me now?" I met him in the middle of the room. "What happened?"

"It's nothing you need to be concerned with, really. We had a minor disagreement over the current management of the guardians."

Did he really think I was going to fall for that? Putting my hands on my hips, I gave him the royal glare I had seen my mother use so often. "Since the *current management* is you, I would say that is certainly something. How bad was it?"

He waited to speak until the guards carted off the ice chimeras. Then Kato's demeanor changed alarmingly fast. If his chest were a balloon, then someone had let all the air out. His shoulders slumped in resignation and his head drooped. He looked like he hadn't seen any rest for years as opposed to days. "First, Grifflespontus altered the lava flow in my room, since that's where he thought you'd be. Then he attacked me with about five other chimeras. It was close; let's leave it at that."

"What are you going to do now?"

He growled a little. "Much as I loathe to admit it, I won't be able to keep him frozen indefinitely, even though I boosted the ice with life magic. Your Emerald flames might be useful as a last resort."

I frowned and helped shore up his wings, since he was having trouble walking. "I already gave you my answer."

"I know, and I refuse to accept that one."

Sparks shot off from the tips of my hair. "Look, you stubborn ogre…"

I was so busy scolding Kato that I didn't notice Rexi barreling into the room. She didn't notice that the floor had spots of ice. Without a tail to help steer her sliding, as Bob had done, she bowled right into us, and we ended up in a big, tangled ball of limbs and fur on the floor.

"Why do you people keep landing on me?" Rexi moaned from the bottom of the heap.

Expecting to see a comical sideshow, I looked at our reflection in one of the mirrors lining the walls. My chest tightened, and not just from Kato's weight. In our reflection, I didn't see the Chimera, but the rugged *human* prince from the ballroom—dark, mussed hair; bronzed, dirt-smudged skin—lying on top of me.

Kato followed my gaze and peered at us in the mirror. Our eyes met for a moment, making me feel even more uncomfortable. No, that wasn't right. I couldn't exactly place how I felt, since it was so foreign. It was sorta like leaning out of the highest window of the Emerald tower. Cool view, but it still made my stomach do queasy flips.

"Any day now, people," Rexi hollered from beneath me.

Kato blinked and backpedaled off like I'd bitten him.

"Thank Grimm! I thought I was gonna suffocate." Rexi stood and saw our reflections for the first time. "Hey, who's… Why is… Well, I'll be spelled."

Rexi's knapsack had gotten tangled up in Kato's horns,

hanging like it was on a coat rack. The reflection showed the bag hovering over his head, held up by an invisible pointy bit of the horn.

"That's just weird." Rexi rescued her bag.

Kato seemed to be entranced by his human reflection. He raised a paw to his muzzle, and the mirror image raised a hand to his cheek. He continued making motions, the human counterpart doing the same.

I was getting impatient for an explanation. "Enough of the mime act. Is this an enchanted mirror or what?"

"Wouldn't it be freaky if one of these times the mirror guy didn't move?" Rexi said.

Both Katos huffed and stared up at the ceiling. "Yes, Rexi. That would be freaky. And no, Dot, it's not. I think that magic doesn't show up in a reflection anymore."

"That can't be right." I knocked on the mirror, trying to get it to work right. "My reflection is still on fire."

"Maybe because that's who you really are," Rexi said quietly.

I started pacing across the floor, and when I opened my mouth, all my fears tumbled out.

"I think I might be evil. Verte's dead, and it's all my fault 'cause I broke the barrier and let Griz in, and then Kato bonked me on the head with the potion, and voilà! Girl of Emerald bathed in flames bent on world destruction. Or at least the destruction of Black Crow, 'cause I felt all-powerful and angry there for a second and she needed to pay, but then I didn't mean to, but then I did anyway, and then she was all melty and…poof! She was a scarecrow. But the power felt good, which is bad, so I can't do what Kato asked 'cause I'm afraid if I hurt someone else, I'll tip the scale over to total badness and end up exactly like Blanc."

I forced my jaw shut before any more spilled out.

"I thought you said a house fell on Crow," Rexi said, completely missing the emotional point of my ramble.

Kato sent her an icy glare, so she raised her hands and backed off.

I took a few measured breaths before trying to be coherent. "Kato, I can't help you with Blanc. I can never use whatever"—I pinched the green, curly, crackling ends of my hair—"this is again. The last part of the curse can't come true, not if I can help it."

"I understand, I think." Kato still looked disappointed, despite his words. He whistled sharply, and Bob came trotting without delay—as in he must have been eavesdropping outside the entrance.

"Please take them to my mother's old room. I'm sure they could use the rest." Kato's tone of voice basically added *whether you want to or not.* "When you're done, Bobbledandrophous, join me at the White One's cell."

Bob bowed and shuffled Rexi and I out in a flurry of his feathered wings.

"And, Dot," Kato called just before I reached the exit. "While I don't agree that destroying evil would somehow make you the same as her, I won't force the issue. For now."

"*Rule #68: When you're afraid, hold your head high and whistle a happy tune. This remedy is also known to increase dwarf productivity by a multiple of seven.*"

—*Definitive Fairy-Tale Survival Guide, Volume 1*

21

We're Off to See the Wizard

Time to greet the suns, Priestess," a very chipper voice cut through the fog of slumber.

Prying my eyes open took some effort, but when I finally succeeded, Bob's smiling face took up the whole door frame. Morning people should have to live in their own country or something and not bother the rest of us.

"Unh, need…more…sleep." To say that I'd had a restless night would be a gross understatement. Between Rexi snoring and grunting in her sleep and me worrying that one of Griff's cronies would do the volcano thing in my new room, I hadn't actually had any peaceful rest.

"Apologies, Priestess, but my lord instructed me to wake you. He and the rude human are waiting for you."

Rude human? He must mean Rexi. She wasn't kicking me out of bed, so she must have already gotten up.

I stumbled to the door and shooed Bob away. "I'll just change and be right there." Luckily, the late queen and I were the same size—coincidence, not a sign. We certainly didn't share the same taste in fashion. I threw on a blue gingham frock and headed out.

Rexi sauntered down the hallway, her knapsack bulging to capacity. "I've found all sorts of useful supplies around this dump, so I'm all ready to go."

I quirked an eyebrow at her. "Where are you going?"

"We are going to go see your stalker wizard whether he wants the rest of us or not."

I wasn't particularly happy our plans had been changed without me. "I thought we were going to the spring some-where over the rainbow?"

"Kato says without the help of the Emerald Sorceress…" Rexi trailed off.

"We'd never find it." Kato came toward us from the other direction. Instead of continuing the thought, he stopped. "That dress."

That's all he said—then stared, making me self-conscious. "Is it okay if I wear this? It was just lying there, and my other one's toast so…" I waited for him to say something.

He smiled, then quickly coughed. "It…suits you. If you don't mind it being simple and used, you're welcome to keep it."

I couldn't tell if that was a compliment or another dig. "Well, vintage is in this season, so it'll do."

"Yeesh," Rexi groaned. "Just get to the whole homicidal rainbow sprite."

"Excuse me?" I asked.

Kato straightened, turning royal know-it-all again. "The spring Verte wanted you to go to has special powers that might be able to undo the wish. But the spring is invisible. It moves so no one knows where it is, and it's guarded by a sprite that uses deadly rainbow sorcery."

If that was true, how did Verte ever expect me to be able to find it? "Are you sure?"

"I spent most of the night doing research," Kato said. "I also poured through the chimera archives and found lots of references to a *Book of Making*. Supposedly, you can use it to bind or bend magic to create what the user imagines. We don't have anything like that here anymore, so the most likely place I could think of was the wizard's workshop at the Ivory Tower."

An image flashed into my mind while Kato was explaining. A book I'd seen before. "Is the cover engraved with a quill and sparkly red ink?" I asked.

"How did you know?" Kato countered, his furry forehead all crinkled.

The morning sluggishness gave way to excitement. "When I watched Blanc's story, the Maker used a book like that. And I saw one at the Maker's workshop that popped up in the forest. If you want it, we'd better hurry because that bibliobug was chomping it down pretty fast." I smirked at Rexi. "See? I told you we were supposed to be there."

She pursed her lips. "I still think you're delusional. I vote we go see the wizard."

Kato wiggled in between us. "We should do both. If the book is there, we will need someone who can read the spells."

"So Maker hut first, then Wizard of Oz," I said with finality.

"Oz?" Kato and Rexi asked in unison.

I waved them off. "Griz and Crow were talking about keeping me away from *Oz*, so I figured that's the name of the realm where the wizard lives."

After gathering a few provisions, Bob escorted the three of us to the secret exit, also known as the way out for people without wings. He couldn't come with us; he was in charge of everything until Kato came back—preferably on two legs again. After a quick private conference between the two of them—no, I didn't eavesdrop—Bob came over and lowered his muzzle to my height.

"My lady, please continue to look after Lord Kato in my stead. He tries to hide it, but being the Beast King is not an easy task, and I worry his heart will harden to obsidian because of it. But already, I can see he has grown from his time with you."

"He's grown because he eats nonstop—"

Bob cut me off and swiped a giant paw across the floor, literally sweeping me off my feet and into a crushing embrace.

"May your embers burn ever brightly and warm the hearth until your return."

A sizzling sound came from the top of my head, and a big, wet drop landed on my shoulder. I couldn't help but think that while it was really nice to be cared about, it would really suck if he cried me to death. But my hair was still flaming when he gingerly set me back on my feet and gave me a watery smile before flying back to keep his own hearth safe.

"Are you coming, Dot?" Kato shouted when he and Rexi reached the end of the obsidian tunnel.

I jogged the distance and joined them outside in the lush rain forest. "Wow, what is this place? It's amazing." For the first time in days, I felt at peace. Maybe because I was surrounded by so much green and it reminded me of home, but even our forests were nothing compared to this jungle.

"These plants are huge!" Rexi went to examine a red hibiscus that Bob would have had to stand on tiptoe to sniff.

I was not a small girl—I've always been tall for my age—but this place made me feel like a Munchkin.

Kato's forehead creased, and the lines around his muzzle drew in. "It's not supposed to be like this. Last time I was here, it was just an ordinary forest. It's like somebody went around and sprinkled Miracle Grow Dust on everything."

A strong gust of wind threatened to blow my skirt into a compromising position. Peering up at the shadow that crossed the sky, I discovered the source of the wind. A creature twice the size of Kato streaked across the first sun, long and wormy with all-encompassing butterfly wings. I dubbed it a butterpil-lar given the combo of the wings and eight-dozen hands and feet. It settled down in an open spot not too far from us and started smoking a hookah, blowing gray *O*'s with the puffs.

"Is that normal?" I whispered, still staring in awe.

"No," Kato answered in equal awe. "I can't say I've ever seen one of those before."

As we tiptoed away, the butterpillar eyed us with curiosity, but he made no move to either eat or halt us—just slightly tilted his head in acknowledgment.

This time we actually had a map, so we headed northeast, back to Sherwood Forest.

"All this fresh air and walking can't be good for me," I said well into the afternoon, after continuous hours of trudging. The distance went by much faster by Air Chimera. Kato had insisted we go on foot, since a huge flying beast would be an easy target for the storm-cloud riding Griz.

For the first time, I really wished Verte had gifted me slippers rather than heels. "I think my blisters have blisters," I complained.

"I know!" Rexi said, brightening. "We've got a beast of burden right here we can ride."

The temperature around us dropped at least ten degrees, enough that my breath became visible.

"Guess that was a *no* on the 'loyal steed' thing."

"Never," he growled. "And even suggesting that I'm a horse or mule makes you an—"

Rexi drowned him out with the clinking sound of rummaging through her knapsack. She pulled out a small piece of chrome, a crinkly gold leaf, a seashell, a crumpled parchment sheet, some hot-pink panty hose, then finally, apparently, found what she was looking for—a teacup that looked exactly like the ones at Crow's.

"Why do you have that?" I asked as she dipped the cup into the stream to fetch a glass of water. Just seeing that tacky porcelain rose again gave me the shivers.

She shrugged and sipped without looking my way. "I like to keep the realm clean by picking up and recycling things that people carelessly leave behind. You know, one person's trash is my souvenir."

"In other words, you have Obsessive Compulsive Klepto Disorder." I sighed.

Kato stuck his nose in the bag while Rexi wasn't looking. "Hey, that's the snowman figure my mother gave me when I was a kid."

Rexi snatched her bag back, hugging it to her chest. She looked ready to protect her *treasures* to the death.

I patted Kato on the head. His horns were frosting over. "Let it go, snow boy. Let it go."

"You know what this trip needs?" Rexi asked, completely changing the subject.

"One less member?" Kato mumbled.

"A traveling song to make the journey go faster. I'll start." She coughed in a few weird pitches, presumably to warm up her vocal chords. "Heigh ho! Heigh—"

"NO!" Kato and I shouted in unison.

"Fine." She rolled her eyes and clomped off in silence.

Of course that couldn't last too long. Soon, she fell into step beside me, munching on something that vaguely resembled a sandwich. With a full mouth, she said, "So this decrepit wizard really has the hots for you, huh? What's he like?"

"Hard to say, really. He didn't really talk about himself in the letters. They were mostly poetry and nonsense about undying love. But the gifts he sent were nice. And he's actually not your typical gray-bearded, hunched old man wizard. He's very handsome."

"Well, rich, good-looking, and powerful." Rexi clucked her tongue. "Guess your love triangle is going to be a bit lopsided."

Up ahead, Kato rumbled low in his throat.

"You're cracked," I said and shook my head at Rexi. Whispering, I added, "There's no triangle, circle, or any other shape. One thinks he loves me as a replacement for someone else I happen to remind him of. The other needs me but doesn't even like me."

Rexi clucked her tongue. "Later, when we're alone, we need to have a chat. Your cluelessness is bordering on a crime, and friends don't let friends be as dumb as you."

Friends? Is that what we were? Weren't friends usually um… friendlier? Rexi reminded me of a marshmallow that'd been burned to a crisp: acrid and a tough-to-swallow exterior but all ooey gooey inside. I know we hadn't really seen the gooey part, but I was nearly positive it was there.

I stopped for a second to stretch. When I looked back up, Kato wasn't in front of us anymore. "Hey, did he ditch us?"

"Guess so." Rexi pointed. "He's over there and walking the wrong way."

She was right. He'd shifted south.

"Where are you going? The forest is over there." I jogged over to him and yanked his horn, but he didn't stop.

Kato jerked his head to the side, like he was trying to get water out of his ears. "It's Rexi's blasted whistling. It's messing with my head." He kept walking.

"Nobody's whistling." I was starting to have a really bad feeling about this. Instead of yanking on his horns, I grabbed them both and planted my heels in the grass. They left a rut as Kato dragged me with him.

"Rexi, help! Something's wrong."

Even with both of us hanging on, we couldn't keep Kato from moving forward. It was like he was in a trance; he didn't even acknowledge we were tugging on him. His icy blue eyes were just empty puddles.

Looking across the lake, I could see what had to be the China Isle. Even in its current state, I recognized it from pictures I'd seen. Something was making the cup-shaped houses spin and twirl, dancing in a frantic tea party around the Town Hall Teakettle. The kettle was bubbling over with, well, bubble tea.

"Oh, pix." As if to emphasize my point, the wind kicked up and carried a small stray bubble so that it popped in front of me. A splash of tea landed and sizzled against my hair. I doubled over like I'd been punched.

Rexi stayed with Kato, but cursed and twisted her upper body to try and get away. "Can't stop. The music…"

I could hear just the faintest tune on the wind. Kato, with his sensitive ears, must have heard it before we did.

As the third sun sunk, the last bits of light shone down on the lake where a tea saucer served as a boat for five figures on top. No larger than hand's height, a small band of metallic bugs played a myriad of instruments. They were being conducted by my least favorite Bumpkin.

"Glam it all. What do you think you're doing, you pixing stick?" I shouted to Moony.

"Do you like my cousins, the Jitterbug Band? The Pied Piper loaned them to me for this one-night-only engagement. The Gray Witch has offered a bounty and a place in the New World Order to whomever captures you. Double if you're dead." This time, Moony's smile no longer threatened retribution. It promised it. "Enjoy the music while you drown like rats."

22

Ashes, Ashes, We All Go Down

I wouldn't drown; my flaming hair would go out long before that. The end result would be the same though, so it wasn't worth arguing semantics. Except…my feet had no problem staying still.

My shoes!

No wonder Verte insisted I hang on to them. They hadn't stopped me from getting dusted at Crow's because I ate the stuff. But I was willing to bet that since they'd protected me from the fire flowers, they would protect me now.

"Yoo-hoo! Little fairy," I taunted Moony. "Notice I'm not moving? And if I stay back here, your bubble bombs can't reach me. So give up and paddle away now or spend the rest of your life under glass."

I was hoping Rexi had swiped a bug jar somewhere along her travels.

"Fairy-farting pox-ridden princess," Moony swore. "I may not be able kill you, but I can hurt you."

"With what?" I sneered. "By blinding me again with your full moon?"

"By taking what you care about. And without your bumbling bodyguards, you'll be easy pickins'." He grinned wickedly.

Though I'd stopped, Kato and Rexi kept marching forward. They were at the lake now, with the water up to their ankles. If I didn't do something quickly, they'd both become more casualties of the wish.

A minefield of bubbles peppered the air between us.

I ran to my friends, weaving and dodging the bubbles the best I could but still got some back spray. If I held on to Kato, he'd pull me down with him. Instead, I grabbed Rexi by the shirt, yanked her back to the shore, and sat on her so she couldn't go anywhere.

One down, but Kato…

I felt the answer within me. The fire burned just underneath the surface my palm, fueled by the voice in my head. *Take their life and power. Like shooting frogs in a barrel.* It would be so easy. The metallic bugs would melt and Mooney would go up like tinder.

"No," I ground out between my teeth. "There has to be another way."

Rexi squirmed beneath me, still trying to answer the music's call. I didn't need to stop my friends; I needed to stop the music. Ignoring Rexi's shriek, I grabbed the knapsack out of her hand and looted her stash of stolen goods.

I didn't even bother checking what I was throwing. As soon as my hand held on to something solid, I pulled it out and chucked it at the Jitterbugs. I wasn't even close for the first few, but I got better, and even when I missed, I made waves. And that was a very big problem for a very little tea saucer.

Moony and the Jitterbugs swayed and staggered, trying to keep their balance while ducking to avoid an incoming snowman figure.

"This ain't what we signed up for, cuz," said the bug playing the upright bass.

"That's right. Keep y'all's money. We quit." This bug threw down his pipe and jumped into the water. The rest of his band abandoned their instruments and made a break for it too. They swam for the nearest gravy boat.

"What'sss goin' on? Why'm I wet?" Kato slurred, waking up slowly.

The reprieve was short. Moony ignored the deserters, picked up the panpipe, and began to play.

Kato pitched forward again, his belly now brushing the water. I reached into the sack but came up empty.

Hopping off Rexi for a moment, I retreated back to the

road to find some rocks or something. A giant bubble hit me in the face, stealing some of my flame, making me wobble and fall.

"Dorthea!"

I was too dizzy to answer, but even through blurred vision, I could see Rexi's feet were scooting for the water even though she was still sitting on the ground. Worse, Kato was close to going under. I staggered into the lake, climbed onto Kato's back, and shoved my fists in his ears. He'd grown again to be the size of a court stallion, so I couldn't cover the entire hole.

The water was up to his chin and my waist. Moony somehow played with a smile on his face and increased his tempo—and the pace of Kato's death march. Unbidden, the image of Blanc's drowning prince came to mind. She hadn't been able to stop it.

But I could.

Makers forgive me.

I shut my eyes, but even behind closed lids, I could *feel* where the Bumpkin stood. Bringing my flames to the surface of my palms, I held them there. Then let them go.

The music abruptly stopped.

Smoke and ash filled my lungs, making me want to throw up. I thrust my hands in the water to put out the flames because holding the power in my hands felt good.

That did make me throw up.

My vomit barely missed hitting Kato's wing as he flapped back to shore, wet but no worse for the wear.

We all looked at the fiery green glow on the lake.

"Is that… I thought you said you'd never use it," Kato said sluggishly, clearly peeved. "What happened?"

"She saved your hide while you dozed through the epic battle and barbecue, Sleeping Beauty." Rexi pulled herself up out of the shallow water. "Warrior princess here and her flames—"

"I don't want to talk about it," I croaked and moved to slide off Kato's back.

He shoved me back on with his wing and covered me from an oncoming bubble. "Ride up there for a while."

"Why?" I asked. He'd made it clear before that he was not a beast to be tamed or ridden.

"Because you need it," he answered quietly. "Let's go, Rexi." He turned in the direction of Sherwood Forest and ambled off the shore.

I buried my face in his fur, partly because I was cold and felt like I'd been drained of all my energy, but it was more to try and stop the tears from coming. It would've been easier to stop the suns from rising. It felt like little splinters stabbed inside my heart. Moony's revenge maybe. I couldn't get his voice, his face, or the taste of his ashes out of my mind. If I thought about it, I'd go mad, but it was hard not to, since to my eyes, the whole world still looked tinted in green flames. I wanted the world black, so I closed my eyes and sank into oblivion.

I must have fallen asleep, because when I opened my eyes again, I was on the hard ground instead of soft fur. The flames were gone, but the world hadn't returned to the right color. The lake and giant flowers were all a muted gray. Rexi lay on the ground, curled up, probably passed out from exhaustion. I didn't see Kato though.

My skin prickled with cold. And it was far too quiet. Not a single cricket chirped. Maybe they'd all been eaten by the ironwood trees. Turning in a circle, I tried to get my bearings to figure out if we'd reached the workshop yet. The forest was a short ways off, but a full-length mirror stood much closer, out of place.

I stared into the mirror, surprised this time by my reflection. A girl stared back at me. She looked lovely and innocent, and was dressed in long, white robes. She held the *Book of Making* and ripped out a page. It floated out of the mirror and onto the ground. The page was an illustration. A portrait of my parents. They didn't look like themselves, dressed in foreign clothes in a seemingly foreign land.

Seeing them again made my chest hurt. I reached out to grab the picture to look closer, but the wind kicked up and stole it from my fingertips. I chased after it in a circle, the page whisking away like it was taunting me. I screamed my frustration into the sky.

The sky screamed back.

Kato crested a hill of wildflowers, but he wasn't my cute little fluff ball anymore. He was a beast that could have swallowed the Emerald Palace whole. He reared back and roared again.

Spelled

The ironwood trees shook in fear and the ground quaked.

With a crash, the mirror splintered into countless pieces. Each shard showed the white-haired girl, now grown into an evil empress.

Kato was drawing closer. His black claws gleamed, his eyes no longer ice blue but dark bottomless pits. There was no humanity left in him. He was flanked by flying puppies.

"I've found you, my pretty." Blanc spoke from the mirror shards. "We are connected and you can't escape us."

I reached down to grab Rexi and run. Up close, I could see that she wasn't sleeping peacefully. Her face stiffened in pain as red-orange tears fell. Before hitting the ground, they turned to swirling stones.

Blanc's voice came again, soft and lyrical. "Once upon a time, there was wretched girl who brought pain and misfortune to all those around her. But you won't have to worry about that anymore."

The silver pieces of mirror melted and oozed together, forming the mercurial shape of the Gray Witch. "And the princess died unhappily ever after."

The silver coalesced into a giant stormball and hurled itself at me. A shiny glob landed on my chest and spread. Its weight forced me to the ground. Nearly every inch of my skin was coated with the icy, silvery liquid. Then it spilled into my mouth.

I couldn't breathe.

"After a one-hundred-year nap, I like to think of myself as a bit of an expert on dreams. For starters, you never want to die in one. That would be bad luck."

—*Sleeping Beauty's Dream Dictionary*

Dream a Little Nightmare for Me

A freezing chill spread throughout my body from within. Silver frost formed along my skin. The wound from the wishing star pricked and ached.

Right as a glittering icicle started to burst out from my palm, I bolted awake from what had—hopefully—been just a nightmare. My mind must have thrown together every fear I had into one nightmare, mixing Blanc and Griz together. But it wasn't real, even though the cold followed me from the dream world, making me shiver. My palm really hurt too. A faint line of blood dribbled down from a puncture wound.

It was just a dream, right?

Besides the sound of my teeth chattering, I heard a small squeak beside me that was much too quiet to be a chimera.

I wiped the dream monster out of memory and looked down at the small gray creature. The rodent had prominent features from several different animals. It had the body and ears of a mouse, but its tail was wiry and tufted, while its face was tough, not fuzzy like the rest of it. And the nose elongated to a tusk.

"Did you wake me up with that tusk, little, um… Rhimouserous?" I whispered.

The animal, if possible, glared as it nodded its tiny head. Then it jerked its tusk, as though saying, *This way.*

"You want me to follow you?" When I stood, it scampered off. I got a few yards, but the night was too dark, and I lost track of where it went. I *absolutely* did not lose sight of it because I got distracted by a certain prince.

Kato sat by the lake, staring at his reflection. Like the throne room's mirrors, it too showed his human nature. Sad and pensive lines marked his face even among the slight waves in the water. He jumped when my image joined his.

"I didn't know I was that scary," I mumbled and plopped down next to him.

He grinned. "No. I was just surprised, that's all. After you fainted, we walked for hours, but you never even stirred. I thought you would never wake up."

"Bad dreams." I shivered, only half from the memory of the cold.

Kato nodded over to a daffodil. With feet. "You're not the only one it seems."

I recognized Rexi's breeches and ugly brown shoes as she tossed fitfully in a flower bed and moaned in her sleep.

"Should we wake her?" I asked. I almost wanted to check and make sure the fire gem tears had stayed in the dream.

"No." He shook his head, and the dewdrops on his mane flew everywhere. "Bad sleep is better than no sleep."

I wasn't so sure about that. My subconscious definitely had some serious issues.

Kato stared absently into the lake.

"Are you thinking that maybe if you stare long enough, your real body will match your reflection?" I asked.

"I'm not sure I'd want to."

"What do you mean?"

He stared at me from the water. Kato's human face was much more expressive, what with it not being covered in fur. An eyebrow quirked and he frowned slightly. There was a dimple in his chin that I hadn't noticed before.

"He looks so arrogant. The Beast King. I thought I had the power and the right to command anything. I thought I knew the best way to save everyone, and I never even once cared how it might affect you. Finding a way to end Blanc and secure my title was the only thing that mattered. So when the Emerald Sorceress suggested the alliance—"

I jerked in surprise. "This was all *Verte's idea*?"

He sighed. "Your wish turbo-charged the process, but the

flames that imprison the White One have been slowly going dim for the past seventeen years. Some factions of my kingdom suggested we flee our duty, and without officially being king, it grew harder to control them. Verte came to me a week or so ago and told me about a girl that could solve all my problems. When I met you, I couldn't see how you could possible help me and thought you'd be a burden." He had the decency to blush, the color showing even in the watery image. "The sorceress assured me she was never wrong, so I approached your parents and demanded your hand because I wanted to get it over with."

"Gee. Thanks." I blew a few fiery strands out of my face. Since I was calm, they weren't too bright.

"But I was wrong." Kato placed a paw in my lap, but in the reflection, it looked like his hand brushed my knee. "Verte saw something that I was blinded to."

He wasn't the only one. I didn't know what she had seen in me either. "I wonder what mischief she was up to. I suppose we'll never know."

"She knew you best, knew the parts no one else could see. And I don't think it's a coincidence that the girl from the story looked a lot like you, Dot."

I stilled. "Blanc?"

"No," he answered. "The princess who rejected the Beast King, then helped fight and bind the White One."

I'd been too preoccupied by the story to even notice. Who was she and why was she special enough to earn the trust of both a Storymaker and the King of Beasts? Searching my reflection in the lake, I hoped for a glimmer of insight. All I could remember were Blanc's words from my dream. I chucked a nearby stone into the pool, rippling the water and distorting the image. "Well, you're wrong. I think we've established that my best intentions and wishful thinking do nothing but put people in danger."

"It can save them too. After you fell asleep, Rexi filled me in on what happened, on what you did for me."

"Oh," I said and looked at the sky because its darkness didn't remind me of white. Or green. Or wood.

Kato hooked a wing around me and turned my head back to meet his reflective eyes. "I understand the price you had to pay—are still paying—to save me. I thought your empathy was a weakness. But it's the proof you will never be *her*. It's just not possible."

What would he think if he knew that, even now, a small part of me craved to hold the fire in my hand, to banish this feeling of helplessness. He'd probably push me in the water himself. I kept my feelings to myself and watched the wind distort our watery, mirrored images.

Our reflections looked like the cover of a fairy tale—a simple prince with his arm around his princess. Both our reflections reddened and turned away at the same time.

Kato flapped his wings and hovered around me before flopping back down to the ground. "You know, your wishful thinking hasn't been all bad. I love the feeling of flying. I'm kind of getting the hang of it. I don't really mind being a chimera." He poked me with his tail. "Even if it makes me a disgusting beast for real."

Now it was my turn to be embarrassed, being reminded at just how un-princesslike I'd been at the ball. "Sorry about that."

He settled back down next to me. "No need. We both made mistakes. But I hope you feel a little differently now too."

I did. I wasn't sure exactly what I felt, but it definitely wasn't the visceral dislike I'd had for him at the beginning. I knew I should probably say something, but no words came.

The first sun began its ascent into the sky. Its fiery hues painted the clear water in oranges and pinks. With the dark lifting, my surroundings became clear. The forest stood behind me in a familiar semicircle. The clearing was empty.

"So I guess the workshop has a habit of disappearing too." I could feel the frown weighing down my face. "I bet Rexi was pretty happy last night getting here and finding out I was wrong…again."

He sprang to his paws. "That's right, you were asleep and wouldn't know. The workshop was gone, but the trees still stayed back because there was still one thing in the clearing. The book."

I gasped. Something had gone as planned. Mostly. We had a chance, which was better than we had yesterday. "Where is it? Did you read it? Does it have the uncurse?"

"Well, not exactly." Kato winced. "The book has the cover

described, but it won't open. It's sealed, glued, locked, or broken, and we can't get to the pages. And the way magic is working, I'm not sure we want you to touch something so flammable."

Having it so close, yet out of my grasp, pixed me off and made my hair spark. So Kato was probably right about the no touching.

"You never said where it is now," I said.

Kato sighed. "Rexi has it."

"Seriously?" I asked, shocked he would trust her. "Is that a good idea?"

He chuffed. "With those sticky fingers? She'll guard her treasures better than any dragon."

So true.

"Well, all right then. We need someone who can magic that sucker open," I said and brushed off my dress. "Let's go wake snoring beauty and find the Ivory Tower?"

He offered me the tip of his wing. "I suppose we have to since she's got the book."

Before we got close, the daffodil bolted upright. "Son of mrph murphen. Get this…off me!"

I lifted the flower off Rexi. She had her arms wrapped around the *Book of Making*, hugging it fiercely like a teddy bear. Her blond hair was wild on a good day, going in every direction, but bed head covered in pollen took it to a whole new level.

"What are you two laughing at?" She looked around self-consciously, then checked the side of her mouth for drool.

Forcing myself to straighten my face, I shook my head. "Not a thing. We're heading out to find the wizard."

"We can't!" Rexi jumped up in a panic, the yellow pollen dandruff flying off. "I had a dream that something bad happens there."

"So now you're an oracle?" Kato scoffed.

"Better than being a fur coat." The two continued bickering back and forth.

So this is what it must be like to have siblings. I'm glad I'm an only child.

I started to walk to the meadow on a carpet of petals. Either they'd follow or they wouldn't. Both options had their pluses and minuses. Taking out my frustrations, I pushed several fallen flowers out of my way. I must have gone several hundred yards before the two even noticed I was missing.

"Hey, where are you going?" Kato flew up next to me. "What happened to the flowers? Why are they squished?"

Squished? I hadn't noticed, but he was right. Petals lay broken and folded on the ground. Stems were bent low at odd angles. And the path wasn't straight. It curved, almost like a footprint. But that's ridiculous. Even trolls didn't have feet that big.

I figured it out at the same moment I saw the tin leg.

"Hide!" I yelled in my most whispery voice.

Kato disappeared into the unbroken flower stalks while Rexi and I hid under a fallen bluebell. The ground shook beneath us with each step the Tinman took. Small tremors at first; then the impacts made the ground tremble harder.

He was getting closer. I didn't hear any creaking though. Someone must have oiled his joints.

A shadow moved in front of the light filtering in through the petal.

"Look harder! She was here. I know it. I saw her."

I knew that voice. It was the one that had haunted my night. Griz had found us.

The Tinman spoke to Griz, I think. It sounded like grinding gears.

"Yes. I'm sure."

Grind.

"Because the runt bears my mark, that's why."

Grind.

"I don't care how. Just find her."

Griz's shadow passed our flower as she continued her search.

How did she know where we were? Then it hit me like a ton of gingerbread cookies. The nightmare. Had it been more than just a dream? My insides grew cold again at the thought.

"It's gonna happen, just like I saw it." Rexi let go of the book and put her hands over her ears, mouthing, *no, no, no.* Her rocking back and forth made the flower twitch every time she accidentally brushed it.

Her level of fear was extreme. She needed to calm down or the big gray wolf would come over and blow our petaled house down.

I gathered Rexi onto my lap and smoothed her hair.

"*Shhh…shhh.* We'll be fine. Nothing bad can happen to us." I spoke so softly into her ear that I could barely hear my own voice.

"Yes, it can. There are no Storymakers," she sobbed quietly.

"Storymakers or not, the bad guy never wins. It's in the rules," I said in my softest reassuring voice.

Instead of having the calming effect I had intended, Rexi's body shook harder with her silent screams. I took her head between my hands and turned her face to me. Her eyes were huge circles. Her lips stopped quivering just long enough to mouth, *You broke the rules.*

"If it looks too good to be true, it probably is."

—Gretel from *Candy Kills: A True Story*

Welcome to the Land of Ozmosis

With nothing left to reassure her with, I protected her with the only thing I had—my body. I draped myself over Rexi, using my weight to push her into the grass. Once I'd had seen a mama unicorn do something similar to her colt—push him against the fencing, the pressure grounding the frightened foal. It worked with my frightened filly. Rexi stilled; her breathing evened out.

Lying down, I noticed that my hair wasn't as bright as it had been. Barely the slightest burning green sparked along the tips. They flickered to the time of my heartbeat. Since I was trying to force Rexi to be calm, I had slowed my own heart rate. Breathing deeper, I tried to bring it down even more. Sure enough, the ends died down to merely embers. That was a useful skill. The last thing I wanted was for my hair to light up like a signal flare and give away our hiding spot.

"Dot…" a whisper.

The voice came from outside the flower.

"Where are you?"

It could be a trap. Did the Gray Witch have a talent for imitation? Because I would bet that voice belonged to Kato. But was I willing to bet my life? I lifted the bluebell an inch and looked for the telltale paws. A wet nose slid under the gap and flipped the flower over.

My hair flared to life as my heart rate tripled. Kato shielded his eyes with his paw.

"Don't do that!" I hissed. "You scared the fairy dust out of me."

"Sorry," he said, still squinting. "I think she's gone. We need to move, in case she comes back."

I reached out my hand to Rexi, who was still lying prone on the ground. She took it and pulled herself up.

"What's her—*ow!*" Kato lifted and licked the paw I had *accidentally* stepped on.

We weaved through the stalks as delicately as we could. If we brushed one, it would wave a great big hello to Griz on a fly by. She was still out there. And the acid burns among the flowers made me think she had her puppies with her too.

I heard a buzzing sound.

Rexi squeezed my hand in a panic. "She doesn't have killer bees does she?"

"I don't think so." I looked around but didn't see anything. We all looked up in time to see a basket fly by.

"What in Grimm's name was that?" I asked.

"Don't know. The question is, do we want to find out?" Kato answered.

Rexi spoke, her voice stronger than it had been. "It's probably better to know what's after you than to be surprised by it."

We made our way to the edge of the flower forest, so we could get a clear view of the sky. It wasn't a basket but more like a gondola suspended by ropes. The ropes hung from a golden bicycle contraption that, in turn, hung from a balloon. On the bicycle was a man wearing a flight helmet with goggles. His pedaling made the oars—in the place of wheels—move, directing the balloon. The pedaling was also the source of the buzzing noise.

With a soft thump, the gondola set down in the open. "If you're coming, you'd better hurry. The witch has probably seen me by now."

As if to confirm this, lightning split the sky, along with Griz's scream. "What are you doing? You can't have them, Mick. They're mine!" Her puppies howled and flew toward us from their varied locations. They were closing in from all sides.

The wizard! We didn't have the book open yet, but we also didn't have another choice. Rexi and I piled into the gondola, but there was no way that Kato, who had grown even more since yesterday, would fit.

"What about our friend?" I called.

He started pedaling and hollered down. "He has wings doesn't he? Make the beast fly!"

As the balloon rose, I called out to Kato, afraid he still couldn't fly. His massive feathered wings stretched out. The wingspan surpassed that of the pegasi back home. He flapped his wings, and the resulting wind blew my hair in every direction. I didn't need to worry; he had it under control.

The man yelled down to me again. "Tell the beast to follow us and stay over the water. The witch won't cross it."

I didn't bother yelling back that *the beast* could understand him just fine. "Why can't she cross the water?" Last time she had chased us, she'd stopped at the cliff's edge too.

"Afraid she'll fall in. She's allergic to water; plus all the lightning and such would electrocute her." He adjusted his glasses and leaned in to the handle bars. "Now hold on and make sure to duck."

At that precise moment, a lightning bolt sailed between the ropes holding the gondola.

"I won't miss next time," Griz shouted. "Last chance to give them to me."

The man spoke in a most gentlemanly voice. "Thank you for your offer, but I'm afraid I must decline." Then he pedaled faster, and the balloon lurched.

True to his prediction, Griz pulled up short—right at the

edge of the lake. The Tinman stopped as well, probably afraid he'd get rusted.

Griz threw stormballs and lightning bolts at us furiously. Kato had more maneuverability and dodged them effortlessly. It's much harder to maneuver a flying balloon bicycle. One of the balls took out our left oar. The uneven rowing had a rolling effect, making our flight seem more like a ride on ocean waves. But soon Griz's stormballs landed harmlessly in the water. We had gone past her throwing distance.

"Where are you taking us?" I called to our rescuer.

"To my home, the Ivory Tower over there." He pointed to the horizon, but all I saw was more water. What I had thought was a lake was merely an inlet to a sea.

Rexi raised a hand over her brow and squinted, searching for the tower as well. "I don't see it."

"That's because it's invisible, you buffoon. What good is having a magnificent secret island tower if everyone knows where it is?"

"Ohh," I yelled up. "The Emerald Sorceress's main specialty was creating big barriers. So is the disappear-reappear thing your main magic as the Wizard of Oz?"

"I'm afraid you've got my name wrong again, darling. It's the Wizard of *Is*, my dear. Not Oz."

Pretty sure I heard Oz. But I had been coming down from pixie dust, so it's possible I misheard.

"Oz is not a person or place," he continued, correcting me. "It's another name for the nonsensical and disorderly magic that disappeared from the world of story many years ago. Although, if I'm not mistaken, your wish has started the process of ozmosis."

"Ozmosis?"

"What I call all this magic running amok. All the very reliable rules and order are becoming chaotic and unpredictable, and it's only going to get worse." When he paused, I could feel his disapproval even if I couldn't see it. "Very inconvenient, if I do say so myself. And of course had you not wandered off at the ball, we would have been able to avoid the situation entirely. I hope you've learned your lesson."

Well, he'd certainly reminded me of *why* I'd "wandered off" in the first place.

"I've learned quite a bit actually, including something that might be able to help. A *Book of Making*. But it's sealed shut." I poked Rexi to lift it up so the wizard could see.

The air bike wobbled as he leaned over and gasped. He quickly corrected the dip. "That," he squeaked then started again in a normal tone. "That is most certainly a rare find. We will go to my workshop right away and see if we can't crack the spine."

We slowed down and Kato flew past. The wizard waved his hand in front of him, like wiping a windshield. "*Abra cabis,* the Ivory Tower of the Wizard of Is."

Suddenly, the tower blinked in front of us. One minute it wasn't there; the next minute Kato flew right into it.

Rexi winced and puckered her lips. "Oohhh, that had to hurt."

The wizard set the balloon down, but I was out of the gondola before it touched ground, running over to Kato. "Are you okay?"

"That's a dumb question. I ran into a wall. Of course I'm not okay," he snapped at me grumpily. I let it slide because I would be grumpy too if I had just flown face-first into a wall.

The Wizard of Is perched atop his bicycle seat and pulled off his riding gloves. "I think his horns have damaged my tower." He climbed off his bike and took off his helmet and goggles, peering up at the impacted section. Sure enough, there was a Kato head-sized hole in the wall.

I winced and forced a smile. "It's a good place for a window, don't you think?"

"Perhaps." His disapproving frown transformed quickly into a sparkling smile. "Maybe I will leave it if it would make you happy." He walked away and gave orders to a servant who was trying to tie up the balloon.

We both stared at the wizard while he showed his servant what he wanted done. He was still as gorgeous as I'd remembered him. Even his hair had the perfect wave rather than what should have been a tragic case of helmet head. And his clothes were divine and clearly magically tailored to accentuate each and every muscle.

"You were right. What a hunk." Rexi sidled up beside me and elbowed me in the ribs.

"You're drooling, Rexi," Kato said drily.

Rexi blushed up to her hairline. "So are you. And you smell like wet dog."

I laughed. I couldn't help it; it was funny. Kato didn't think so. He sniffed and stalked off.

A hand brushed against my back, and the sandalwood and rose scent filled my nose. "Anything I should know about?" The wizard gave me a winning smile again.

"Have we ever met? I feel like I've seen you before," Rexi said, her face perplexed.

It was probably just my imagination, but I thought I saw his thousand-watt, dimpled smile slip just a little before answering. "Perhaps at the ball. Or I must just have one of those faces. Let's go inside and take a look at what you've brought me." He led us around the side, to a gilded door.

Inside, everything within sight was cream colored with sharp angles. There were prismatic ivory spindles on the winding staircase, and the floor was marble with gold inlays. As far as towers go, it was grand and opulent but not what you'd call warm and inviting. The wizard was guiding me up the stairs when I heard Kato growling behind me. Several guards barred the doorway into the foyer, forcing him to stay outside.

"It's okay; he's with us," I said, ducking under the wizard's arm.

By the time I walked back to the door, the guards still hadn't budged.

The click-clacking of the wizard's shoes echoed off the

marble. "I'm sorry, Princess. This tower simply was not built with such a...magnificent chimera in mind. I think he'd be better off with the other animals, don't you agree?"

Okay, the wizard was starting to sound like a used carriage salesmen.

I slid away from his attempt to put his arm around me again. "No, I don't agree. Kato's not an animal; he just looks like one temporarily."

The wizard covered his tracks and made a broad gesture with his hand, like he hadn't intended to touch me at all. "Yes, you're right of course, but think of his comfort. His claws would slip all over the tile, and there's no room to stretch his wings." He walked over to a window and pointed outside. "There's a lovely courtyard in the rear where he could stay. You could visit him whenever you wish. But for now, I would think you'd be anxious to examine that book of spells and see if we can't find a way to bring back your parents."

And those were the magic words—it was what we had left chimera mountain to do in the first place. It was also probably the only thing that would make me leave Kato, aside from the promise of a bath. I no longer had to kneel to look directly into Kato's eyes. He was now as tall as me. "Will you be all right?"

"Yes, but be careful. Don't eat or drink anything," Kato whispered so our host couldn't hear.

"Don't worry. I'm not about to get dusted again," I whispered back and gave his mane a ruffle.

The wizard clapped his hands. "Nikko!" My favorite gorilla butler in his trademark golden fez came out of the side room. "Escort our esteemed furry guest to the courtyard," the wizard ordered dismissively.

Nikko bowed low to me, then shooed away the guards and led Kato outside, shutting the gilded door behind him. The thud hammered at me. My hair popped and cracked with my unease at being apart from Kato. But knowing that he had Nikko to look after him helped—assuming Kato didn't try to eat him.

The wizard coughed into his hand, drawing my attention. "My workshop is just up the stairs on the fifth floor, past the room with the spinning wheels. I'll be right behind you. Just have a quick snippet of business to take care of." The wizard click-clacked into the side room Nikko had come out of.

Rexi and I climbed the stairs. There were a lot of them. Somewhere around the third floor, Rexi snapped her fingers. "I've got it!"

"Got what?"

She looked at me and rolled her eyes, exasperated that I wasn't following her random topic change. "I figured out where I've seen him before."

"At the palace during the party?"

"I was too busy being a frog to notice." She nodded knowingly. "He was on the cover of one of Verte's magazines. Ummm…*Sorcery Illustrated*, I think."

My jaw dropped. I was shocked Verte would have *that* kind of magazine. And that Rexi would look at them—and probably add them to her *souvenirs*.

"What?" Rexi responded to my look with a sheepish one of her own. "You're not the only one I had to stock snacks for. They were under her bed, which made them fair game." I was still staring, and Rexi shifted uncomfortably. "It's not like they were *my* magazines," she muttered.

"I'm sure she only read them for the potion recipes," I grumbled, trudging up the stairs again.

When we reached the fifth floor, the wizard was already waiting for us on the landing. Creepy.

He held his arm out to the side, indicating a door on the right. "Your place is through there. Please have a seat."

I walked in, but the wizard stopped Rexi at the door. "Just the princess and the book, if you don't mind. I have some news she should hear alone."

Rexi stepped back awkwardly from the wizard's palm facing her chest. "Um, sure, here," she said and reluctantly parted with the book. "I'll just wait—"

"Right there is fine. Nikko will fetch you momentarily." He shut the door in her face.

My earlier relief was turning into worry. He was snooty and treated everyone around him as inferior. Except me. He treated me with deference because I reminded him of that girl he used to love. Or because he knew about my power. I caught him eyeing my hair.

"Please take a seat in the chair." He plucked a brass tray off the desk and offered it to me. "Refreshment?"

I sat in the plush chair next to a giant bouquet of poppies. I politely refused the tea and crumpets. "So what did you want to tell me that Rexi shouldn't hear?"

The wizard gave a little frown, like he was disappointed that I was cutting to the chase. "I thought you should know that I've found the Emerald Sorceress."

"Alive?" I moved to the edge of my seat.

"Yes, actually, that's what my business was downstairs, contacting her to let her know you are all right." The wizard walked closer to me. "Don't these flowers have just the loveliest fragrance?" He pushed the bouquet in my face so that the pollen went up my nose. The smell actually made me sick, like the wizard's cologne, but one hundred times stronger.

"Achoo!" The second sneeze turned into a yawn. "Fabulous, now what were you saying?"

"About your friend coming to meet you here and what she wants you to do."

"Really?" I yawned loudly and completely inappropriately. "Excuse me." I was mortified, but I couldn't seem to help it. I was just so tired. Verte was okay. I should be jumping for joy.

"Yes, she should be here in the morning. Any other questions, dear?" He looked at his watch.

"Yeah." I bit back another yawn. "Why're you called the Wizard of Is? Why not the Ivory Wizard, or Gold… yawn…Guy."

"It's an appropriate title for one who can master all that Is in the world. You look a little wilty, Princess. Is everything all right?" His face didn't match his words.

No, it wasn't. But my head wouldn't shake like I wanted it to. "I don't know what's wrong."

He turned his lips in and nodded sympathetically. "Well, it has been an emotional and difficult few days. You can rest now. I just wanted you to know about your friend. Tomorrow, she and I can work together to craft a spell of reverse ozmosis."

My eyes were closing without my consent. "And then my parents will be back?"

"Everything will be exactly the way it should."

Ain't Never Had a Friend Like Me

My eyes felt glued shut. I needed my hands just to pry them open. I got one open. Then the other. I was in a bed with red poppies everywhere. Took a deep breath. Smelled sweet.

Sleepy now.

I wanted to wake up. But it was too dark. *Must still be bedtime.* I rolled over to go back to sleep.

Thud. Splash. Sizzle.

My eyes popped open. Why was my face wet? Why was my hair popping like firecrackers? So confused. One piece at a time. I was on my back on the floor. There was a vase with wilted flowers tipped over next to me. I had probably knocked them off when I rolled out of bed.

Upsy daisy.

I used the four-poster bed to support me because my legs didn't want to. It felt like I hadn't moved in days. And my head was fuzzy, like it was filled with cotton candy. Looking around the room, I saw vases and vases of wilted flowers.

Weird, random decor.

I had no clue where I was. Worse than that, I had no clue *who* I was. Maybe taking a walk would help me see if something looked familiar. My feet were cold against the floor. Where were my shoes? I thought I remembered liking shoes. Well, that was one thing at least.

Outside the room there was a long hall of mirrors. I walked down it, not really recognizing the girl walking next to me in the mirror. She was barefoot and wearing an ugly dress. I'm pretty sure I wouldn't be caught dead like that—and something was wrong with her hair.

The mirrors must be broken.

I heard scraping behind me and spun around in time to see a small puppy run into one of the rooms. Instantly I felt a visceral gut-clenching hatred. See, there was another clue. Apparently I was more of a cat person.

Did I have a cat? Or a pet? I willed myself to remember and caught fragments of memories. A little fuzzy thing in a basket. Toto or something. That must be it.

Satisfied, I continued down the hall. The door to the room at the end was cracked open. People were talking. A man and a woman.

Spelled

It would be bad manners to interrupt. Someone once told me to always wait outside until they're done. But who? Maybe they were inside. I would listen and see if I recognized the voices. Maybe get a better idea of who and where I was.

"...poppies aren't working, are they?"

"If they were, I wouldn't have had to transport you here, now would I? I've removed the shoes, but she's got the magic of Oz in her blood now," said the man.

"What's to stop me from killing her and torturing you? Giving my sister your head on a silver platter would be a very nice start to make up for your double-crossing us."

"That wo-would be unwise," the man stuttered. "After so many attempts, you know very well you don't have enough power to kill her. But with my help, we would be able to contain her."

The woman sighed. "I'm listening."

"The princess brought me the book. It's yours if you help me keep her here. And when your sister is free, she can use it with the power of Emerald and have none of the risk. Surely with that, the empress will forgive me."

"Why would you want to keep her here?" She clucked her tongue. "Don't tell me you've fallen for the little twit. Are you trying to replace the first Emerald with this one?"

"What concern is it of yours? As long as you know where she is, you won't ever have to worry about your little mistake coming back to burn you."

The woman growled something low, but I couldn't make it out.

Pushing my ear tighter to the door, I fell into the room and collided with a blond man. I started to apologize to him but realized I'd been confused. It wasn't a man at all. It was a green woman. An ugly green woman.

Why was I crying?

She offered me an emerald staff to help myself up. I took it and got to my feet. Then I hugged the woman fiercely, already forgetting what they were talking about.

"I don't know who you are, but I think I am very happy to see you." I sniffled and wiped my nose against her sleeve.

"You don't recognize me, Dorthea?" the green-faced woman said, her eyes searching me over.

"Is that my name?" I turned it over in my head, tasting it to see if it felt right. "I don't remember. There are holes in my brain, and my memories keep falling out."

The other person in the room scoffed and turned her eyes up. The green-faced woman glared at her and wrapped an arm around me. "My name is Verte, and you have been very sick with the curse. We had to leave the Emerald Palace to get help from a special, magnificent man named the Wizard of Is." She pointed her red-tipped fingers to the other girl. "This is Rexi. She came with us from the palace. Does any of this sound familiar?"

The name Rexi did ring a bell. The girl's hair looked like she'd put her finger in a lightning bug jar and got electrocuted.

I looked back to Verte to answer her question. "I think so. I remember that girl being really rude. And there was this boy. Mother wanted me to marry him." My heart started beating faster. There was something I needed to know, something just on the edge of what I could see. Teardrops fell onto my hands. "Are my parents here? I think I need to see them."

Verte patted my back. "Hush now, child. They're still at the palace, but they're coming for the wedding. You were right; you are getting married. In fact, it's to the wizard I was telling you about earlier."

Rexi made a strangled noise in her throat and looked like she'd swallowed a bug. A really gross bug.

With effort, I tried to recall the boy I was supposed to marry. I think I was upset at first, but now he gave me warm, fuzzy feelings. Even if I couldn't quite remember what he looked like. I could have sworn I had heard a man's voice, but only the two women were in the room. "Can I see him now?"

Verte got a strained look on her face. "Not right now, dearie. You are still very sick, and if you want to be all better for your wedding day, you'd better get your rest. Rexi will take you back to your room."

The young girl sighed and helped me up. I was still kind of light-headed and leaned on her for support. We left the room and headed back down the hallway of mirrors.

I pulled myself back, so I could get a good look at Rexi. "Are we friends?"

She smiled sweetly. "Of course, the very bestest. Why would you ask?"

"Because if you were my friend, you would tell me if something was wrong."

She batted her eyes and smiled brighter. "Absolutely."

Rexi opened the door to the room. While I had been gone, all the dead flowers had been cleared away and replaced with new ones.

"So you think it's okay to marry this wizard guy?" I continued my earlier point while Rexi helped me back into bed and under the covers.

Her smiled tightened, and when she spoke, her voice sounded odd, like she had stuffed something up her nose. "Fairy-tale wedding and happily ever after. Isn't that what every princess wants?"

"I guess so." I yawned. "Hey, Rexi," I called sleepily.

She was out the door but poked her head back in. "What?"

"Will you tell Verte the mirrors are broken?"

"What do you mean?"

"They…*yawn*…have the wrong…*yawn*…reflection. Yours is really pale with silver hai…" I trailed off into sleep before I could finish.

"*Rule #71: When making the seating chart for your royal wedding, don't put dwarves near the champagne fountain.*"

—*Definitive Fairy-Tale Wedding Survival Guide*

Something Borrowed, Something Blue

"Today is a magnificent day."

I opened my eyes but immediately had to squint because of the bright light streaming in from the window.

"What day is it today?" I croaked. My throat felt dry, like it was out of practice.

"It's your wedding day—the most important day of a young princess's life." Verte bustled around the room.

My heart nearly exploded. "I'm getting married?" I squeaked.

Verte clucked disapprovingly at me. "Don't you remember? We had this conversation already. You've spent all this week getting better for it."

I vaguely remembered the conversation now. But wasn't that yesterday? My sense of time was completely wonky, and I couldn't remember a single thing in between that chat and this moment, let alone a week's worth.

Verte continued to flit about the room, finally going to the corner and opening an armoire. Inside hung a dress that sparkled with diamonds and emerald beading. "Your mother sent it. Something came up at the Emerald Palace and she won't be able to come. She left you a letter. Would you like to read it?"

Somehow I wasn't surprised that my mom wasn't coming. For some reason, I couldn't even picture her ever leaving the palace. Still, what kind of mother didn't show up at her own daughter's wedding? "Yes, please." I swung my legs to dangle off the bed and greedily waited for my letter, since that was all I could have of her.

Dearest Princess Dorthea,

I am so sorry your father and I cannot be with you today. Horrible beasts are threatening to take over the kingdom. That's why this marriage is so important. Once we enter into an alliance with the wizard, the Emerald Kingdom will be safe. Then we can see each other again. Isn't that what you want?

I've sent you the dress I wore at my own

wedding. Wear it for good luck and think of me. Your father sends his love. We're counting on you.

Many happy returns on this most blessed day,
Queen Em

"Are you all right, my dear?" Verte sat down on the bed next to me.

I attempted to summon a smile. It would have been easier to tell the suns not to rise. "It feels like I haven't seen my parents in ages."

Verte patted my hand. "As soon as today's important business is settled, everything will be exactly as it should." She got off the bed and opened the door. Rexi stood in the doorway with a tray of food. "Eat your breakfast," Verte said as Rexi brought it in. "Every bite. Once you're married, you'll need all your strength." Verte cackled at her own joke and hobbled out of the room.

Rexi set the breakfast tray down on the table and motioned for me to take a seat. The tray was brimming with all sorts of goodies: mini cheesecakes, burrberry croissants, chocolate wands, and an apple. They looked and smelled delicious. Adorning the tray was a white agave lily. All of my favorite things—and I was extra pleased that I remembered that these were my favorite things.

I looked around the room to see what else I could glean

about my life. The walls were bare and sterile. The nightstand held a single vase of gardenias. The room seemed…empty. "Weren't there a whole bunch of red flowers here earlier?"

Wearing the tight smile again, Rexi plucked a flower from the nearby vase. "Yes, but I find white to be much more appropriate for a wedding." She started plucking the petals off to emphasize each word. "It symbolizes new beginnings, a blank slate, if you will." Her smile got big and toothy, like she was doing a commercial for sparkle toothpaste. I had the urge to say, *Grandma, what big teeth you have.*

She called for Nikko, who had brought a satin pillow. On it was a silver hair comb adorned with a large, white flower. She clapped in pleasure. "Let's get you ready for your big day."

A loud commotion came from outside my window, and I peeked out to see what was going on. People were running around yelling like Munchkins while some kind of animal roared and reared up. The huge beast was being led by chains—kind of. Even with ten men, they had a hard time getting the big, winged creature to cooperate.

"What in Grimm's name is that?"

I wondered if that was one of the beasts threatening my kingdom.

Rexi looked out the window too, her face set into hard lines. "*That* is dinner for the feast." She stomped to the door. "Nikko, help the princess get dressed and make sure she eats. Everything. I'll take care of preparations for the barbecue."

She stayed by the door for a minute more, watching me

expectantly. Picking up one of the chocolate wands, I took a bite. Apparently satisfied, she turned and left.

As soon as she was gone, I pulled a face and tossed the wand back on the tray. The candy tasted sour and a little funny, like maybe it was stale or had gone bad.

Nikko set about pinning my hair into some intricate style. He was surprisingly nimble, considering he had big apelike hands, and but he probably got a lot of practice since he so much hair of his own—all over his body, not just under a hat, which looked like some kind of upside-down takeout food box. In fact, I didn't want to be rude, but he looked rather much like a gorilla. While he worked on my hair, I gingerly examined the flowered headpiece he'd brought up. I'd never seen anything like it. Delicate white petals shot up through the middle and seemed to cascade over like a waterfall.

"Mind the thorns, Lady Emerald. Sometimes even the most beautiful things can bite," Nikko whispered. It was the first time I had heard his voice. It didn't really match the oafish old man.

Following his warning, I looked closer at the bloom. Sure enough, hidden beneath the flower's head were sharp, spindly thorns.

"It's called a lotus rose." He continued to whisper as if he were afraid to be overheard even though we were the only two people in the room. "It used to be the symbol of a powerful sorceress. I haven't seen one in many years. Did you know that if you tried to grow it in a garden, it would never bloom? The flower only blossoms in the most horrendous conditions. But when it does, it's strong and almost nothing can kill it." Nikko gently took the flower from my hand and pinned it into my hair. "There. All done."

"Is there a looking glass handy so I can see it?" I asked and glanced around the barren room.

"I'm sorry, but the wizard has sent away all the mirrors. They had some sort of magical malfunction." Nikko pulled the wedding dress out of the armoire and laid it on the bed. He looked from it to me, then back to it again, blushing.

I took pity on him since I didn't think that *ladies hand-maiden* was in his typical job description. "You really don't have to stay while I get dressed. I'm sure I can manage myself."

He looked around, distressed, probably worried his boss would yell at him for leaving me alone. "I don't—"

Placing a hand softly on his arm, I gently nudged him out. "You can stand just outside the door, and I'll knock when I'm ready for you to come in."

Looking relieved, Nikko bowed and scurried out the door, closing it. I think I heard the snick of a lock. Honestly, what was everyone so jumpy about? Worried that I would become a runaway bride or something?

My memories were starting to come back to me. I remembered bits of my childhood, like tagging along with Verte because everyone was always too busy for me. And the desperate desire to please my parents but always falling short.

Well, not this time.

I picked up the dress and thought of my mother's wedding portrait that hung just outside the ballroom. Hopefully, the borrowed dress looked half as good on me. Slipping it on felt, in some small way, like she was here with me. This was what she wanted—no, *needed* me to do. But I would have been lying if I had said I didn't have cold feet.

Speaking of, where were my shoes? I opened the armoire to check and see if my mom had sent some. When I bent over to look along the bottom, I got dizzy and sick to my stomach. The piece of chocolate wand I had earlier came back up.

Yuck. It tasted even worse the second time.

It seemed important to both Rexi and Verte that I eat, and it was clear from the sampling of my favorites that they had put a lot of thought into preparing it. I didn't want their feelings to get hurt, but I was too nervous to keep anything else down. And throwing up on my intended's feet would not make a very good impression.

I looked out the window. The beast and his handlers were gone. The only thing directly below was a litter of golden retriever pups.

"Here, puppy puppies," I called, rapping on the open glass.

They all looked up, ears perked, tilting their heads.

"Are you hungry?" I held the tray out the window and tipped it over, allowing the food to fall to the dogs below. They gobbled it rabidly.

With that little piece of ingenuity taken care of, I set the tray back down and restarted my search for shoes. There was one thing I knew for sure: I had a lot of them. "One pair must be around here…"

A twinkle under the bed caught my eye. There's no elegant way to squat down in a wedding dress, but I managed. Aside from a few dust gerbils, there was a pair of silver slippers with two-inch ruby heels. I loved them on sight.

"They're gorgeous." I stroked the sides and felt a little electric charge run down my spine. Setting down the shoes, I lifted my gown and stepped into them. Immediately I felt better; my head even cleared a little.

I lowered my dress. The hem barely grazed the floor, meaning the shoes would stay hidden and no one would see that the ruby clashed with the emeralds sewn onto my dress.

A tepid knock on the door. "Princess, all your guests are waiting. May I come in?" The quiet voice was muffled even further through the wood.

"Yes, Nikko. I'm ready." And I was. I felt better than I had in days—I think. Putting on those shoes had clicked something into place. Things were going to be all right. I could feel it.

Nikko stepped in the room and gasped.

I chuckled awkwardly and toyed with my skirt. "Hopefully that's the good kind of shock as opposed to the 'emperor's new clothes' kind."

His eyes brightened and the corners crinkled in. "I see you found the shoes I snuck in for you." He stared at me for another moment before his eyes clouded over as if he remembered something. "Have you finished your breakfast?"

I proudly pointed to the empty tray. "Every bite."

"Then there's nothing left to do, is there?" Nikko chewed his lower lip, like he wanted to say something else. "I really wish I could be of more help." His golden bucket hat flashed a bit.

Taking a deep breath, I rolled my shoulders back. "It's okay. I'm ready. Let's go."

Nikko still looked hesitant but held out his arm to escort me. "As you wish." He led me up the stairs to the top of the tower. Off to the right of the landing, there was a large hole in the marble wall. And just underneath the hole was a single tawny feather.

I picked it up and twirled it through my fingers, playing with the soft, downy end. "What the hex made this hole?"

Nikko stumbled slightly, tripping over his shoelace or something. When he straightened, he said, "A bird, Your Majesty."

Must have been a big bird.

"There you are! What took you so long? Everyone is waiting." Rexi hustled toward us. She couldn't go very fast since she had somehow squeezed herself into a little silver lamé cocktail dress—that was two sizes too small.

"Rexi, please don't take this the wrong way, but is there any way you could change your clothes? That dress looks really tacky, and your opal necklace, while lovely, is a little much, and the bright red clashes, don't you think?" I tried to put it as nicely as I could, but still, it had to be said. After all, it was my wedding—the only one I was ever going to have—and I didn't want anyone looking like they got dressed at the Three Blind Mice Boutique.

Rexi's jaw dropped so low she looked like a boa constrictor. Nikko turned paler than Snow White's tuchus and slowly backed away.

She snapped her mouth shut with an audible click. "I'm sorry but that's not possible; there is simply no time. Here." Shoving a bouquet of flowers into my hand, she next turned her anger to the man at my side. "What are you staring at, Nikko? Go outside and check on our other royal pain." Her curled lip attempted to smile sweetly. "I mean *guest*." Then she stormed back in the direction she had come from.

"She is so not my maid of honor anymore," I muttered, fluffing up the flowers in my bouquet. "Ouch." Blood welled up on my finger from the thorn.

"I did try to warn you, Highness," Nikko said but wouldn't look me in the eye.

I shrugged it off. "It's no big deal. Just a little blood. But I did just think of a way you can help. If there is another royal guest, will you please send them up?"

A smile broke across the gentleman's face. "Yes, Your Majesty. I can do that." Then he bounded down the stairs, some two at a time.

Rexi gestured impatiently from the double doors at the end

of the hall. No reason to delay the inevitable. As I walked down the hallway, the old superstition entered my head. *Something borrowed, something blue. Something magic, for love so true.* I had the borrowed dress and I had the magic shoes. I didn't have anything blue though.

Wait, maybe I did. *I think my fiancé's eyes are blue, a lovely but unusual shade.* I remembered the first time I had looked into those eyes, and with a deep breath, I pushed open the doors.

Inside was a grand ballroom, everything opulent to the point of excess. There were floating chandeliers, a champagne waterfall, even a five-piece orchestra that was playing itself.

The guest list was small and intimate, just the major heads of the fairy-tale families. Cinderella sat with Charming. Behind them was Jack with his plus one, the goose. Beauty sat closest to the door.

That wasn't right. *She shouldn't be here…* I just couldn't put my finger on why.

My stomach twisted and coiled like a snake ready to strike. Now I was extra glad I had chucked the food. Clutching my bouquet for dear life, I walked toward the man standing in the front of the room. His cream-colored tux had twice the amount of diamonds that mine did. It attracted the light and made him difficult to focus on from far way.

Staring down at my bouquet, I kept walking. The satin ribbon that bound the flowers together had crimson spots from my pricked finger. The stark contrast of red against the white was unsettling. It reminded me of another party.

I heard the chandeliers shatter onto the floor. But when I looked up, they were still floating. I stared back at Beauty, but the Beast was wearing her yellow dress. I blinked and Beauty sat there again.

Looking now to the front, there were two thrones with a crown resting on one. My breathing quickened. I looked up into my groom's eyes. They were deep sapphire—the wrong color blue.

My bouquet went up in emerald flames.

I remembered everything.

"I would rather face down a swarm of fireswamp rats than one pixed-off princess bride."

—Prince Humperdink

Princess Bridezilla

My fury reigned unchecked, and green flames rolled down my arms.

Burn it. Burn it all. Leave nothing but ashes.

The voice grated, like it left splinters of wood in my mind. I didn't care.

The magical five-piece orchestra was still playing Tinkerbell's "Canon in D." They were the first to go. I shot a fireball to the corner and blasted the instruments into toothpicks.

It was immensely satisfying. And there was so much more to come.

I advanced on the wizard with both hands fisted at my

side, glowing with emerald flames. "Do you have Verte and my parents?"

His chest rose and fell rapidly while treading backward until his heels hit the dais. With nowhere left to go, he pointed at Rexi. "It was her idea."

"Wrong answer." I aimed the flames for his head, but he fainted, so I only singed the top of his pompadour. The power inside me was disappointed I had missed. But the wizard's head did make a pleasant crack when it hit the throne.

I rounded on Rexi and snarled. "Why did you betray me?"

She smirked. "Because the Gray Witch offered me a better deal than following after you like a handmaiden."

She's the worst of them all. Making you believe you could trust her. The punishment for treason is death.

My anger smoldered at the traitor. "I will ask you once. Where are they?"

"Rotting in—"

I threw the flame, but she deflected it up with a platter. Too bad for her, she was standing under one of the chandeliers. It crashed on her head, and she crumpled onto the floor.

Not enough. More.

"Who else…" I spun around, ready to face any attackers in the audience, but no one was there. Little voodoolike dolls sat toppled in the chairs, the magic that animated them gone. I walked down the aisle, torching each and every one as I went by.

More.

Spelled

Outside the ballroom, a litter of puppies sat in the hall. There was the sound of tinkling crystal behind me.

"What are you waiting for? Fry her!" Rexi screamed to the dogs.

The lead pup burped a small flame, but that was it. They looked drunk. No, not drunk—drugged. One of the dogs still had burrberry sauce on his snout from the food I'd tossed out the window. I took out the leader of the pack with a single throw, the blast throwing the others to the side of his ashes.

Each time I used the flames, I felt my body getting weaker and colder. But still, the power inside wanted more.

It was hungry.

Rexi shrieked from behind me. I blindly threw a flame in her direction. The resulting explosion took out the door and crumbled most of the wall. I staggered and caught myself with one hand on the ground. The flames were dancing in front of my eyes, turning the world to bright green.

Behind the barrier of rubble, Rexi was throwing a temper tantrum. From the crashing sounds, she would be out here soon. The dogs on the ground weren't stirring yet, but I heard more claws scratching their way up the staircase. Those puppies would be normal again and fully lethal in a matter of minutes, and if my dimming vision was any indication, I didn't have enough juice to take them all on.

There was no time to track down Verte or my parents, and I suspected they weren't here anyway. I had to get out, and there was only one exit point and I only had a slim chance of surviving. I climbed through the hole and called for the one who had made it. "Kato!"

A blast from behind forced me off my ledge and into free fall.

Seconds went by, and I wondered if I would have been better off fighting my way through the puppies.

A streak of brown shot from around the side of the tower, and Kato snatched me out of my descent.

For a moment, all I could do was memorize his features, from his whiskery chin to the ice water in his eyes. "That is the right color blue."

I laughed when his face crinkled up in confusion.

We were gaining altitude when the top of the tower seemed to explode outward.

"Dorthea!" Verte stood in the center of the blast. "Hurry!"

Kato angled to make the turn back and swoop her up, but I stopped him.

"It's not her." My heart shattered all over again.

"How do you know?" Kato flapped his wings just enough to keep us in place, like treading water.

"She called me Dorthea," I whispered sadly.

"Pum'kin, I've missed you." Now my father stood in the center of the room.

Oh Grimm, this hurt. This treachery was worse than being drugged, betrayed, and burned—it was the loss of hope. I nudged Kato. "Let's go, please."

As he turned, I saw my mother blink into place where

my father had been. "You come back here right this instant, young lady!"

I buried my tear-stained face in Kato's fur. I couldn't bear to see any more. He put his back to them and started to fly away.

"No!" Rexi screamed from the tower, and I looked up just in time to see the explosion of feathers as Kato's wing was obliterated in a flash of lightning. His face screwed up in anguish. The remaining wing flapped furiously to make up for the loss of its pair, but it was no use.

Once again we were falling. We had flown far enough away from the island that we were over the water. Usually crash-landing in water is better than solid ground. Except my life depended on my hair not getting wet.

"Get ready!" Kato called and banked left.

"For what?" I flipped over and saw what he was aiming for. There was something floating in the water that looked like alphabet letters. But we were diving too fast. We were going to miss them.

"You can't mean to…"

"Yep," he said and dropped me as we passed over.

I landed with a squish and my hair sizzled against the slimy letter *C*. Seconds later, Kato hit the water with a giant splash. The drops rained down on me, making my hair crackle more, taking my breath away.

With effort, I pushed up from the *C* and looked forward. The letter *B* blinked while the *A* was sideways, like a snout.

I must have been riding BeC, the mythical ABCserpent. Though I was pretty sure it was imaginary and shouldn't really exist.

Wonder gave way to panic when Kato didn't resurfaced.

No, no, no, no. He couldn't die now. I'd finally figured out that I liked him—the "more than my shoes" kind. "Excuse me." I patted the *C* insistently to get the serpent's attention. "Helllooo?" I knocked harder.

What were my options? I couldn't just jump in the water. According to Crow, if the flames went out, I'd die. I considered a swim anyway.

"What?" The voice gurgled and sounded like it came from underwater.

My voice was breathy, and I was practically jumping out of my skin. "My friend. Please use your snout and pull him out of the water."

The serpent turned away from the spot where I had seen Kato land. "No. Why?"

"Because he'll drown." I panicked. It had to turn back—I had to make it turn back. I let the flames return to my hands. "If you don't pull him up I'll…"

Kato flew up from out of the water and landed with a wet squish on letters *D* through *L*.

The voice spoke from under the water again. "No. *Y.*" It shook the *Y* at the end of its tail. "No need for threats."

I crawled my way through the slime to check on Kato and ran my hands over nearly all of him. His chest moved up and down, but his side oozed blood from where his left wing used to be. "Grimm save us. Are you okay?" *Please be okay.* When he didn't move, I called louder. "Can you hear me?"

"Yes." He groaned and opened one eye. "My wing is busted, not my ears."

I gave him a huge hug, and he winced beneath me. "Sorry." I shifted slightly, still not willing to let him go. It felt like I had lost everything all over again today. I would hold on to the one thing I had left to my last breath—and then some.

My hands continued to search around his body for signs of any more damage. I lifted his paw and counted his nails. He still had seven left. "Why didn't you call Bob for help?"

He raised his head slightly to better see me. "They knew. As soon as I was out of your sight, they muzzled me, put iron thimbles on my claws, and tied me down with chains. I stayed bound in a well for nearly a week not knowing what happened to you."

I dropped the paw in surprise. "A week?"

His head fell back down with a slurp. "Yes, but it felt like years. What were you doing, and why do you look like you're getting married?"

There was no way to explain that well. I didn't really under-stand most of what had happened myself. My head was foggy as I tried to figure out what was poppy-induced dream and what was real.

"Long story. Short version, I took a nap and Rexi elected herself Team Villain MVP." I could feel my temper rising.

"I know," he said, curling his lip. "She came down and personally tied me to the roasting spit. If that servant ape hadn't let me go, I would have been barbecue."

That surprised me. "Nikko? See, aren't you glad that I didn't let you eat him?" My arm grazed Kato's side, and he hissed in pain. We could go over our little travelogues later. Right now, we needed help. "We've got to find someone to bandage you up. I'll ask the serpent to take us to land. Then we'll call Bob, get you home, and I'll take care of Blanc." I paused and let the emerald flame come to my hand again. *Yessss.* I cared a lot less about the curse than I used to, and the inner voice had taken on a softer, almost fuzzy quality. Almost comforting. In fact, I couldn't remember why I'd refused his request in the first place.

I crawled back toward the head. The serpent continued swimming while I checked on Kato. It traveled quickly; the island was nowhere in sight. The sea had narrowed and we were cruising down something more akin to a river, with high cliff walls on one side, thick Ironwood trees on the other.

I patted the brow of the *C* again. "Excuse me. Thank you for saving my friend, but he's really hurt. Can you take us to land?" The ABCserpent didn't answer. I had the feeling I was getting the silent treatment. "And I'm really sorry I threatened you. It's been a rough few days."

"Apology accepted," the serpent gurgled. "Remember that nice girls use their heads and their words. Not their hands."

Great, I was stuck on a pacifist serpent.

"I'll keep that in mind. About finding a spot to land…"

Glug glug. "Yesss. I know someone who will help. We're almost there."

"Thank you!" I turned to get Kato ready, but he was already limping my way. The serpent giggled under the water. I thought Kato's nails may have been tickling it.

"We're going to somebody who can help," I said to Kato and crawled back to him.

We couldn't get there soon enough—Kato wasn't looking too hot. He swayed on his feet, more than just being on the water would cause. And he was shaking his head and laughing in a delirious sort of way.

"We're here," the serpent singsonged from the water.

I looked away from Kato and saw that we'd pulled up to a beach. A very familiar beach—with a weedy garden and a shack with shutters stuck on with gum.

I knocked on the *C.* "No, no, no. You've made a mistake. There's no one here to help us. Just a blind head hunter."

"Hydra has many spare parts. She will help your friend."

She had lots of heads, but what were the odds she had wings too? Or that she wouldn't just try stealing Kato's good one?

"But she's creepy." My voice turned down at the end. I knew I was whining, but the image of the heads was still fresh in my mind. Maybe she was just a harmless old lady with a morbid hobby because she got tired of collecting spoons. After all, she had tried to warn me about Black Crow.

Hydra ambled out of her shack. She was being led by a girl in trousers with pokey blond hair. Rexi.

Kato roared. "Why?"

"Okay," the serpent gurgled. The tail poked out of the water, slid under Kato and I, and deposited us, roughly, on the beach.

"Thanks," I muttered.

A watery, "You're welcome," came as it sped away down the river. We were marooned, but I was ready to fight. Ignoring BeC's advice about words versus hands, I readied my flames to take Rexi out, but Kato was already bounding up to her.

Kato cornered her against the house and growled. Then he collapsed.

"True love can overcome anything. Even fish breath."

—The Little Mermaid, from
Pea Soup for the Fairy-Tale Lover's Soul

Spare Parts' Dealer, Make Me a Match

I rushed over to Kato. "Help him, please," I pleaded. Hydra and Rexi spurred to action. I snatched Rexi's ankle, allowing my palms to keep just a flicker along the skin. "You've done enough. If you move, I will end you."

She started shaking. "I couldn't help it. She wouldn't let me go back."

Rexi seemed like a completely different person from the one who had conspired with the wizard at the tower. All the bravado, not to mention the tacky dress and ugly fire opal necklace, was gone. Right now, Rexi was either scared hexless of me or up for the best actress award at the Grimmy's. Something wasn't right, but my brain was still too muddled to sort through it. I released her leg and let her cower under the window.

Hydra emerged from her shack carrying a head by its red hair. She yanked off her own and tossed it. Rexi caught it and turned a distinct shade of "I'm going to throw up" green.

There was that squishy plop sound and bippity bob's your uncle, Hydra was a redhead with a white streak down the side—like a skunk. She blinked her green eyes a few times. "Ahh, that's better." Now she spoke with a bit of a twang while smiling a crooked and yellowed smile. The shack behind her shuddered and folded in on itself—all the way down to a square the size of a tinderbox.

What in story was going on, and how was packing all her junk up going to help Kato? Now was not the time for redecorating.

Hydra sensed my impatience and held up a hand. "Wait fer it."

The box wiggled and jumped, then opened back up and expanded until it was a light blue stucco building with a blinking neon sign out front that said "Spare Parts."

By far the coolest thing I had ever seen. If I ever got home or had a chance at a normal life again, I was so ordering one of those from the Castle Shopping Network.

Hydra grabbed Kato's back legs. "Don't just stand there. Help me git him inside."

I grabbed his front paws, and we heaved, moving about a dwarf's length before we had to set him back down. I grunted and tugged while Kato groaned, not entirely conscious. "If you can hear me, you are officially on a diet." While I was in the Ivory Tower, he had doubled in size again. And weight.

Hydra snapped at Rexi. "Git over here."

Rexi shook her head emphatically. "Nuh-uh, she'll—"

"She'll behave on accountin' her friend is gonna be just fine. Provided we git him inside…" Hydra finished.

I didn't look at Rexi, so the lack of evil glare must have been her signal to go ahead. She lifted under Kato's middle. Together we hefted, but there was no way the three of us would be able to move him through the door. Cursing, Hydra let go, and Kato fell down again, trapping my legs.

Please, I prayed, no longer sure if anyone was listening. *There has to be a way to get him inside.* I struggled to get free and felt my heels click against his claws. Within the space of a blink, Kato was gone. Before I could wail and rev up my flames, he reappeared inside on the stainless steel table. The two other conscious people present looked at me, one with trepidation, the other with thoughtful consideration. If Hydra knew something, she wasn't sharing. Quietly, she went into the back room to search for something.

I didn't really care how Kato got inside; I was just glad he did. It was probably something with this magic house. I mean, it obviously had power since the inside of the building had changed just as dramatically as the outside. It was an odd combination of doctor's office and carriage body shop. There were grease spots—at least I hoped they were grease spots—on the floor, but nearly everything else was clean. The wall of shelves containing all of Hydra's other heads was the only thing the interior had in common with the last time I'd stepped inside.

Amid the clanging and banging from the back, I held on to Kato's paw. He was going to be all right. His breathing had leveled out, so it would be okay. The more I kept telling myself that, the more I hoped I would believe it.

Rexi stood nearby with a conflicted look on her face. Her head was down, but I could see her reflection in the stainless steel table. Her normal reflection. Everything between the Ivory Tower study and the wedding march was pretty much a drugged, blurry mess. But unless it was a dream, I recalled her having a silver-haired reflection.

I sighed wearily, tired of nothing being what it seemed. "It wasn't you at my wedding, was it?"

Rexi's eyes nearly bulged out of their sockets. "Holy toad. You and Kato got married?"

"Not Kato, the wizard."

"You married the wizard?" Her mouth popped open wide to match her eyes.

Hydra shouted from the back. "I know a good divorce demon."

"No. It was a trap. It's…really confusing." I had no idea how to explain it coherently. It was still jumbled up in my own brain. "The demon puppies were there. And Verte and Rexi were there, but I don't think it was really them. I just don't know who's who anymore."

I let my head hit the table with a bonk.

"Ain't really *that* confusing. You was at the home of the Mimicman." Hydra emerged from the back holding a black raven's wing and held it up against Kato's body. "Nope, too small." She headed back into the storeroom to try again.

"No, I was at the Ivory Tower with Mick, the Wizard of Is." Exhaling loudly, I rolled my head so that my cheek rested on the cold metal table.

Hydra stuck her head back out. "Pish, is that what he's calling himself now? Bah, he got more names than I got fleas. But ever since he turned human, he's been the Mimicman, master of illusions. He can cast a few parlor spells, but his only real source of power is shape-shifting himself into anybody."

Turned human? Not sure I wanted to know exactly what kind of thing he'd been before that. I thought back to the scene in the blasted tower. "So he pretended to be Verte and my parents."

This time, Hydra came back out with a much bigger white wing. "Yes, ain't that great?" she said, chipper, and held the wing up against Kato's body again. "Right size, wrong color. Oh well, it'll have to do. Hold this." She shoved the wing in my face.

I spit out the feathers that got stuck between my lips. "Why is that great?"

Hydra rummaged around in a drawer that was full to bursting, tossing random junk over her shoulder until she found what she was looking for. "Aha!" she exclaimed, holding up a jar of spider glue. She went over to Kato and slathered it on the raw part of his shoulder where the wing was destroyed. "Because the Mimicman can only mimic what *is*, what exists in this world. He don't got no form of his own anymore, and you cain't imitate death, so any shape he takes—"

"Has to be alive," I finished. "So my parents and Verte are alive and well somewhere." Hydra took the wing from me before I dropped it as I jumped up and down with excitement.

Rexi poked me. "I told you he looked like the guy from the cover of *Sorcery Illustrated*." She smiled just a little, like she was testing the water with a big toe to see if I were a ticking crocodile that would bite.

Still aligning the wing, Hydra perked her head up. "The Fourteenth Swimsuit Edition?" Rexi nodded, and Hydra's face brightened with an expression of nostalgia. "Yeah, that one were pretty yummy. But just to clarify an earlier point— hold his wing in place please—your people is *alive* somewhere. I ain't say a thing about them being *well*."

Hope is like a balloon. It seems like it swells up just so someone else can pop it in your face. I would have smacked my head again, but I was busy holding the wing in place so the glue could dry. Oh well, alive was good, and I would take what I could get at this point. But something still bugged me. "So best guess is that the McWizard made Griz a Rexi suit. Right?"

Hydra shooed my hands and moved the wing up and down to check its range of motion. "Or she done made it herself. Were the Fake Rexi wearing an opal necklace, by chance?"

My insides shuddered just thinking about her and her horrible fashion sense. "Yes, and it did not match her tacky silver dress."

"Were it a black opal or a fire opal?"

I thought back. "Fire. Why does her bad taste in jewelry matter?"

Hydra sat back in the chair next to the table. "Because a fire opal holds someone else's life essence. She done gone used their life to power her spells and do the replication."

"That's horrible." Rexi turned pale and green again. "Is there any way to give it back to the person it belongs to?"

"Nope. Once it's agone to a new vessel, no exchanges, no returns. Then it's only matter o' time afore it's used up." Hydra nodded to me. "Your emerald flame is the exception. The more yous usin' it, the more you gots to be rechargin' it. 'Cuz each time you is chuckin' fire, it sucks *your* life instead of someone else's."

Now it was my chance to turn pale and slightly green. At my wedding—and how surreal is that to say?—I had been in a blind rage, ready to burn down the world because it deserved to fall to ashes. I hadn't yet come to terms with how much I had used the flames or how much I enjoyed it. Worse, I was afraid I already knew how to recharge the life magic.

"So if Griz was pretending to be you, Rexi, what the pix happened to you?"

Rexi busied herself checking the new wing. "I waited for you outside the study. Then the cover model clone came out and said he had something to show me, said he knew how to spin straw into licorice. I touched the spinning wheel and…"

She got really quiet, probably embarrassed about falling for one of the oldest bad-guy tricks in the book.

"She washed up here yesterday," Hydra said, filling in the rest of the details. "I told her to wait fer you here. I is wearing my oracle head at the time, so I knows you were coming." She went to the door and picked up the old blind lady head and put it back on the shelf.

And there she stayed, doing nothing in particular, except maybe giving me a minute to make amends with Rexi. I guessed that because she kept moving her eyes from me to Rexi and puffing her cheeks out like blowfish.

"I'm sorry, Rexi," I said quietly. "You're my friend, and I sure as spell should know better than to trust what my eyes tell me. I should have known that you'd never betray us."

"Stop." Rexi looked really uncomfortable. "I need to tell you—"

Kato's groan interrupted her. He was coming to. Thank Grimm. I helped him roll onto his belly. He rotated his shoulders, moving each wing up and down. I think it was kind of an auto-reflex thing, because his eyes were still closed. When he did open them and saw Rexi standing next to him, his entire body vibrated in a growl.

I stepped in front of Rexi, blocking her from his view. He still looked like he was going to plow through me to get to her. I had to talk fast, like the guy with the magical disclaimers on late-night infomercials. "The bad Rexi was really the Gray Witch with a Rexi mask on because this Rexi got duped and dumped in the sea, and she's been here ever since with Hydra." By the end, I had run out of breath, so the last few words were a little strained.

He stopped growling but still didn't look convinced. "How do we know this is the real Rexi?"

"Reflection test." I grabbed a startled Rexi by the scruff of her neck and positioned her close to the shiny table. "See, all blond, not a speck of gray or silver."

Kato grumbled and hopped off the table. "Fine, but only because I trust Dot. I won't eat you...*yet*. But I'm keeping an eye on you."

Holding a roll of gauze, Hydra returned to wrap his wing, binding it to his side. "Why just one eye? I gots more in the back iffin you want to make a few alterations." She tapped the middle of his forehead. "Right here might look nice." She scurried into the storeroom and came back with a jar of eyeballs and a broken unicorn horn. "We is having a special. Buy one get a half one free."

Kato slyly scooted away from the googly eye jar. "No thanks, but I was wondering about a different kind of body alteration. Can you make me human again?"

Hydra put the extras back and watched Kato carefully. "Human? But why would you want to trade in the freedom of them skies to trudge along the ground?" She jerked her thumb in my direction. "Changin' yourself fer somebud else cain't work. Specially fer a high-maintenance ball and chain that ain't worth it anyway."

"Hey! I'm didn't ask him to change."

"Well, isn't that what this is all about?" she said matter-of-factly. "Personally, I like my men with a little chest hair, but I can see how difficult an interspecies relationship might be fer someone like you." She stuck a finger in my chest. "Can you honestly say you is willing to put up with his shedding all over the furniture? Is he yer one true love?"

How had this become about me? My cheeks heated and I stumbled through my feelings for some sort of rebuttal. "Love isn't just something that happens at first sight. It, um, takes a while and, uh, grows with calcium and thorns and, um, might bite until you teach it to fetch." I tried to remember everyone's love talks, but I'm afraid I got them mixed up. "Oh hex."

Hydra took my disjointed answer as answer enough and went back to addressing Kato. "See? You is better off finding a nice chimera to nest with. The cost to change are too high, especially iffin you is only changin' fer the affection of someone who cain't care for the real you."

Kato looked me over, much like he did the first time we met. This time, at the end of his search, there was no look of disdain. Or confusion. He stood up and went to Hydra. "I want to be human. I don't care about the cost. She's worth it."

Everything a girl's ever wanted to hear, and I had no idea what to do with it. What could I say to that? My feelings were stuck in the jumbled mess of my brain, playing peeka-boo, trying to hide from me.

Pulling a sour face, Hydra threw her hands up in the air. "Bah! You is dumber than I thought. And I gots no use for romantic fools. Be gone, all of you. I done everything I can. There ain't no solving stupid." She turned and walked away from us.

Rexi headed out the door, and Kato padded behind her.

My temper and hair crackled, and I wasn't about to let that wench get the last word. I stalked after Hydra and turned her around. "Hey. You don't know jack sprat. Kato could be puce with green stripes that clashed with everything I owned. He could turn into a mountain troll and eat nothing but goats. Wouldn't change a thing. And you're right; he might be stupid for wanting me, but for some reason he does—curse, shoe addiction, and all. So a little thing like being furry won't stop me from falling in love." My face grew even hotter than my emerald flames. "Not that I am or…"

A slow smile spread over Hydra's face. "And that were exactly what I needed to hear." She grabbed a new head off the shelf and pushed us out the door. "Out, out, unless you wanna git squished." An excited shiver shook her body. "This is gonna be good."

"*Rule #92: Need to wake a sleeping cutie or transform a frog into prince charming? The best magical cure is always a kiss.*"

—*Definitive Fairy-Tale Survival Guide, Volume 1*

29

A Spoonful of Sugar...

Hydra yanked off her current head and tossed it to Rexi again.

"*Yech.* Throw one of these at me again, and I swear I'm gonna chuck it like a golden ball into the river," she said, holding the head as far away from her as possible.

Kato shook his head. "Dot was right. You're too wussy to be an evil villain mastermind."

Hydra ignored us all and positioned the new head. It was dark skinned with sharp bones piercing the bridge of her nose. Small opossum-ish creatures hung from holes in her earlobes. And her hair was shaped and colored like a lemon afro. Once the new head connected to Hydra's body, the parts store closed itself for business and folded up.

We all watched Hydra's multiple personality disorder in action. Kato looked elf-struck, since he had been passed out the last time. Even for those of us who had already seen the show, it was impressive.

The tinderbox reopened and became a grass hut with a conical stick roof lined with wendigo horns. This time, the outside was decorated with dragon hides and chupacabra skins. Hydra looked at the hut expectantly, like something was missing. She muttered and kicked the door. A small sign rolled down: The Witch Doctor Is In.

Apparently satisfied with the transformation, Hydra opened the door and invited us in. Curved shelving lined the walls from roof to dirt floor. Aside from the heads, the shelves were stuffed with jars of all sizes and contents. I read a few of the labels: lizard breath, spider's shoes, pickled pixie pops, rotten beetle juice.

In the center of the floor was a big black cauldron boiling over with purple mist. Hydra went to the counter, picked out a little recipe card, and traded it for the head in Rexi's hand. "You be makin' yaself useful now and be gatherin' ingredients." Her voice was smooth and reminded me of caramel. It was different than it had been earlier. Come to think of it, the body shop voice was different than the blind hag too. I suppose it made sense in a "not really at all" kind of way.

Rexi held up the list and groaned when it folded down like a Jacob's ladder, tripling her work.

Kato sauntered over and tapped me on the back with his tail. He was grinning so wide you could see his back fangs. "So…love, huh?"

High up on the ladder, Rexi reached for the jar of newt nuts but couldn't resist getting in a jab. "She's been hit on the head multiple times and drugged. Her judgment is clearly impaired."

I didn't have a mirror, so I couldn't tell if my flames were burning the tips of my ears or not, but it felt that way. My pronouncement had been made in the heat of the moment, and now I was in the awkward *after* moment. What had I just done? Thoughts zip-a-dee-do-da'ed through my mind. I very carefully replayed every word Kato said. Not one of them was *love*. Or even *like*. He said, "She's worth it." Maybe he was thinking of my political value. Or the worth of my new powers. Maybe it had nothing to do with me as a person at all.

Instead of just asking him how he felt, I took the coward's way out. "What was that, Hydra? I'll be right over," I said, cocking my ear to the imaginary call. I ran over to the small prep table where Hydra was making some calculations. Kato followed me but didn't say anything more; his smug, satisfied look spoke plenty.

Tugging on the tiger-print tablecloth she was writing on, I got her attention. "You spoke about costs earlier. I don't have anything on me right now other than the jewels in the dress. Will that be enough? Or do you need more?"

Her face smoothed and got very serious. "Costs not be in da terms of jewels nor gold. Cost be comin' from ya life."

"Are you talking about a sacrifice? Because if so, I nominate Rexi," Kato said, trying to take a peek at Hydra's notes.

Rexi made a rude gesture with the chicken's foot she was holding.

"I be needin' ya life magics. A nail from da boy, and some hair from da girl." Hydra finished writing what she was working on and asked us to sign. It was completely illegible.

"What does it say?" I asked.

She held the document out in front of her. "It be sayin' I's not at fault if de spell don't be workin'. Dat ya dun broke da magic rules and dis is bein' da bestest I can do. An if he be dyin', ya's not be allowed to be comin' afta me."

I turned to Kato, giving voice to the alarm bells ringing in my head. "Maybe you shouldn't. There's really nothing you need to be human for. Plus, we haven't had a very good track record with magic lately. Think Black Crow. Do you want to become a stuffed lion or something?"

Hydra put the paper on the counter and turned back around to counsel us, her face grave. "She be havin' a point. But ya should alsa know, if ya be growin' inta a full beastie, der be no changin' back for ya."

Kato huffed, the air ruffling his auburn mane. "So try to be human and possibly blow up, or be stuck as a Chimera and lose my ice magic for all eternity. That about right?"

"Dat's abut da sum of it. I be lettin' ya decide." Hydra went over and helped Rexi with the ingredients.

"Don't do this, Kato," I pleaded. "I'll still help you figure out a way to keep Blanc imprisoned."

"It's not about that." His whiskers twitched, bristling with agitation.

I raised my hand to his face and stroked the fur on his cheek. "I meant what I said. I will still like you if you stay furry forever."

Kato's muzzle quirked to one side. "Like me? A minute ago you said you loved me."

My face heated. "Not exactly. Listen, about that—"

Kato stopped me. "No, you listen." He moved his head close, resting his brow ridge on my forehead so I could see nothing but those ice-blue eyes. "At the tower, it was obvious that the wizard wanted you. And he was very handsome, so I was jealous."

I tried to interject, but he kept right on going.

"And when they locked me up, I knew something was wrong. I had nothing to do with my time but worry about what he was doing to you. Had he put his hands on you? The thought made me want to rip that tower down brick by brick. I realized it wasn't just because I was concerned for your safety, but because *no one* should be allowed to touch you but me."

My hair was still more or less bound in the intricate style, but the few strands that were loose glowed and popped with the pounding of my heart.

"I need to be with you," he continued, backing up a step. "I would rather blow up than live a lifetime without being able to kiss you. It may be unreasonable, but I won't settle for anything less than living happily ever after *in love with you*." He gently took the pen from my hand with his mouth and signed the paper. "Okay, Hydra, I'm ready," he called and walked over to where she and Rexi were dicing the ingredients.

I stared down at the paper he had just scribbled on, and I knew I couldn't sign it, because if anything happened to him, no force in story would keep Hydra safe from me.

"Mix da ingredients togeda, child." Rexi headed over to dump the handfuls in the cauldron. Hydra panicked and caught the ingredients before they hit the water. "Not der! Dat's da battub. Put dem in da Crock-Pot by Dotea." Hydra shook her head and muttered something I couldn't make out.

"You spell in a Crock-Pot and bathe in a cauldron?" Rexi asked in disbelief.

"Would be pretty hard to be doin' da reberse now wouldn' it?" She turned her attention to Kato and I. "Okay, yas two lovebuds. Come on ober here so I be collectin' da life magics."

She took a snippet of my hair. The emerald tip popped and hissed in protest at being cut away. Even more than that, I felt its loss, like I was weaker somehow. Next, she took a hammer and chisel to Kato's paw and chipped off one of his nails. He only had six left. It made me ill that he had used three out of his lifetime quota of ten since meeting me. At this rate, he'd use them all and be dead in a month.

Hydra stirred the potion and frowned over it. "Sumthin' be not quite right." She looked around and tapped her finger thoughtfully. Her gaze stopped on me. "Could dat be a lotus rose in ya hair?"

I felt in back. Sure enough, it was still there. Kind of surprising that it had survived everything. I pulled it out of the comb and held it out to Hydra. She looked it over and nodded her approval. The flower might have been missing one or two petals, but it was still largely intact. Instead of taking it, she pushed the flower down into my palm. The thorns under the petals pricked me, drawing blood—exactly as Hydra intended, no doubt. She plucked the flower from my hand and tossed it into the Crock-Pot.

Nothing happened.

Rexi peeked into the top. "Shouldn't you say a rhyme like, *Double bubble royals are trouble?*"

Leaning back against the counter, Hydra calmly folded her arms. "No, but yas betta be standin' back if yas wantta be keepin' yas eyebrows."

Rexi jumped back right before green and purple flames burst upward from the Crock-Pot. "You might have said that before I stuck my head in there."

Hydra shrugged and found a jar. Dumping out the little worm in the bottom, she went to the Crock-Pot and ladled out a scoopful. It did not look appetizing. Her sniff and resulting look of disgust verified my opinion. She ran over to the side counter, where the tea set was, and dropped in a sugar cube, then handed the jar to me. "Ya can help him drink it." She grabbed Rexi and moved to the other side of the cauldron. "We's be ober here."

Good to know she was confident in her work.

Putting a hand under Kato's mouth, I readied the potion jar. "Last chance to change your mind."

His eyes burned into mine, his features set. "Nope. I know what I want."

"Then open wide and start praying." I dumped the contents down his throat. He stuck out his tongue and screwed up his face. Apparently the sugar didn't help the medicine go down. He started trembling. No, it was more like convulsions. His horns shrunk down to nubs. The process wasn't going to be easy, and Kato roared in pain.

Rexi grabbed my arm and dragged me behind the cauldron. Feathers popped off Kato's wings and started floating around the room. He roared again, standing on his hind legs, the top of his head bumping the ceiling. Then he collapsed on the floor, the cauldron blocking him from my view.

I started to run to him, but Hydra pulled me back. "How many times I be sayin', *wait for it*?"

The space of a few heartbeats might have taken centuries for what it felt like. Then came an explosion of smoke and fur. A few more beats later and a tanned hand gripped the rim of the cauldron. Then another hand grabbed the rim—a very pale hand.

Rexi scrunched her face. "What the spell?"

My thoughts exactly. I prayed even harder that the boy about to stand up looked mostly like the prince I first met in my palace—including the appropriate number of appendages.

With a groan, Kato pulled himself up to standing. His fur was gone, replaced by a head of auburn hair and tanned skin. All except for his left arm, which, starting at the shoulder, was stark pearl white.

Oh, and he was completely naked.

I closed my eyes and used my hand to cover Rexi's.

"What are you doing that for? The cauldron hides all the good parts anyway," she complained.

"Well, they're not yours to see," I snapped. Rexi snickered. Then I realized what I just said and what that implied. *Ah Grimm, can the earth just swallow me up now?*

I felt a hand brush against my arm. It wasn't a delicate hand like Rexi's. And it wasn't wrinkly like Hydra's. It felt rough and callused. And it gave me goose bumps.

"You can look now. I'm decent."

I opened my eyes and found myself looking into Kato's very human face. "Hi," I said dumbly.

"Hi, back."

Rexi made gagging noises and pushed my hand away. "Nice skirt, Tarzan." Kato had the tiger-print tablecloth wrapped around his waist.

He didn't snark back or give any indication that he'd even heard her. Instead, he took my face into his hands and kissed the top of my head.

I didn't know how it happened or how it even could happen, given how much we had hated each other at first sight, but all at once, I knew exactly what all those *talks* from Mom, Dad, and Bob had been about. I kept my eyes closed and waited for my very first real kiss.

His lips didn't feel like I thought they would. They were cold and a little leathery. The kiss wasn't very good, to be honest. I opened one eye to peek and saw that I was kissing the back of Hydra's hand. I backed away and rubbed my lips against my arm, trying to get the old lady taste out of my mouth.

Rexi fell to the floor laughing.

"I wouldna be doing dat if I's was ya."

"And why is that?" Kato stopped clawing at his own mouth and noticed his hand issue. "And why is one arm a different color?"

"Jus be grateful it dinna stay a big white wing. An as fo da kissin'—da rules of fairy tale be broken man—"

Rexi sat up and waved her arms frantically. "Ooh, ooh, let me. The frog prince. If she kisses him, he'll probably turn back into a chimera." She fell back over again, laughing.

The temperature in the room lowered about ten degrees. Kato had gotten back his command of ice.

Hydra swatted Kato. "Stop dat, horny boy."

He colored and tried to stammer some sort of rebuttal. Hydra pointed to the top of his head. I went over and ruffled Kato's hair. Lo and behold, a pair of nubby horns.

Kato took a turn patting them and swore.

Rexi looked like she was in the final death throes on the floor. "Horndog takes on a whole new meaning."

Even I couldn't hold back a chuckle. "It's no big deal, I promise. And we can figure out the whole kiss thing as soon as we fix the rules. So let's figure out how we're going to do that." Then I noticed that my hand was on his bare chest. My face heated again. "But first maybe we can find something for you to wear."

Hydra tossed Kato some clothes. "Dese belonged to me fourt husband. Mebe dey be fittin' ya."

I turned around but noticed both Rexi and Hydra were still watching. Grabbing them by the hand, I hauled them outside. "We'll just step out for a sec and give you some privacy." I closed the door and hit my head against it.

Rexi pouted next to me. "Come on. Aren't you just the least—"

"No!"

"I tink we's bess go back inside."

I groaned and trudged myself around. "Not you too, Hy—"

Something was stepping out of the water. They were short, blue-gray, muscled guys with hammer heads. I didn't need to wonder if they were friendly or not, because the wizard was leading them from his flying balloon.

"The Rule of Duty: Always ask someone else to do, so you won't have to do for yourself."

—*Thomason's Tips to Ruthless Ruling*

Head in the Clouds

We've got company," I said breathlessly, rushing inside and slamming the door.

Kato was in the middle of buttoning his shirt. "What do you mean?" He ran over and took a peek out the door—then slammed it shut, quickly putting his weight against it. "That doesn't look good."

"Is there a back door or a secret exit or something?" I asked Hydra.

"No in so muny wordins," she replied.

Someone pounded on the door. "Ozma. I know you're in there. Just hand over my princess and I'll leave you alone."

Hydra leaned her mouth near the door crack. "Sorry, wrong numba. Der be no Ozma here."

"I don't care what you're calling yourself now. Just do your-self a favor and stay out of it like you have the last two hun-dred years."

I really hoped she didn't hand us over, but you don't get to be that old by taking risks for near strangers. She didn't owe us anything.

Hydra pursed her lips and seemed to think over his pro-posal, then shook her head—the opossums swinging wildly. "No tanks, dat would be borin'."

I wanted to cheer, but the door pounded against my back. "Let. Me. In."

"Not by da hairs of me chinny chin chin."

"Then I'll huff." The voice behind the door started changing. "And I'll puff." Getting rougher and gravelly. "And I'll blow your house in." When the wizard—no, Mimicman finished, I can only imagine that his body had shape-shifted to match his voice. There was a big bad wolf outside our door.

I took a deep breath and called the flames to my hands. It wasn't hard to summon hatred for that man. He'd tried to use and manipulate me. And Grimm knows what his plans were for after the marriage. My body shuddered, and my hair flared bright in anger.

Hydra put her hand to my heart. "No child. Dat is not da way. Using it will only feed da hunger inside until da mad-ness gobble ya whole."

The power gnawed inside right now, trying to claw its way

to the surface. The wind and something worse howled outside. "I don't think we have a better option. Can you freeze them all, Kato?"

He thought about it for a moment. "Not with my normal powers. Maybe if I used my life magic."

"No," Hydra said. "Between da two beasties, I's not sure you be winnin'."

I really didn't like that idea either. He was burning through those way too fast, and our enemies just kept growing in numbers.

Rexi ransacked Hydra's hut, pulling boxes and jars off the shelves, opening drawers and looking under the counters. "Where is it?"

I couldn't help but notice she hadn't frozen up with fear like she did any time Griz was around. Maybe that's because she had a trick up her sleeve—or under Hydra's cauldron or something. "Where's what? Do you have a huntsman stashed somewhere in here?"

The howling outside increased, and there was the sound of knocking coming from the walls—probably the hammerheads looking to do a little home remodeling.

Rexi yelled at Hydra over the din. "Where does it go? The black hole, wormhole, or rabbit hole that your houses keep disappearing into? Can't we just escape through that?"

"That's brilliant, Rexi!" I cried.

Hydra shook her head. "It only opens when I be puttin' on a new head."

Kato's back bucked against the banging of the door. "So switch already."

"I neber doned it while inside. Even with a transmigra-mogr-whosa, we's might be gettin' squished."

Rexi grabbed a random head off the shelf. "I think the house is comin' down either way."

"Okay. Donna be sayin' I dinna warn ya."

The tip of one of the hammerheads broke through the back wall.

"If it doesn't work, we'll be dead. Then we won't be saying anything." Rexi yanked the voodoo head off by its yellow afro and placed the new head on Hydra's shoulders.

"Wait for it," I whispered to Kato. He grasped my hand and squeezed.

The hut shook fiercely, making my shoes click together. Up above, the ceiling started to crack. The walls buckled. Pressure built up in the room, making my head ache and my ears clog. Just when I thought my head would explode, there was a loud pop.

We were no longer in the hut, but pieces of it were strewn all around us. Not only that, but we were surrounded by mountains of, well, junk. Old rockers, bed frames, doors, a giant shoe—all piled high in some kind of warehouse.

"Where are we?" I marveled.

Kato still had his back up against the door, but instead of the door to a wooden hut, it was now heavy, riveted steel. He pulled on the handle and opened it with a loud creak.

Hydra wrapped a purple shawl with clinking coins around her shoulders. "Should I read you your fortune, or perkhaps you might just be taking clue? Ve are in the cloud storage, da?" The new head had more wrinkles than smooth, while her nose and chin looked like a withered squash. She spoke like a native of the Old World, from the times when Grimm was the only Storymaker. They weren't spoken of in polite conversation, but from everything I'd heard about them, they made Rexi seem like a ray of sunshine.

To emphasize the point, she chucked a dead rat at Rexi, making her drop a pocket watch she'd been looking at. "Little thieves have a tendency to lose little hands."

I ignored Rexi's shoplifting attempt and subsequent rodent freak-out to look over Kato's shoulder and out the front door. The beach was gone. Thankfully, so was the Mimicman and his hammerhead soldiers. The ground had been replaced by white, fluffy clouds. Up above, the sky was dark, but the clouds were backlit from below, like the three suns were shining underneath the clouds. So while it was day down there, it was night up where we were.

"Is it safe to step on?" Kato asked and gently placed one bare foot outside.

"Why don't you try it? If we don't hear you plunging to your death, we'll know it's safe." Rexi batted her eyes and gave Kato an innocent, toothy grin.

Kato got a mischievous look on his face. "Watch this," he whispered and cupped his hands in front of his mouth. He took a deep breath and blew. Snow built up in his hands. When he had enough, he chucked the snowball at the unsuspecting Rexi.

She wiped the snow off her face. "That's it. The abominable snow boy is going down." She lowered her spiky blond head like a ram and charged full speed at him. With an *oof!* he doubled over, clutching his stomach, and fell out the door. He landed on his back, the fluffy clouds holding him up.

I smacked Rexi. "He doesn't have wings anymore. You could've killed him."

She waved me off. "Nah. I've been up here before. I knew it was safe."

That was news to me. "When?"

"The Emerald Palace has storage up here someplace too." My face must have shown my surprise, so she continued. "Think about it. You've ordered enough stuff from the Castle Shopping Network to clothe every storybook character ever written. Your closet's big, but not *that* big. It all has to go someplace."

She was right. I hadn't really thought of it before. I guess I hadn't really thought about a lot of things.

"I think I'm stuck," Kato called and waved his arms, having trouble getting out of the squishy clouds.

Rexi and I ran outside to get him out.

He grasped both our hands. "You know, we've had a rough day. I think you deserve some *down*time."

Instead of pulling him up, on the word *down*, he yanked us to him. Soon, we were all rolling and playing in the clouds' banks, making cloud angels. It reminded me of winters in the courtyard when I was a kid, but this was so much better. For one, it wasn't cold and wet. And for another, I wasn't playing alone with palace guards standing watch. Aside from the hair and layers of grime, that was one of the biggest changes from the Emerald Palace: I wasn't alone anymore.

I had friends.

And now that I knew my parents and Verte were still alive somewhere, I was glad I'd stepped out of my Emerald Palace. Seeing the world up close looked a lot different than from my gilded window.

I had a whole new perspective.

Though I still believed in the Storymakers, I'd started to question how much control I had on how this story turned out. Maybe it was me and not the curse that would determine the kind of person I became. The power alone wouldn't make me evil. It all depended on what I did with it. But that didn't mean I had to be helpless either, waiting for someone else to solve my problems.

Hero or villain—it was up to me to decide.

I let the flame come to my hand. The power was sluggish, sleepy without having an immediate target. I thought back to the times I had used it, especially at the Ivory Tower. That voice, guiding me to burn it all. And the feeling of being invincible, being powerful—of having control. But who had really been in control? That was the question. If I didn't use the power in anger, if I only gave it my life to eat, was I strong enough to harness the flame and use it to my benefit? I'd used it to save Kato once…

Let's hope that in addition to my mother's temper, I also got her strength.

Leaving Kato and Rexi to finish their cloudball fight, I went back in the storage unit to find Hydra. "What do I need to do to put back the rules of magic and set everything right again?"

"Iz bout time you grow brain and stop vith the froo froo and play. Iz like carryink fire in one hand and vater in other. Maybe vere you to listen to me first time, you vould not have been burned, da?" Hydra spoke to me but didn't bother looking up while she sifted through piles of her things. She tucked the strands of her new salt-and-pepper hair behind her big gold hoop earrings.

Squatting down to her level, my dress pooled around my feet. "No offense, but you smelled and looked like the headless horseman's long-dead granny."

Hydra muttered under her breath. "Vise men say to never judge book by cover." She tossed a cannonball over her shoulder, narrowly missing me.

I cocked my head to the side and chuckled. "Hello…princess here. My whole life was about the cover—the clothes, the wrapping on the package." I put a hand on her arm, stilling her search. "But I was wrong. And I'm ready now to hear what you have to say."

She cocked her head to match mine and searched for the truth in my words. Apparently satisfied, she pulled her hand out of the pile. Opening her fist, Hydra's palm held a wishing star. Not just any wishing star—my wishing star.

What Goes Up...

I hadn't thought I'd ever see that star again after I'd left it at Hydra's house the first time. "But I've already used up the wish. I've tried unwishing on it. Nothing works," I protested.

Hydra grasped my hand and placed the star in it. "Vish is not gone, just stuck inside. Vere you to find some magic bleach to be unstickink it, perkhaps vish would be *dasvidanya*."

Rolling the star in my hand, I contemplated what that might mean. "As in never happened? Or everything just goes back to normal?"

Hydra shrugged. "Oy! How I be knowink? Pig might fly.

Might be breakfast. *Nyet*. All my years, never see big mess as this." She stood, her back cracking underneath her shawl and floral housecoat.

Great. If the wish had never happened, I would be the same shallow princess I was before. But it wasn't like I had a whole lot of options. I would do whatever it took to make things right. "Okay. So where do you keep your strongest cleaners?" I started, looking through the piles for a big bottle of bleach.

"Say I be havink? Is not been made for hundred years or more." She shook her head and made a face, showing a mouth full of sharpened teeth. "Case of cure being more trouble than the curse."

I threw my hands up in sheer exasperation. "First, there was a killer rainbow that no one could find. Then we got the *Book of Making*, just to have it swiped by the wizard and Griz. And after all that, we're back to page one again."

Hydra clucked her tongue at me. "In sense. Book would be helpful, but that is flown coup, so back to plan A and finding of glasses."

And I used to think it was tough to get a straight answer out of Verte, that it had to be something with being incredibly ancient. The cobwebs built up in the brain and got their thoughts tangled or something.

Hydra harrumphed around the storage, opening baskets and boxes, and crawling under tables until she spied a leather sack. "Ahh," she said, opening the satchel. Then she frowned and shook it upside down. Nothing came out.

She stormed out the door, grabbing a walking stick and miniature suitcase on the way.

Rexi and Kato were outside, breathless, but still in one piece. I was glad that the play fight hadn't turned into a war. With those two, you never could tell.

Whistling through the points of her front teeth, Hydra caught Rexi's attention before sweeping under her legs with the walking stick. "If not vanting to be made into soup, then save rotten tuchus and give back spectacles."

Rexi opened her mouth to protest, looked again at the pointy stick, and thought better of it. Reaching around to the back of her shirt, she pulled out a pair of goggles with multicolored lenses.

Hydra inspected them and nodded. "*Da.* Will do job, but better to be goink at once. A little late is too late in this cases."

She unlatched the small suitcase and set it on the cloud. "Vait." Like a miniature version of her house, the bag suddenly expanded and left a carriage-sized mortar with chicken feet.

"What's that?" Rexi asked, staying well away from it.

"Have never seen RV? Running Vehicle. Is somethink I von from Baba Yaga playink roulette." She climbed in the bowl and gestured to the little bit of space left behind her. "Comink?"

Even Kato eyed it with a leery expression. "We'll walk, thanks. But where are we going?"

"Hopefully not there." I pointed east, to the extremely

large house made of stone and metal—with a bean stalk in the garden.

"*Nyet*, but if hungry, giant make very tasty golden egg omelet." Hydra put on the colored goggles and rotated the pestle, heading out at a brisk pace across the clouds.

"I'll pass," I said and looked at the bean stalk again. Instead of going down, the bean stalk started in the clouds and grew upward, higher than the eye could track. Guess we weren't getting down that way.

We followed after Hydra, but walking on clouds was nothing like walking on air; it was like walking in snow. Maybe those big chicken feet acted like snowshoes, but my heels kept getting stuck. The darker clouds were especially gooey.

After a few hundred yards, the chicken bowl stopped. Hydra pulled off her head, tied it to her walking stick, and thrust it down through the cloud cover. "What are you doing?" I asked, hoping she knew how to tie a good knot, because if not, we'd be going head hunting.

Hydra's body hoisted the stick back up, her head still on it, and moved the bowl to a new spot. "What look like? Head periscope plus color-spectrum glasses find invisible rainbow. Is not rocketink science," she said before plunging her head down under the clouds again.

The grayish clouds beneath our feet rumbled. Or maybe that was Kato. "You can't be thinking about using the spring," he yelled loud enough so Hydra could hear.

"*Da*. Unless you are havink better plan," she hollered back, her head still out of sight.

Wanting answers and to see for myself, I crouched down and poked my head through the dense clouds. From so high, I could see the patchwork of kingdoms, each setting so different from the next. But no rainbow. Then again, I didn't have the glasses on. "When Griz attacked the palace, the Emerald Sorceress said my only hope was over the rainbow at the spring. What's the big deal?" Being so high—and upside down—was making me a little dizzy. As I started to sway, Kato's arms circled my waist, keeping me steady as he pulled me up.

My hair cracked and hissed from more than the condensation in the cloud.

Once Hydra got her head back on straight, she launched into a long, extremely hard to follow history lesson on the springs. *SpiffNotes* version: Guy named Rainbow Sprite found a magic spring and had issues sharing, so he made it invisible, built a killer rainbow to guard it, and moved it regularly. Don't ask me how.

"So in other words," I said, trying very hard to control my temper even though I was really pixed at Verte. "Last week, when we started looking for the spring without the glasses, we wouldn't have seen the rainbow—unless we walked into it, and then *poof!* Princess Crispies."

Hydra popped her head off for another rainbow fishing expedition. Before she went under, she said very matter-of-factly, "If was easy, das Gray Vitch have given sister spring vater shower a goat's age ago."

"What?" Kato roared. If I had closed my eyes right then, I would have thought he was still a chimera.

At the sound, Hydra's bird-legged RV took off like, well, a chicken with its head cut off.

"Hydra, please wait." I had an unpleasant feeling that I knew what she was talking about. Grimm, I hoped I was wrong. "Are Griz and Blanc sisters?"

"How did I not know this?" Kato put his head in his hands, causing his ill-fitting shirt to flap open.

"Bah. Is obvious. You must have memory vorse than Anastazia. Vhite Vitch. Gray Vitch. Das entire line have the boring colors with silver eyes." Hydra glared down her lumpy nose at me. "Just who are you thinkink have put curse on high and mighty House of Emerald in first place?"

I had already figured it out a while ago; I just hadn't wanted to believe it. The story of the sisters and the Emerald curse, my dream—all the pieces came together, and I didn't like them.

"No wonder you look so much like the princess from the book. Your ancestor must have been the girl who helped the Beast King lock Blanc away," Kato said, his face weary.

"Is true." Hydra hopped off her chicken bowl, walked over, and put a bloated and clammy hand on my shoulder. "Beast King double-cross vitch sisters to make little Emerald princess happy. Gray Vitch vant to beat two birdies one stone. So she try make your great-great-great-great vhatever elder burn him to crisp along with whole world. But Griz is just a hatched chickie then. Not even finish her curse school. She made mistake in spell so is skipping down generation."

Everything from the past seemed to come together to create this storm of craziness. Griz's curse, the chimera's Fire Priestess, Blanc being nearly indestructible—and I was sitting smack in the middle of the tornado.

"So I just happened to pick the short wand?"

"Perkhaps it is pickink you." Hydra flung her hand out dismissively. "But that is nother bowl of goulash." She jumped way too spryly back into her bowl and started the chicken feet power walking again. "As sure as bears relieve self in vood, Griz is knowink Dorthea's power can be turnink sister into charcoal, so vill not vait for magic prison flames to go out. Best ve hurry and beat that vitch to the spring. I must say it vill feel good to see her, how you say, get hers." She grinned, and I could see her tongue moving between the gaps of her teeth.

"So you think we'll be able to beat her?"

"Is fifty-fifty. I vould have better idea if had crystal ball." My face fell. "Pardon, me. I am not realizink I vas supposed to lie. This head has not been vorn for century and out of practice. I vill try again." Hydra cleared her throat, touched her fingers to her temples, and stood up a little taller. "*Da*. I am seeink it now. Ve vill win."

I wonder why that didn't make me feel any better?

Kato caught up to us and grabbed my hand, giving it a

reassuring squeeze. "They were beaten by the Beast King and Emerald Princess once, so you and I can definitely do it again."

The clouds in front of us thinned out, becoming wispy enough to see through.

"Is there!" Hydra cackled, pointing down to a lush green spot of land.

"Great. So how do we get do—" I shrieked as my foot went through the dissipating fluffy floor.

Kato, still holding on to my hand, snatched me back.

That had been close. I'd been saved by the chimera a few times, but being rescued by the boy felt completely different.

"My hero," I huffed and put a hand to my chest to keep my heart from bursting out of it.

He brushed his hand along my cheek. "My lady."

"My village idiots," Hydra snapped, completely ruining the mood. "Clouds no longer safe. Unless vant to arrive on ground as pancake, am suggestink hurry."

"After you," I grumbled, then paused. Something was missing. Rather *someone* was missing. No way Rexi would have let the mushy stuff go by without a snarky comment.

Kato, on the same wavelength, looked around. "Where is she?"

Parts of the cloud floor had thinned, while others had turned dark and stormy. A thunderous rumble vibrated through the ground beneath our feet.

At the same time, a loud bellow echoed through the air. "Fe-fi-fo-fum. Leave right now or turn to crumb."

Kato groaned. "She wouldn't."

"Gold-laying tweety bird?" I thought it over for a millisecond. "Yeah, she would."

Kato and I started for the giant's house, but it didn't look right. I put my arm in front of Kato, making him stop. "Does it look like that house is shrinking to you?"

"Not shrinking. Sinking."

"Let thief have vhat comink to her. Must make escape now, before we go kaput in more cloudquake," Hydra mumbled and cursed.

I crossed my arms defiantly. "She may be a thief, but she's our thief."

"*Nyet.* You have got to be pulling legs."

"I mean it." I pointed out the tilted house that looked like a ship after hitting an iceberg. "Rexi is probably in there, and we can't leave her behind."

"Thief will be fine. Have strong self-survival sense, like cockroach. You...not as much." Without warning, Hydra grabbed me by the ear and hauled me back to her chicken bowl. She'd wrangled Kato too. "I am meaning literally pull off legs."

Hydra took off her head and set it on the ground, then had her body jack up the underside of the chicken bowl onto her shoulders so the little chicken feet had no weight on them.

Kato shrugged at me and started yanking the left chicken leg, so I got to work on the right. Hydra's head supervised. Both gangly legs came off from the bowl with a pop. After setting the legless bowl back on the darkening cloud, Hydra's body retrieved her head, then took the drumsticks off our hands.

"Good. Now have less than two minute to make RV into ATV, Air Traveling Vehicle."

"Two minutes!" Another rumble shook the clouds, making me hang on to the sides of the bowl.

With a crash, stone and metal crumbled off the giant's house to the ground below.

Hydra climbed back into the bowl and put the legs inside, feet end up. She fussed and fiddled, spit and mumbled until the combination of legs and bowl somewhat resembled a whirligig.

Kato scoffed. "There's no way that thing will fly."

With a smug and defiant snort, Hydra pulled her scarf off from where she'd tied it around the legs, and the "propeller" began to spin.

"I smell storm comink. Get on or all fall down," Hydra said as the chicken-copter started to hover.

My stomach was in knots, worrying where Rexi was and if she was okay.

"Dead princess have hard time savink realm from Blanc. So move!"

Kato put his hands on my waist and hoisted me into the getaway vehicle. "Have faith."

That was asking a lot, considering that, right then, the house groaned and plummeted through the air.

Let Go of Me Lucky Charms

The giant's house broke and fell to the ground. It actually held up better than I had thought it would. Only a few big cracks and… Oh, never mind. The stone walls fell inward, crumbling worse than last year's solstice fruitcakes.

Someone had managed to flee to the cloud from the house at the last moment, though it wasn't Rexi or a normal giant either. It bellowed, sounding like a giant, but then, why did he have furry, purple polka dots? I stopped caring because no one else was on the cloud with him.

Crossing my fingers and toes, I prayed Rexi had escaped death at the last possible moment in some odd or unlikely way that no sane person could ever imagine.

The wind shifted slightly, blowing away the rapidly dissipating wisps of cloud. I could hear more thuds as things fell from the sky.

"Must go to rainbow now." Hydra hooked the goggled spectacles around her ears and blinked. The fractured pieces of glass made her look like a bug with multicolored eyes. She pulled her head off her shoulders and lowered it by scarf this time, rotating it for a three-hundred-sixty-degree view.

She gave her body directions to steer the pestle toward the right spot. "Oy. Right there."

"The rainbow?" Kato asked.

"Think smaller and more trouble."

The bowl tilted as I ran to the side and leaned over. Not too far away from the decimated and pointy stick remains of the giant's home, Rexi ran around like a pokey-haired Chicken Little screaming that the sky was falling. And, well, it was.

The chicken-copter landed right beside her, not nearly as gently as I would have hoped but without breaking any bones.

Excited to see Rexi alive, and pixed she'd disappeared in the first place, I tried to jump out of the bowl without watching my feet. I tripped and ended up flattening her.

"Ugh. Do we really have to do this every day?" She shoved me off her with a grunt. "It wasn't enough to try and drop a house on me. You had to make sure I busted a rib or two?"

Kato freed himself as well and joined us. "You were already down here? We thought the giant had ground your bones to dust. Did one of the clouds drop and take you down here?"

Rexi got a weird, frozen look on her face. "Yeah, something like that." Her eyes darted away, a guilty look on her face that made me want to check her pockets.

"See? Vhat I tell you? Like cockroach," Hydra said as she walked past Rexi.

I waited for the requisite snarky reply, but Rexi was quieter than the Little Mermaid after she'd lost her voice. Maybe it was the shock of nearly having a house fall on her. She was probably silently picturing herself squished, with only her feet sticking out from under the house.

Hydra pulled off the goggles and flung them at me. "Your turn to find rainbow spring."

I put on the goggles and looked around, but I still had trouble finding the rainbow, and not just because the world through the stained-glass lenses looked like a paint factory had blown up. I stood on my tiptoes, but it was no use.

Just when I was about to pull the goggles back off, hands gripped me from behind and lifted me higher. Kato set me on his shoulder and kept one arm around my lap. The emerald tips of my hair sparked like fireworks. He chuckled, aware of the effect he had on me.

Yeah, it sucks to have hair that emotes along with you.

I got myself back under control and looked again. The extra height improved the view, and just above the Sherwood Forest, something sparkled and moved up. A lot of some-things. It was kind of like looking at a waterfall going in reverse. I took off the spectacles, and the sight disappeared.

Kato set me down. I tossed him the goggles and rounded angrily on Hydra. "That's not a spring. A spring is a bubbling brook or fountain-ish thing. That is a geyser."

It might have looked like I was overreacting, but I sure didn't think so. If I got anywhere near that thing, water was sure to fall on me and put my hair out. And I wouldn't even see it coming, because it was invisible.

Hydra shrugged off my mini-tirade and put the spectacles back on. "You paid to have palm read, no refund if not likink your fortunes." I interpreted the gypsy speak as, *Your wish, your problem.*

There was a rumble in the clouds followed by the booming of blood thumping in my ears as my heart beat in alarm. Was it thunder, heralding the return of our least-favorite wicked witch? It sounded again, and Rexi's head turned to look so fast that if she'd been Hydra, her head would've come clean off.

I looked at the sky where I thought the sound had come from, searching for Griz and her flying puppies. Wasn't her. With a resounding crash, another building fell from the sky. The Mimicman Wizard had lied through his perfectly capped teeth about glammed near everything—except ozmosis, it appeared. I could almost feel the magics moving around me, like it was alive. It was chaotic, and that made it dangerous, because there was no nursery-rhyming reason to it, no way to guess which part was going to fall apart next—with you standing on it, under it, or in it.

The closer we got to where I figured the spring must be,

the slower and more careful each step got. I was excited, nervous, anxious, and relieved for what was to come. The star would soon be unmagicked or disenchanted or…whatever. I imagined what would happen when I tossed the star into the water—from a very safe distance, mind you. Would all the rules just start working again, or would it be like hitting a rewind button on the magic mirror remote?

First thing I planned on doing was apologizing for every rotten thought I'd ever had about my mom and dad. Then I was going to take a bath. I had more layers of grime on my skin than the pea princess had mattresses.

Hydra interrupted my musings with a hand, pushing me to a stop. Though with her hunchback and lumbering mass, she was about as stealthy as a Minotaur, Hydra got down on her stomach and motioned for the rest of us to do the same.

"What the pix are we doing?" I asked.

"*Shhh,*" hissed Hydra. "Rainbow spook easy. Is moving the moment ve are gettink close."

She passed the spectacles down the line, so I could take a peek. Without the glasses, it looked like any of the other countless rainbows I'd seen from my room at the Emerald Palace. With the glasses on, I saw not one arch, but three, forming a deadly triangle around the spring.

Kato took the glasses back, so he could have a closer look. "Sprite must be using the light from the three suns to reflect the water spraying up and create the barrier."

"So how are we going to get close?" I asked. "And then, when we do, how do we get to what's over the rainbow?"

Hydra stood slowly, making no sudden movements, and put her back to the rainbow. "Ve approach very slow. No lookink at straight." She reached inside her housecoat and pulled out a piece of glass she must have swiped from the giant's house. When the sun hit it in just the right way, you could see a reflection of the rainbow—all three of them.

Gotta say, out of all the rules that wish had broken, the reflection one was certainly turning out to be useful. So we all turned around and started walking backward, Hydra going first since she had the glass.

Beside me, Rexi tripped over a rock or something and fell on her rear. "This is by far the absolute dumbest thing we have ever done. And that is saying something." She thumped the ground with her fist in frustration.

And with that little tidbit, things felt normal again—at least normal for our little band of misfits.

As I back-walked past her, I noticed that she hadn't tripped on a rock. It was sparkling. Being very careful not to acciden-tally catch a glimpse of the rainbow head-on, I bent down to take a closer look. The rock was actually a golden horseshoe. I picked it up and, nearly immediately afterward, got a sharp bang against my shins.

"Get your greedy little mitts off me lucky charms." A little orange-skinned, green-haired leprechaun stood in front of me—and kicked me in the shins again before I had a chance to give the horseshoe back. So I dropped it on his head, which was just below my waist.

After rubbing his noggin, he carefully placed the horseshoe exactly where it had been. "This here's a piece o' me fairy ring. I've got the wee rainbow surrounded now, so it can't escape." He laughed giddily, rubbing his little orange hands together.

"Does that mean we can stop walking backward now?" Rexi asked wryly and stood up, brushing at the grass stain on her trousers' behind.

Apparently it did, because the leprechaun hurried straight toward the rainbow, only stopping a few feet away. The rainbow didn't move. Either blarney boy had really trapped it with a ring of lucky charms, or ozmosis had taken its toll again and was keeping the rainbow from running away. At this point, one seemed just as likely as the next.

Kato's face darkened with worry. "What interest do the wee folk have with this rainbow?" Did he suspect the leprechaun of being an agent of Griz?

"Do na be daft. The wee folk have claim to *every* rainbow. But this pot o' gold is mine. And you canna have it." That said, the little man ran around us in a circle, moving faster than my eyes could track.

"Look, you've—" I went to walk toward him but found that I couldn't. The clover in the ground had risen up and entangled my feet, tying them to the earth. My friends were snared as well, but their bindings moved well past their feet. The clover and vines dragged them to the ground and coiled around their bodies, even covering their mouths. All of them were making angry, muffled cries.

I didn't take it for granted that the clover couldn't reach above my shoes, and not for the first time, I blessed Verte's good taste in enchanted footwear. My mouth was free, and by Grimm, I would use it. "Wait…please. You don't want to go near that rainbow." I put every ounce of sincerity I had into my voice, pleading that he would listen to me. If the leprechaun was telling the truth and not working for Griz, then he was about to make a lethal mistake. I couldn't let that happen.

The little orange-and-green man was intrigued by my plea—and probably by the fact that his fae bindings weren't working. He scooted a little closer, making sure to stay out of arm's length from me. "And why wouldn't I be wantin' to do that?" he asked.

"Because there's no pot of gold at the end of the rainbow," I said, pointing through his white panty hose–covered legs to the point where the colored arch met the grass.

He leaned forward, bending down to where I lay on the ground. "If there be no gold, what be there?" His eyes squinted as if he were really listening and considering the possibility.

Um, I had no idea what to tell him, so I stuck with the truth. "A special spring. But you can't see it because it's invisible." This was my chance to convince him, and it sounded bad to me, so I know it must have sounded even crazier to him.

He flopped his hands dismissively at me and straightened

again. "Now you're just blowin' a bunch of blarney. Next, you'll be tellin' me there be silver-winged unicorns and the spring's really a fountain of youth." He turned away from me and headed back toward the rainbow.

"I'm telling the truth," I pleaded. Tears of frustration welled up in my eyes. He wasn't going to stop, and there was nothing I could do. What would Mom say? She could make anyone listen and obey. "That's not a normal rainbow. It's going to kill you if you touch it. Please." My voice hitched with a sob.

It was enough to give him pause, but only just. The others were still wriggling in their viney cocoons. He looked at them and then me, a puzzled look obscuring his face. Still, it wasn't enough. He sidestepped slowly, inching under the rainbow.

I called again for him to stop. I prayed that the magical mishaps had already struck the rainbow, making it harmless. But when his hand crossed under the arch of the rainbow, I saw that it hadn't.

I closed my eyes so I didn't have to watch him die.

"You never know what you're gonna find when you look under those covers—Grandma or the wolf."

—Little Red, excerpt from *Tales from the Hood*

Frozen in Time

In the past few hours, my emotions had been all over the map—from the heights of hope, to the lows of loss. And of course, the highs made bottoming out that much rougher.

So I lay there and cried. When my throat was so raw that it hurt to breathe, I let the sound stop but kept my mouth frozen in a silent scream. Why hadn't he listened? I didn't even know his name, so I only had his face to add to the growing list of things that would haunt my waking moments—to say nothing of the sleeping ones.

Someone wrapped their arms around my body and gathered me into their lap like a small child. I finally opened my eyes and looked into Kato's. He held me in his arms, smoothing my flaming hair, murmuring things in a language I didn't understand. My heart recognized them as tender reassurances, but my head rejected them as lies.

It was not okay. I should have been able to make the wee man stop. My mother would have been able to do it. She once convinced an evil genie to seal himself back into the bottle. With only the power of her words, she was able to inspire, lead, or instill the fear of Grimm into a man. Once again, at my opportunity to follow her example, I failed. And I didn't even have the courage to watch, to witness his last moments.

I would look now. Kato tried to stop me, tried to shield my eyes, but I would see the consequences of my failure.

The prone form of the leprechaun lay next to the rainbow. The vines and clover had abandoned my friends and gone back to their master. They covered the body like a death shroud. There was no menace; the vines were gentle, almost caressing as they wrapped around the leprechaun. Once finished, they pulled the body down, entombing it in the ground, returning it to the earth.

Hydra watched the funeral solemnly. Her normally animated face looked worn, showing each one of her two hundred fifty-plus years.

I wanted to stay in Kato's arms and sleep for centuries, be like Rip Van Winkle and let the world continue to spin around me. A harsh sound hit my ears and intruded on my attempt at oblivion. Rexi was retching into a nearby bush. When she straightened, her arms shook and her face was pale, bordering on phantomlike.

Seeing her suffer gave me a jolt. If I laid there and did nothing, I would be failing her too. She deserved a chance to have her old life back—or a better one, if I could manage it. To not be chased from one corner of Story to another, looking over her shoulder for the boogeyman. This needed to end, and the answer was right there. We just needed a way to get to the other side.

I wiped my tears and summoned the bravest face I could, pushing myself away from Kato's comfort. "We need to get to the spring. It's time to write a big *the end* and, with any luck, a *happily ever after*. Hydra, do you think my flames could break the rainbow?"

Hydra considered and then shook her head. "*Nyet*. Rainbows all the same. Nothing solid to hit. Now if sprite vere to be hit…" Apparently, this head was not a pacifist, like the witch doctor one.

Even if she approved, it wasn't an option. For starters, I didn't know where this Rainbow Sprite character was. And second, I didn't want any non-Griz cronies getting hurt if I could help it. There had been enough of that already.

Kato looked glum. "If I still had wings, I could fly over and drop the star in." His broad shoulders slumped inward in defeat.

"Maybe, but who knows how high the barrier reaches?" A

thought was beginning to snowball in my mind. "We can't go under, over, or through the rainbow. And we can't get the sprite to break the magic tied to it." I paused to finish working out the details in my head. "Hydra, if there were no rainbow, would there still be a barrier?"

Hydra stroked her chin and pulled on a lone hair that was curling along the bottom of it. "Is possible. No rainbow. Nothing for sprite magic to be magickink."

"How sure are you?" I asked, grabbing her arms.

She smacked her lips and used her tongue to fish something out of her tooth. "Is fifty-fifty."

Rexi threw her hands in the air. "What's the pixing point? You can't make the rainbow disappear. And even if you could, there's a fifty percent chance we'll all die crossing. Please, let's just go."

I shook my head emphatically, surer than ever of what we had to do now. "I can get rid of the rainbow, but we're all going to have to work together. Here's the plan."

I laid out everything that was racing through the jumble of my brain. Kato had said earlier that the rainbow was tri-angled, because of the three suns' light passing through the moving water. So what if the water stopped moving?

Kato needed to use his ice magic to freeze the water.

His eyebrows shot up. I think he was a bit skeptical. "I'm not sure I can freeze the whole thing at once. Especially if I can't see it."

I pushed the glasses at him. "Now you can. As soon as the

spring is frozen, the rainbow should fade, hopefully taking the barrier with it."

Hydra moved her jaw like she was a cow chewing her cud. "That is big whopper of chance."

"I'm not done yet. Hydra, you're in charge of the sprite if he comes out. Talk to him, distract him, whatever."

"And vhat is it I am be distraction of?" she asked, winking one eye down.

"Rexi," I answered.

At the sound of her name, Rexi jumped and put her hands to her chest. "Why shouldn't he see me? I haven't—"

I walked over to her and grasped her hands. "You have the most important job. Kato is going to be freezing the spring, but I can't drop the star in ice. And when he unfreezes it, I won't be able to get close enough in case the spring unmagicks me." I took the star from the pocket of the sack dress and gently placed it in Rexi's hand. "As soon as the spring is liquid again, you run and toss this in."

She shook her head, her spiky hair waving back and forth. "I can't. You don't—"

"Yes, you can," I said with the utmost confidence. "Kato will guide you while he's wearing the glasses, so you'll know where to drop it." I took a deep breath and turned to Kato. "Are you ready?"

"No. But I get the feeling this isn't optional." Worry clouded his features again.

I kissed the wrinkles on his brow. "It'll work." It had to.

He pursed his lips and huffed through his nose, unhappy, but still he nodded and put on the spectacles.

Magic was happening, even though you couldn't see it directly. The temperature dropped, and my breath turned to foggy mist in front of me. There was a crackling and tinkling sound, like when you swish a drink with ice cubes. I could see Kato's eyes focused intently through the lenses. His lips quivered, and a bead of sweat rolled down the side of his face, then froze before it could drip off.

The rainbow faded from view.

Rexi took a tentative step. "Did it work? Are the barriers gone?"

I took a deep breath and steadied myself. "Let's find out." I walked toward the bright green patch of clover that marked the leprechaun's final resting place.

"Wait!" Kato protested.

I'd left out my part of the plan on purpose because I knew Kato wouldn't go along with it if he knew that I was going to be the one to test the barrier. But I couldn't ask any of them to risk their lives for my crazy idea.

There were more cracking sounds ahead of me. I called back to Kato. "Focus only on the ice. If you don't, I'll get zapped and soggy."

He set his jaw and stared ahead with a single-minded purpose.

I needed to make sure it was safe for Rexi to cross. That meant I needed to stretch my hand across where the barrier should be but hopefully wasn't. I stuck out my arm and inched forward. Then a little more. When I was ten paces past the clover patch without getting electrocuted, I finally exhaled the breath I'd been holding. It was probably safe to call for Rexi.

To the side of me, there was a shimmer in front of a tree. My eyes refused to focus on the glitter, blurring the outlines of the bark. A seam of light formed a door in the trunk of the tree, and out stepped a tall, thin man. He had a hard gleam in his eyes that matched the razor-sharp, rainbow-colored tips of his Mohawk. His face and body were dotted with metal spikes and balls that hooked through and pierced his multi-colored skin. With a name like Rainbow Sprite, I had been expecting a small, winged, fragile creature, not the sharp and very angry man in front of me.

Hydra remembered her role just in time. She tossed her head at the sprite, and he, acting on instinct, put his hands out in front of him to catch the projectile. When Verte told me to use my head, I don't think this was what she'd had in mind. The sprite didn't expect it either though, and so, understandably surprised at holding a head in his hands, he didn't pay attention to where he put his fingers. Hydra bit him. And her teeth were wicked sharp.

The sprite yelled in pain and tossed Hydra's head away from him. Hydra yelled as her head flew past me. I yelled for Rexi to run and for Kato to let go of the spring. Kato yelled at me to watch out.

The sprite stopped yelling when a stormball crashed into his back.

A lot of things happened at once. I saw Griz, the Tinman, and a few demon puppies on the other side of the clearing. The spring became visible between us even before the sprite hit the ground. Kato released his control of the ice magic, allowing the water to move again, spitting droplets of disenchantment. I ran as fast as I could, but some still landed on me. It felt like I was being stabbed in the head with a pickax.

I made it to Kato and looked back at Griz. She was throwing stormballs, but when they hit the water, the balls dissolved. She couldn't attack or come any closer with the water between us. The same applied to me; I couldn't blast her with emerald flame and I couldn't get any closer either.

When I had played chess with Verte, she'd called something like this a stalemate. But I still had a pawn on the board. Rexi stood at the edge of the clearing, doing her best impression of Pinocchio before he came to life. I couldn't even see her breathing, she was so terrified.

Come on, come on. Move. I willed it silently because, if I called out to her, it would draw Griz's attention.

Finally, Rexi took one step. Then another. I could see the bulge of the star in her pocket. If she would have ran, she might have gotten rid of it before Griz noticed her. But she kept advancing slowly, and Griz and I both watched in complete silence.

Rexi made it within throwing distance of the spring and

stuck her hand in her pocket. But instead of pulling out the star and tossing it in, she turned and looked at me. Her face had droplets of water running down it and maybe a few tears. Her eyes were wide with sadness. She opened her mouth to speak but closed it again without uttering a sound.

Then she dropped her head and kept walking.

To Griz.

34

Gone with the Storm

My knees sank into the ground. There had to be some explanation for what I was watching. Rexi wouldn't betray me. She was my friend. Surely I was watching the Mimicman. But if so, why had she looked at me like her heart was breaking?

She handed Griz the star and then stood there, head down, unwilling to meet my eyes.

Griz tossed the star in the air and then caught it. "It was so kind of you to show me this little spring, but I'm afraid I can't let you use it." She threw the star up again, and this time let it fall to the ground. "You see, I rather like the chaos. Stories are so much more fun when you don't already know the ending."

Griz's chunky boot heel came down on the star with a stomach-churning crunch. "Don't you agree?" The pieces of bone and hair that used to be the wishing star rose again. She tugged on one side of her fitted vest and the pieces tucked themselves inside.

"Why?" I croaked.

Griz looked confused for a moment. "Because the Storymakers never let us win. Our defeat is predeterm—"

"I wasn't talking to you, hag. I was talking to her." I pointed to the betrayer. The wolf in my friend's clothing.

Rexi didn't respond, but everything about her looked miserable.

Good.

"The why is obvious. Isn't that right, dear?" Griz took the back of her hand and ran it down the side of Rexi's face. Rexi turned a shade whiter and looked ready to puke again. "Basic survival instinct."

Reaching down her side, the Gray Witch produced a tasseled satchel. With great flourish, she tugged the drawstrings open and removed a large empty glass vial that looked a lot like the ones from Crow's house. She handed the vial to Rexi with a little smirk. "Go, little Jill, fetch me a pail of water."

Rexi stared down at the vial but didn't budge. Griz moved her hand to under her shirt and pulled out her necklace—and squeezed. Gasping sharply, Rexi staggered and a bright red-orange tear leaked from her eye.

"The opal." Kato had finally taken off the goggles and apparently figured out the same thing I just did.

Griz's opal necklace pulsed orange with opalescent flecks. It pulsed with life magic. If I didn't miss my guess, Rexi's life, to be exact.

But when? Did Griz catch her after the clouds? Perhaps, but I think it started earlier. I replayed events in my mind, going in reverse. Her acting weird. The overwhelming fear anytime Griz was near. Disappearing from the Ivory Tower just to be replaced by Griz. Maybe I'd seen Rexi's life force actually sucked out in the nightmare. Had she ever really been my friend, or was it all an elaborate ruse to do the bidding of the Gray Witch? Rexi's every action from frog until now was suspect.

I wanted to hate her. Watching her bend down to scoop up the spring water made the human flamethrower in me want to come out and play. Cold emanated from the boy beside me. I put a hand on his arm. "Don't." Kato gave me a puzzled look but obeyed.

Rexi's hand trembled as she put the stopper in the vial and walked back to Griz. I wasn't sure what to believe anymore, but everything about her right now screamed that she was not happy being a de facto member of Team Evil. Villains took pleasure in causing pain; they didn't tremble with their own. I wouldn't harm her and neither would Kato. It was probably my fault that Griz got her tacky nails on Rexi anyway.

Griz very carefully took the vial from Rexi and stuffed it down her dress. "Now, I would love to stay and chat, but I have a bit of a family reunion to attend." Griz conjured a thundercloud and hopped on. She floated into the sky, high above the spring.

It was probably too much to ask that ozmosis would kick in and drop her into the water.

Griz snapped her fingers. "Bring the girl. We'll need her to get into the mountain." Several of the flying puppies picked up a squirming Rexi and took to the sky. "As for the others... *bon appétit*!" She flew away on her cloud, the sounds of thunder and Rexi screaming trailing behind her.

And we watched them go, because there wasn't a pixing thing we could do about it.

"Makers help us, she's going to set Blanc free. I have to warn Bob; they're going to need help." Kato chewed the last nail off his left hand and phoned home.

"And what about us?" I asked worriedly. Griz had left behind three demon puppies and the Tinman. With just me, Kato, a dead sprite, and Hydra's headless body fumbling around, I was not liking our odds.

The puppies circled to the left of the spring and the Tinman came at us from the right. Kato still had his eyes closed, deep in telepathic communication or whatnot with Bob.

"Umm, Kato..." I started backing up, pulling him with me.

He snapped back to attention. "Right. While I've got the magic boost, I'll work my Beast King mojo. It should be able to control the dogs—maybe the gigan too. You grab Hydra's head and run."

I really hoped he knew what he was doing. Hydra's gypsy

head was still where the sprite had tossed her. I checked back on Kato to see how he was doing. The puppies had stopped their approach and stood still. The Tinman, on the other hand, kept moving. His armor had lots of little rust spots on it though.

The spring water. Wherever it touched the metal, rust holes formed. But not enough of it was falling to make him stop his advance on Kato.

With a deep breath, I told myself, *I can control the fire. The fire doesn't control me.* I let the emerald flames leap into my hands. I forced my arms outward and threw the flames at the Tinman. He barely paused from their impact. I, however, swayed from the amount of effort it took out of me.

"Hey, you big tin can," I panted. "Come and get it." I visualized reaching inside myself and pulling out every last bit of heat I had, then pushing it toward the gigan. The result was a continuous stream of emerald fire that burned through his armor right where his heart would be if he had one. Looking down at the hole in his chest, he staggered backward. Stepping on Hydra's wandering body, he lost his balance, falling into the spring. The Tinman's flailing arm took out the three remaining puppies.

The very definition of a happy accident.

That was the last normal thought I had before my vision clouded with green and the curse took over. I could feel the Tinman like we were connected—feel him rusting from the bottom and melting from my flame on the top. Through the haze of green, I saw something floating toward me. When it hit, my weakness faded. The gigan's strength and life force filled me.

More. You could be so much more.

The voice was right. I could feel the Tinman's power feeding me, making me grow. If I ate more, I would grow stronger. Nothing would be able to take me down. I planted my hands into the ground and searched, using the power. In my mind, I saw the life force of everything around me—the trees, the grass, the boy…everything.

The boy glows with life and power. Take it.

I wanted it. No, I needed it. Without it, I couldn't win. But if I took it, I had a feeling I would lose far more. Inside me with the heat, a cold shell tried to form around my heart. I focused in on the glowing power of the human boy. He was talking to me. He had a name and importance beyond a power source. If I could remember it…

"Kato," I muttered and mentally shoved the power back, rejecting it and the metallic taste in my mouth. The flames left my hands, and I no longer felt all-powerful; I felt like something the Cheshire cat might throw up.

"Are you all right?" Kato's cold hands gripped my arms and helped me up. The icy contrast to my heat helped the world come back into Technicolor focus, ditching the green tint.

No. Once again, I'd stolen a life and a power that didn't belong to me. Good reason or not, I felt a weight from the deaths of Crow, Moony, the puppies, and the Tinman.

Thinking about how close I'd been to adding Kato to this list threatened to tip the scales. I'd managed to control the curse, but for how long?

I didn't want to worry Kato, so I pointed over to Hydra's flattened body and the rusty pile of scrap that clogged the spring well and lied. "Considering the alternatives, I think I fared pretty well." Steadying myself, I picked up Hydra's head. "How 'bout you? Sorry about the body, by the way."

"Vas time to trade up I am thinkink."

I cradled her head under my arm and sighed. Too much had happened in the last few minutes to even process. Our foursome had turned to two and a half, and my hopes for a bright, shiny future had been crushed. Literally. "So, now what? How do we stop Griz? We can't catch up on foot."

There was the saying, *It's always darkest before the dawn.* But the suns always came up.

Didn't they?

Right now, just to mock me, the third sun, Pathos, was setting.

I looked to the sky and called out, "Okay, whoever's there, now would be a really good time to send in reinforcements—a flying elephant or deus ex something or other."

Nothing happened except Kato looking at me like I had burned a few too many brain cells. He didn't understand, so I tried to explain. "You see, there has to be something. I've felt it. I know someone's up there." I let go of Kato's arm and yelled at the suns. The light seemed blurry. "Where are you,

Storymakers? Where's the magic sword in a stone or a lamp to give me new wishes?"

No sparkling dust flew. No sound of wind chimes flitting through the air. No sign at all that anyone cared. I'd been saved so many times, but now at the greatest hour, I'd been abandoned. In my heart I feared I was no longer worthy of saving.

"I've done the best I can and it's not enough." My voice cracked, making it impossible to speak loudly, so I lowered my head and whispered, "I can't do this on my own."

Kato put a hand under my chin and turned my face to his. "You don't have to." His eyes were soft with an unfathomable expression as he placed his hands on either side of my face. "No matter what happens, I will always be here, so you're never alone."

Then, without warning, his lips were on mine—softer than the silkiest mousse and sweeter too. My lungs burned for breath, but there would be time for breathing later. I let everything go and lived in this one moment, this one perfect grain of sand in the hourglass.

I threw my arms around him, dropping Hydra in the process. She landed with a thud and cry of pain. The sound startled me enough to break the kiss. "Pix! I am so sorry." I looked down to make sure I hadn't irrevocably broken anything on her, and then turned back for more kisses.

My prince with the auburn hair and dirt-smudged face was gone. The ice blue eyes still looked at me with what I now recognized as regret while he unfolded his wings—one brown, one white.

"Oh Grimm, you knew…"

His fur rubbed against my cheek. "It's the only way. But at least I finally got to kiss you once." His voice had the rough, grumbly chimera quality to it again.

I nodded, no longer trusting the sound of my own voice. It was official—I had lost everything.

My chimera prince was nearly full grown now. He kneeled and flattened his wings so I could climb on. Hydra coughed softly, showing unusual tact in an effort to not be forgotten.

I picked her up and climbed onto Kato's back. Nobody said a pixing word. There was no need. There was only one place to go and one thing to do.

Save the world before the grains of sand ran out.

"You see that apple, and you know it's poisonous, but it still looks so good."

—Snow White from *An Apple a Day*

Double Bubble, Lots of Trouble

Kato flew like our lives depended on it, which they absolutely did. Griz was the nastiest witch I had ever seen—and she was supposed to be the nice sister. The combination of Blanc and Griz together would make any evil queen quake in her dragon-skinned boots.

Griz only had a ten- or fifteen-minute lead on us, and Kato had warned Bob ahead of time. A whole mountain full of fire-breathing chimeras should be able to hold off one witch, an unwilling accomplice, and six demon puppies, right?

The smoke coming out of the cave opening indicated otherwise.

I knew what was coming; I had been on this ride before.

Flattening myself against Kato's back, I smooshed Hydra under my chest so she wouldn't fall out. She muffled some sort of protest about not being able to breathe, but without lungs, I thought the point was moot.

We dove steeply and spiraled into the mountain. This time it was my coughing that echoed off the walls rather than Rexi's screams. Smoke billowed in big, thick clouds like a volcano was about to erupt. Hopefully Bob hadn't pushed the self-destruct button or something.

He waited for us in the field of fire flowers. Blood stained his muzzle, and more oozed from a gash on his side. He didn't seem surprised to see Kato as a chimera. Then again, I guess Bob never knew that Kato had changed back into a boy.

He galloped toward us as we landed. "My lord. The traitor—"

"We know. Rexi." Kato and I spoke at the exact same time.

"Is jinxed," Hydra said gleefully while I hopped off Kato's back. All the head throwing and dropping might have given her brain damage.

Bob's eyebrows drew closer in consternation while he shook his head. Drops of blood flicked onto my skin. "No, my lord, it's Grifflespontus. He has joined the uprising and—"

"The defenses have been triggered. Does that mean the White One is free?" Kato interrupted.

"Not yet. We have the witch blocked off near the secret entrance. But, sire, Griff—"

"Is right here." Griff stood by the lava flow, blocking the path to the furnace room and looking bigger and scarier than ever. His broken horn dripped with blood and something thicker.

"Stand down." Kato growled and postured himself like a bull ready to charge. Though Kato had grown significantly since the last we were here, he was still much smaller than Griff.

"Thanks anyway, pup." Griff snarled and spat out something globby and red. "There's a new order around here. A human is no longer king of the mountain—especially one *pretending* to be a Chimera." The serpent tail rose up behind him and hissed menacingly.

"So, what, you'd rather take orders from a human in a skanky cocktail dress?" I really should know better than to mouth off to creatures bigger than me.

Griff roared and charged across the large room.

"Freeze him, freeze him," I urged frantically as Griff got closer.

"It's not working anymore."

Kato pushed me away with his wing, put his horns down, and braced for impact.

I cringed at the ripping sound of horn meeting flesh. Bob ran in and gored Griff from the side, knocking him off his collision course with Kato. But Griff wasn't done yet. He reared up and swiped a paw across Bob's wing, the claws shredding the delicate feathers.

Kato bounded over to help and hollered along the way, "Go, Dot! Do whatever you have to. Do not let Griz leave here with Blanc."

Asking me to guess Rumplestiltskin's middle name would probably have been easier. The ground shook and smoke filled the open passageways. I took off down the one that I was pretty sure led to the furnace room. Several chimeras fought in the carved caverns. I didn't know who was on which side. The chimeras weren't wearing team colors or anything.

A barbed tail swung just over my head and hit a stalactite. Pieces of rock fractured off as it hit the ground and bounced into my leg, making me crash. A shock zipped up my body from my right foot. Sitting up, I assessed the damage. The ruby heel had broken off one of my shoes and my ankle throbbed, indicating it was probably twisted. And to top it off, I'd lost Hydra's head in the fall. My eyes burned. I couldn't see it anywhere; it was probably rolling off somewhere. I'd have to find her later, assuming there was a later. To stand, I braced myself against a miniature volcano—the one the Griff had tried to kill me with. That meant I was almost there.

Shoes in hand, I hobbled into the furnace room just in time to see Griz clobber one of the chimera guards protecting the stoic Blanc. Rexi stood in the center of the room, looking like she would run and save her own hide at the first opportunity.

I dropped the shoes so I could bring the flames to my hand. Hoping for a dramatic entrance, I fired a single shot into the ceiling of the cave to announce to Griz that I had arrived. Instantly, I felt the strain of the curse waking up, wanting to be fed.

End this quickly. There is nothing here that doesn't deserve to burn.

I pushed the thought away like I had before, holding on to the name I needed to save.

"Hand over the vial and Rexi's necklace, or the next one goes right into Blanc's prison." I walked forward and allowed the fire to form in my hand again to show her I was ready to do it.

Why wait? Just fire.

I shook my head to knock the voice loose. "Shut up."

Griz leaned to the side and studied me. "Having a bit of trouble controlling it, are we?"

I chuckled. It sounded half-mad to me, so I hoped it sounded just over the edge of desperate crazy to her. "I don't need to control it anymore. I can just let it go and erase you and your sister off the pixing page."

That was not the answer Griz was hoping for. She frowned and yanked the opal off her neck. "We seem to be at a standstill. You are threatening someone important to me, and I have something important to you. What do you propose we do?"

She'd made the right move by holding Rexi's life hostage. Even though she had betrayed me, she was still my friend and I was going to save her life somehow. If I survived the rest, I could beat her senseless later.

A *shuffle shuffle* came from the back of the room. "Do what you were born to do." Verte stood in the left entrance next to the desk. She was a little roughed up but still alive.

My sparks flared up in response.

"Stop." Another Verte appeared in the entrance behind me. She looked exactly like I remembered her from the garden—down to having a little green friend peeking out from under her hat.

My double vision could only mean one thing. Well, two things actually. Verte was here and alive. And so was the Mimicman.

Oh, yeah, and I didn't have a fairy flippin' clue who was who.

I motioned to the Verte behind me. "You, move closer to the other...you." I needed to get everyone in a single field of vision.

"You come to me, child. Use your powers. I will help you control them." This from the beaten-up Verte. "The evil sisters cannot be allowed to live."

The other Verte walked with her back closely to the rounded wall. "Humph. Can't necessarily argue with that fact. But using that abominable curse is not the way. Let it go, Dot."

I didn't know who was real or what to do. Where was a Grimm-forsaken mirror when I needed one?

Logic told me that the battered green witch was the real Verte, because the Mimicman was on Griz's side—he would want to protect her, not tell me to kill her. The other Verte looked too perfect, but she had called me Dot. There was just no way to be sure.

Burn them all.

Both Vertes glowed with magic. The voice was seductive and the power wound its way along my insides. It felt different from the first time I had used it at Crow's. There, it had been a single voice, a single thread. There were multiple voices now, one had a tinny quality to it, another distinctly woodsy. And the thread had grown into a twisted strand. If I focused inward, I could almost see the newest shiny thread, and I still had the metallic taste of the gigan's life magic in my mouth.

Right then, I finally realized the full danger of the curse. At the least, I thought Hydra had been warning me against using all my own life and, at worst, warning me that I would grow to like the feel of power and control and become addicted. Both valid concerns, but I foolishly thought I would be okay—that I could be stronger and tune out the voice if I just used the flames sparingly. But in feeding the Tinman to the curse, I'd taken in more than just his power.

I could feel his mindless savagery fused to the flames within me, the dinner guest that wouldn't leave. Moony too. If I killed Griz and Blanc with emerald fire, they would join in and become my evil Jiminy Cricket consciences. I'd be madder than a March hare in minutes. I would burn down the world and laugh while doing it.

Being lost to my thoughts for just a moment was long enough for Griz to take advantage and hurl a silver bolt my way. One second, I was staring at the silver mercury coming closer, the next, I was staring into Rexi's wide green eyes. She smiled a little half smile and fell forward into my arms.

Her weight dragged me to my knees. The bolt in her back melted and oozed away, losing its shape as it trickled onto the floor. I laid Rexi down flat on the ground, and a mixture of silver and blood pooled beneath her.

My tears were there, but the flames burned them before they could reach the surface. Rexi's final choice answered the questions that had been plaguing my mind about our friendship, and it proved she was not the cowardly lion she believed herself to be.

Griz sighed. "That was…unfortunate." The opal necklace clattered to the ground. Its bright, pulsing light dimmed.

By jumping into the path of the stormbolt, Rexi had not only saved me, but she had also deprived Griz of her source of magic. Unless the Gray Witch had something heavy to float at me, she was out of tricks.

The scuffed-up Verte yelled at me while pointing to Griz, and her green face reddened with anger. "What are you waiting for? Blast her!" In the beginning, she had been hunched over and injured, so I couldn't get a good look at her. Now that I wasn't drugged and had a clear view, I could tell that I was looking at the Mimicman. Even his ability to mimic couldn't copy the emerald eye in Verte's belt. His looked like cheap green glass.

Griz confirmed what I had just figured out. "Don't listen to him!" She put her hands out in defense. There was something in her face that I hadn't seen yet.

Fear.

If the Mimicman wanted her dead as well, the only ally she had left was locked behind a prison of fire and my number of allies had just increased. Kato padded into the room, panting and favoring his left paw.

Perfect timing.

"Kato, will you please go eat the Mimicman? He's the Verte closest to Griz." I pointed him out.

The false Verte looked about to protest, but as Kato drew closer, the Mimicman gave up the game. With a great shudder, the Verte disguise flaked off. Now he was a chimera, with golden horns.

The Beast King.

"It's a lie," Kato growled.

If that was true, then why did it look like Kato was struggling and unable to move any closer?

Griz ran to hide under the golden horns. "You finally reclaimed your first true form, Bestiamimickos. Now is your last chance to reclaim your former glory and side with us. Once the bindings are broken, your powers will be restored and all will be forgiven. Just prove your loyalty and bring this whole mountain down on the Emerald brat once and for all."

The last piece of the sordid puzzle. Apparently some parts of the story get glossed over in the retelling. The noble Beast King led astray by unrequited love was really just a *magnificently* spineless weasel.

He roared, making both Griz and Kato back up. "We both

know the empress would kill me before her bracelet bindings hit the floor. And even if I believed you, it seems I'm destined to make the same choice again and again." Looking over to me, his eyes seemed to burn gold. "In that blaze of green, you are more perfect than you can ever know. I will find you once more. You will love me."

"Only in your worst nightmares," I snarled.

"Finish the empress and fulfill your destiny. I'll be waiting." Abandoning both Griz and me to play out the rest of the story, the Mimicman loped out the side entrance. With him out of sight, the spell he had on Kato broke and the current Beast King bounded after the old.

"You fool," Griz cursed, then realized her mistake in drawing my attention to her again.

The longer the emerald flames danced in my hands, the harder it was to remember why I didn't want to use them. Rexi's body still lay at my feet, so I *really* wanted to use them.

"One down, one left."

"Wait. You still need me. I have what you want." Griz reached into the pouch at her side. Out came the vial in one hand and the *Book of Making* in the other. "What you want more than anything in the world—your parents. They might have been erased from *this* story, but they are still alive in another world."

The dream came back to me, the one I'd had by the lake, the picture of my parents on the gold-leaf page. As my flames went out, my sanity returned.

Griz ran a drop from the spring along the binding of

the book, and the red engraved cover flew open, finally unlocked. She released the book from her hand and floated it closer to me in a flurry of pages. When it finally settled, the pictures moved across the paper, animated like Blanc's story had been earlier. My parents were wearing strange clothing and sitting in rocking thrones on a porch. Dad wore blue pants with something like pinafore top with buttons, and a big straw hat. Mom had her hair in a disarray like I'd never seen, and it was gray. She wore an ugly floral skirt and a white top that had the letter *I,* then a picture of a heart, and then the word *Kansas.* Whatever that was. A little animal ran around their feet. Not a demon puppy, but a small little black dog about the size Kato the chimera had started out as.

I reached out to touch the image, but Griz snapped the book closed. "They're in the world of the Makers. If you join my sister and I, we could show you how to draw out the power in your blood and bring them back from the realm of Kansas." The book dropped to the ground with a clatter, just out of my reach. "But without us, you'll never see them again." She held the vial over the open pages.

Verte approached with a *shuffle shuffle.* There was no *thunk* without her emerald staff. Looking up at her, I longed for home more than ever, to go back to the garden before any of this had ever happened. With the loss of the star, that was impossible now, but I could have at least one thing back.

"Is she telling the truth?" I asked Verte.

She twitched her nose as if trying to sniff out the truth. "Good chance of that."

"What should I do?" I asked quietly.

The emerald eye in her belt clouded over. "You will make a choice and someone will lose." The eye returned to normal and winked at me. Verte hunched over with a groan, a hand protecting her back. "But I already told you that. The rest has to come from you."

Once again, my thoughts went back to the courtyard garden. How much had she seen back then under the harvest moon?

Verte was doing her best impression of a stone wall, and I knew I would get no further help from her. What would my mother do if she were here instead of me?

A memory popped into my mind, something I hadn't thought of in years. I was seven and it was my birthday. The only thing I'd asked for was to spend the entire day with my mother. I planned the whole thing out—a fashion show with my dolls, a tea party, and a mother-daughter sleepover in the palace gardens. But that morning, there had been raiding and a land dispute in some part of the Emerald Kingdom. Instead of being with me, my mother spent my birthday hearing the people, settling disputes, and arranging aid to the village that was pillaged.

I spent the whole day crying in Verte's lap, furious at my mother. She was the queen. She could do whatever she wanted, and she'd preferred to spend the day dealing with other people's problems instead of being with me. That night, when my mom came to say good night, I rolled over and refused to speak to her. She kissed the back of my head and said, "It's not about who I want to be; it's about who I need to be."

I never forgave her. I held that and many more things against her for years to come. She had made her choice: power first and being my mother somewhere way down the line.

I understood her choice much better now; it wasn't power she chose but duty. I *wanted* to be the loving daughter and do what it took to bring my parents home, but I *needed* to be the princess that would keep the land safe from Griz and Blanc.

I had made my choice, and I was the one who was going to lose.

Griz must have seen the decision in my eyes because she turned to the prison of fire, pulling the stopper out of the vial. She was going to free Blanc even though she had to know I would hit her with the flames if I had to.

But I didn't have to. I was never going to feed another soul to this curse if I had any say. The idea didn't even have a chance to fully form before I put it into action. I grabbed the shoe I'd dropped earlier and chucked it at the Gray Witch. The heel hit the glass and shattered it on impact, spilling the spring water down the front of Griz.

A few sparks came from her vest, and there was a momentary look of surprise and horror as her silver, slitted eyes widened to nearly all black. Then her expression became indistinguishable because everything about her turned to liquid silver with lightning streaking through it. The strikes bounced around inside her, melting everything they hit until only a puddle with a few shards of bone remained.

"Rule #1: Every fairy tale comes equipped with a happy ending. You just have to find it."

—Definitive Fairy-Tale Survival Guide, Volume 1

Use Your Head and Be True to Your Heart

Kato flew back into the room. "He escaped. He was just too—" His voice and paws stopped short when he saw all that was left of the Gray Witch. "Is that—?"

"Yes, it is, and good riddance." In the end, I had still taken her life, and that was something I would have to deal with. But at least this way I'd starved the curse for now, and Griz wouldn't be haunting my head for eternity. Looking at Rexi, I was glad the witch was dead. Did that make me a bad person? Maybe. Did I care? Ask me again tomorrow.

As Kato came closer, his claws clicked against the opal necklace. The contact made the stone flash, and a little orange swirl ran through it.

I gasped and clamored over to it on my hands and knees. Sure enough, there were still little flecks of light floating through the darkened and cracked stone. Seeing Kato's life magic collide with it gave me an idea. Maybe there was still a chance. I snatched the necklace off the ground and grabbed a shard of the shattered glass vial.

"What are you doing?" Kato sat and watched my frantic movements in puzzlement.

Verte's smile reached all the way into her voice. "She's doing what I told her—using her head."

Taking the glass in hand, I pricked my finger, then sliced off a big chunk of my hair. Wrapping the blood-tinged flames around the opal, I made sure to press the green spark against the crack.

Please work, please work.

Nervously, I stood watch over Rexi as I placed the necklace to her skin. "C'mon, take it," I urged, pushing the flaming hair harder into the stone, thinking maybe the pressure would help transfer some of my life magic into it. "You take everything else that's not bolted down, so just take it!" The wrapping of hair dimmed, the fiery red strands changing back into the regular old shade of brown they used to be.

Carefully, I pulled the strands of hair away, revealing a bright orange-and-*green* swirled stone. Rexi's chest moved with a sharp intake of breath.

I threw myself down on top of her. "I can't believe that actually worked!"

Rexi mumbled something, but I couldn't understand it.

"What did you say?" I shifted position so I could see and hear her better.

She opened one eye and her mouth tilted into a half smile. "I said, get off, you pixing cow. You're squishing me."

So of course, I squeezed her tighter.

A tear leaked from the corner of her eye. "I'm so sorry. I—"

I cut her off. "Don't want to hear it right now. Let me enjoy the fact that we are, shockingly and against all odds, alive." I kissed Rexi on the forehead.

Next I ruffled Kato's fur and gave him a kiss on his wet nose. And last, I launched myself at Verte and gave her a big smooch on her wrinkly green cheek. Then I hugged and held her lumpy body and let the relief sink into my bones. I had missed Verte so much and couldn't believe that I finally had her back. She was the closest thing to family I had, and if Griz had been telling the truth, might ever have again. "I don't know what took you so long, but I'm so glad you're finally here."

"I had a few technical difficulties. But if I'd rescued you day one, you'd still be a newt-brained brat, so it's better that I waited for you to grow up a bit." Verte lightly pushed me away and waggled those caterpillar eyebrows at me. "Speaking of, think there's something you oughta see." She put her hands on my shoulders and spun me around.

In front of me was a boy with dirt- and blood-smudged tan skin, one pale white arm, auburn hair—with a hint of horns—and ice-water blue eyes. Thankfully, this time Kato was fully clothed, so I didn't hesitate to run into his arms.

"How?" I marveled.

"Must have been your kiss." Kato smoothed my hair and ran a hand across my cheek.

"But that means the fairy tales rules are fixed." The spring water must have disenchanted the broken pieces of the star that Griz had stuffed into her vest. I'd forgotten they were even there until I saw them in the puddle, but it didn't occur to me that, fractured, the star might still have been cleaned of the wish. When I threw the shoe, I'd just been remembering something the pixing wizard had said about Griz being afraid of water.

Wrapping his arms around me, Kato twirled me away. "I guess that means we get the happy ending after all. We skipped this part the first time, but would you do me the honor of being my queen?"

Rexi's moan was cut off by a little kick from Verte. "Shh, this is the best part."

"Yes, for all of ever after."

The words had barely left my lips before he kissed them. If it's even possible, it was better than the first. And this time, there was no Hydra head to spoil it.

I broke off the kiss, startled by the mental image of her head rolling around somewhere after I dropped it in the hazy mess of the halls. "Oh, pix. I forgot about Hydra."

The smoke was still creeping into the furnace room, and a

big puff of it was right in front of me. When it cleared, I was left looking at Kato's unamused *furry* face.

Rexi snorted. "You're right. This is the best part."

Verte helped her off the ground and cackled, "Hehe. Guess the rules aren't as fixed as lover boy might like."

I sighed and rested my forehead on Kato's. Of course it couldn't be that easy. Maybe the star being broken messed the reversal up. Or maybe some of the pieces had fallen out of the Gray Witch's brazier on the ride over. Whatever happened, it meant we still had some work to do.

The ground rumbled beneath our feet.

Kato frowned. "The defenses should be turned off now that the danger's passed."

"Yay. One more thing that isn't working like it should." Rexi rolled her eyes and leaned on me for support since she was still a little wobbly. I suppose being very nearly dead will do that to you.

"Unless you want to see a volcano erupt up close and personal, I better figure out what's going on. It's probably easier to check the defenses as a chimera. But after I'm done, you'll change me back, right?"

"Ooh, she's got you by the short whiskers now, boy," Verte cackled.

Kato shook his head in mock disgust and lowered himself down next to Rexi. "Get on. This is a one-time offer, and if you say one word, I might drop you into the lava," he warned her.

Rexi mimed zipping her lip and collapsed onto Kato's back, then they flew from the room.

"I suppose we'd better find Hydra." I nudged Verte. "Can you use your emerald eye and do whatever it is you do to find me all the time?"

She jiggled her belt. "This can't find anybody. Never has, never will."

"Then how did you know where I was, and how did you know to come here?" I asked.

Grinning slyer than a fox, she pointed at my broken and discarded heels. "I always put tracking spells in all your shoes because they're the only thing I can count on you hanging on to with your last breath."

"That's it?" I asked in disbelief. "That's why you told me, 'Don't lose your shoes'? That's the only reason I've been wearing these blister makers? What about the being enchanted and protecting me from all the dangers I'd run across?"

Verte's eyebrows curved sharply down, meeting in the middle to form a *V* shaped unibrow. "I didn't put anything like that on them. Were they modified by elves while you slept?" She hobbled over to the broken shoe, picked it up, and gave it a good sniff. "Something smells like mildewed doughnuts."

"Excuse me?" I said, more than mildly offended at the foot odor insinuation.

Ignoring me, she turned the shoe this way and that, then finally licked along the broken edge of the heel.

"Ewww."

Verte smacked her lips, savoring the taste. "Yup, I knew that smelled familiar. They haven't been modified. They've been ozified."

"Is that kind of like ozmosis?" I asked.

Verte ignored me, lifted up her hat, and felt around. Finding nothing, her eyes narrowed at me. Or rather past me as she darted to the discarded book and scooped up what looked like a small green creature.

"Crazy unpredictable troublesome wonderful old fool," Verte said in a mouthful. "You've been meddling again." She fought to keep hold of her squirmy prisoner, but her grip loosened as the creature in her hand changed shape.

First I thought that the Mimicman had returned, but aside from his chimera form, Hydra said he could only mimic *people* that existed. That would exclude the mustached bibliobug that grew into a large butterpillar and dropped onto the ground. The change didn't stop there. Instead, it went faster, switching through wild and impossible creations in a blink of an eye—things I'd never seen before and a few that were familiar. A horned mouse. Slimy letters of the alphabet. A polka-dotted furry giant. And finally, a short old man with ink-stained hands: the Storymaker I'd seen in Blanc's story.

"Lovely to see you again. Frank, Maker of Oz, at your service." He coughed and beat his chest, getting out a few puffs of green dust. "Now, my dearest Verte, I promised you I wouldn't meddle. Nudging on the other hand…"

"So what do you call this?" Verte shook my broken shoe at the man's nose.

"Well clearly, they're transdimensional particle-accelerating devices."

"They're what?" I asked.

Verte turned around and sighed. She had that look on her face, like she was trying to instruct ants on how to ride a bicycle. "It channels your will into magic for protection, and clicking the heels on the who-magig connecting to the whatchamacallit allows the shoes to move people from one spot to the next. Or across worlds. But it's controlled by your thoughts to make the magic work." She turned her ire back to the Storymaker and tossed the shoe in disgust. "And you newt-well know that's not what I asked. Giving those to an untrained girl is a clear violation of our agreement."

I picked up the broken heel, again awed by the almighty power that is designer shoes. They'd protected me on my journey and must have moved Kato inside Hydra's house. Maybe that's how we'd all been able to go up to the cloud storage with it. And if that was true, maybe getting my parents back wasn't going to be impossible after all. I slipped the shoes on, thought of my parents and stamped my heel to make it go.

Verte clucked her tongue at the Storymaker. "See, that's what I was talking about." She waddled over and yanked the shoe back off my foot while I was still standing. "I thought you'd learned the lesson to stop messing with magic you don't understand! You broke the wangeroo inside the pointy part. Even if you figured out what you were glammed well doing and got it to work, best it would do is move half of you."

That would be extremely unpleasant. But I still had hope.

Verte yelled at the Storymaker while he tuned her out and stroked the engraved quill on the cover of his book.

"Excuse me." I used the most reverent tone I could, as was appropriate for a Storymaker. He didn't budge so I tugged on his worn-out coat to get his attention. "Would you please fix the shoe so I can bring my parents home? Oh, and put back the rules the way they should be."

"No," he said and slammed the book close. "But…"

Verte's lips wiggled and her wart twitched. The little hairs on her chin stood to attention. "Whatever you're thinking…stop."

He blew a puff of dust up Verte's nose and smiled while she fought a sneezing attack.

"Now, where were we?" he said. "Ah, yes. The rules of story are always changing. They will balance themselves out with time. But I'm afraid even if I fixed the shoes, you wouldn't be able to harness enough of the power in your blood to reach the other side."

I was about to beg again when he handed me the book with a wink and said, "Not unless I teach you, that is. Destruction is only one half of the so-called curse, the flipside is creation. We'll start tomorrow."

Verte cursed a green streak, chasing the man around the

room. He headed for the cave entrance, shouting over his shoulder. "Teaching is not meddling, just training a Maker's apprentice. What could go wrong?"

They were both out of sight, but I could hear Verte holler back, "The last time you said that, I turned green!"

With a smile, I cradled the book that had shown my parents and brushed off the Griz goo that marred one corner. Crazy seemed to be the new normal, but maybe that wasn't so bad.

As far as happy endings go, this wasn't "ticker tape parade ride the carriage off into the triple sunset" material. Magic was working again—somewhat. Kato was human again— sometimes. My parents were alive—somewhere. The bad guys were dealt with—unless you counted the wizard/Mimicman/ Beast King. And I had managed to survive the Emerald curse without turning evil—for now. Still, the good guys won, and for today, that was enough. And for tomorrow…it will be whatever I make it.

B lanc stared stoically ahead as her sister's murderers left the room, but the fools had forgotten something, a rule that the original beast king and mimicking traitor had laid down centuries ago.

Never leave liquid near the water sorceress.

Blanc focused all the energy she had gained since waking and drew the puddle toward the fiery prison wall. It crept and inched toward her, sizzling when it made contact. The spring water extinguished the flames.

Satisfied that Grizelda's death was not in vain, she stepped out of her prison.

"That Emerald brat has no idea what heartache is." Blanc smiled for the first time in centuries. "Yet."

Acknowledgments

An ogre-sized thank-you goes out to my agent, Michelle Witte, for having the same twisted sense of humor and the bravery to take a chance on me. Big thanks to the tinkerers at Sourcebooks, Aubrey and Kate. You guys really helped focus the story and make it true magic. Without great beta readers like Karen, Jessica, T. J., Stacy, Melody, Caleb, Julie, Kari, and the rest of the Wednesday class, this book would have been dragon fodder. Tim, thanks for letting me swipe your weird creatures. A pixie dust of love goes to Alexis C. for giving me the tween perspective. A click of the heels to the real life Dorthea, Misty and your fabulous shoe obsession. And most importantly, I couldn't create without my one true love, Jarom, who makes sure the kids don't starve while I disappear in my own little world for weeks on end.

The Storymakers series continues...

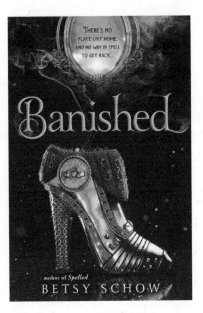

About the Author

Betsy Schow is the *Today Show* featured author of the nonfiction book *Finished Being Fat*; however, she's been mixing up real life and fantasy for as long as she can remember. If someone were to ask about her rundown truck, she's 100 percent positive that mechanical gremlins muck up her engine. And the only reason her house is dirty is because the dust bunnies have gone on strike. She lives in Utah, with her own knight in geeky armor and their two princesses (who can totally shape-shift into little beasts). When not writing, she helps teach kids creative thinking and how to turn their toasters into robots. Catch up and connect with Betsy at www.betsyschow.com.